The Term Between

Also by Brady Harrison

Agent of Empire

All Our Stories Are Here

The Dying Athabaskan

Punk Rock Warlord (co-edited with Barry J. Faulk)

Teaching Western American Literature (co-edited with Randi Tanglen)

These Living Songs (co-edited with Lisa Simon)

The Term Between

Stories

Brady Harrison

Published by Twelve Winters, a literary project.

P. O. Box 414 • Sherman, Illinois 62684-0414 • twelvewinters.com

The Term Between: Stories was first published by Twelve Winters in 2022. It is also available in a digital edition.

Cover and interior page design by TWP Design.

ISBN
978-1-7331949-6-9

Printed in the United States of America

for Emma

Acknowledgments

The author gratefully acknowledges publication of earlier versions of these stories in the following literary journals. Many thanks, in particular, to all the editors and readers for their diligence, good will, and support.

"The Guest" was published in *The Long Story.*
"Stones" was published in *Wascana Review.*
"Robbie" was published in *Serving House Journal.*
"Gone to Ground" was published in *J Journal: New Writing on Justice.*
"Buffalo Jump Brother" was published in *The Big Windows Review.*
"It's Not Like You Think" was published in *Aethlon: The Journal of Sport Literature.*
"Los Borrachos de Donostia-San Sebastián" was published in *The Meadow.*
"The Sumerian in the Driveway" was published in *High Desert Journal.*
"Wreck on the Highway" was published in *Short Story.*
"Working My Way Through High School & College" was published in *Poems Across the Big Sky II.*
"The Pintlers" was published in *La Piccioletta Barca.*
"The Dying Albertan" (Originally "The Dying Athabaskan.") was published by Twelve Winters. (Winner of The Publisher's Long Story Prize.)

Many thanks, as well, to Gabriella Graceffo for proofreading the manuscript—any errors or idiosyncrasies rest with the author—and to Ted Morrissey for his tireless work on and support for this book.

Contents

Behind Me—dips Eternity—
Before Me—Immortality—
Myself—the Term between—
Death but the Drift of Eastern Gray,
Dissolving into Dawn away,
Before the West begin—

Emily Dickinson

The Term Between

The Guest

I.

SHE LEFT THE CLUB just before closing.

In the course of the trial, during an afternoon recess, I drove out to this club, and it was nothing remarkable—a cinderblock rectangle with a façade of neon and burnished aluminum sweeps and curves. Most of the parking was in the back, and to the east, separated by a chain-link fence, was the pinkish back wall, spaced with delivery doors, of a strip mall; to the west was a restaurant, General Hu's Wok, one of those places where customers load up a plastic bowl with meat, noodles, vegetables, and a sauce of their choosing and hand it to a kid who then cooks it in front of them on an immense metal slab, chopping and stirring, while several of his or her co-workers do the same with other people's food, the would-be diners elbow-to-elbow, looking-on anxiously from behind a semi-circular barricade, the cooks elbow-to-elbow around the giant wok, all festive and steamy, joshing one another and occasionally calling out or juggling their spatulas to add to the excitement.

The only thing striking about the club was its name, The Universal Sea.

I was astonished: The Universal Sea! What could the owner possibly have had in mind? A name so evocative, mysterious, promising. But promising—what?—untold depths? the evergreen hope of me-not-me and you-not-you? immersion, then suspension, in a warm, soothing, protoplasmic solution? a primeval commonality, the source, the origin of us all? All that, and certainly the usual, contained in a perfectly ordinary cinderblock rectangle in the absolute middle of the American ordinary!

The name was uncanny, a thing of genius, and so of course I went inside, and even at three in the afternoon the music was pulsing—the beat absolutely metronomic, reverbed, both ear-splitting and hollow—and the air was close with the smell of beer, piss, and deep-fryers. My headache got worse; I could feel hot, bitter sand, though I knew there was none there, clinging to the sweat on the back of my neck.

I thought to inquire after the owner, to ask him what he thought the name meant, but I sat instead at the bar and ordered a beer. Half an hour was enough, my head pounding in syncopation to the machine-tooled beat, and as I rose to leave I asked the barkeep about the name.

He looked at me as if deciding whether I was a reporter, lawyer, or cop—the case was in the news and on TV every day—and shrugged.

When she left the club, she had used her remote to unlock the door to her car, a new, silvery-blue Priam that her parents had bought for her, only a few thousand miles on it, and eased herself into the form-fitting seat. She wiggled into place—you might say zaftig, though that might be too ample a term—and, the temperature having dropped over the course of the evening toward freezing, she activated the driver side seat-warmer and turned on the heater, set the fan to defrost, and then punched the rear-window defroster. Rather than pulling on the seatbelt, she turned on the satellite radio to her favorite after-dance station, and immediately found what she was hoping for: the synth-heavy, drum-machine beats of the club.

I offer these details, gleaned from conversations with her and from the testimony of the forensic experts who later examined her car, to suggest that while she may have been a little high—there had been vague testimony concerning X—and a little drunk, she was not sloppily so and may very well have been under the legal limit, at least in terms of alcohol.

Safely ensconced, she eased from the parking lot onto Cuyahoga, a major thoroughfare in her district, and headed west toward her neighborhood. Although it had begun to snow wet, early winter flakes swaying lazily and melting when they hit the pavement, the roads were neither particularly slick nor treacherous, and the traffic being light, she made good time, driving a little over the speed limit in order to catch the green lights. A few blocks from her house, she turned off Cuyahoga and followed a long, curving feeder street that looped around a community sports complex and high school.

Perhaps by now she was going too fast. There hadn't been any cars for a while, and she was close to home, and had driven this road several thousand times—she had attended Ulysses S. Grant High only a few years earlier—and perhaps wasn't paying as much attention as she should have. Perhaps she was still a little high or sleepy, and the car was warm inside, and if the music was loud, it was nevertheless in the background of her consciousness as she sped along the sweeping, four-lane, median-divided boulevard. At that time of night, in that wide open space, the school and baseball and football fields on one side, the houses set well back from the road on the other, the residential side of the street lined with maples, she would have had little sense of urgency or care.

Slowing a little as the road bent hard to the right, she neared the front of the school, and there, before she had time to react, was a shape, a person, pushing something, a shopping cart heaped with things. She did not have time even to touch her foot to the brake as, in that instant, the shape pulled up short, turning from the shopping cart, turning to face the car head-on. For a moment, the shape, the person, was frozen in the stark white headlights, and then the car struck and he or she was flung into the air, crashing headfirst through the windscreen on the passenger side. The shopping cart, having a little momentum of its own, had rolled forward in that instant and was smashed aside, pinwheeling into the air and away from the windshield on the driver's side. It careened off the roof of the car, gouging deep grooves in the metal, and came to rest, its contents spilling everywhere, amid some bushes in the semi-dark of the lane-away median.

Shattered glass flying inside the car, and the car itself shuddering and yawing toward the curb, now hydroplaning on the thin slush and pulpy debris of leftover maple leaves, she grappled with the wheel, instinctively turning against the skid and back toward the lane even as bits of the windscreen peppered and cut her face, driven into the soft flesh of her cheeks and neck by the deploying airbags.

The car hit the curb, spun, and came to rest facing the wrong way, stalled, in the middle of the road, an icy wind plinking droplets of ice against what was left of the windscreen, the engine cooling and clicking as it cooled.

In shock, she sat as if frozen in place, gasping for air, trying to breathe, shrieks of pain radiating from her face, shoulders, and chest, and for a time she did not know where she was or what had happened.

As she explained in court, she did not know how long she sat there, gasping, trying to force her lungs to work, her face hot and shrieking in pain, as if shredded, unable to see properly from her right eye due to the glass lodged in the eyelid and eyebrow. She remembered trying to brush the glass from her cheek and forehead, the radio still playing, the beats absolutely regular and throbbing with the throbbing in her face until she heard the person, beneath the music, a kind of counter-song, moaning, perhaps whispering, perhaps trying to speak.

Rather than being thrown free due to the centrifugal force of the car spinning out of control, the person had remained embedded in the windscreen. Having slammed headfirst through the glass, the impact had brought the shoulders through the surface as well, pinning the body, torso, and arms, the legs jutting upwards outside the car, the shoulders and head inside, the face pressing up against the dash, the deflated airbag clinging, she said, like a caul.

Blood beaded and trickled down the nylon surface of the bag and pooled on the floor mat and the moaning turned, she recalled, to a whimper, a pleading. Unable to see well, and with the only illumination in the car coming from the dash instruments, she could not tell if the keening figure was a man or a woman and if he or she were speaking words, she could not hear, her ears ringing from the force of the safety-device exploding in her face, the trance-music pounding. The other airbag clung to the face as it pressed up against the glove box door, and he or she was wearing a hoodie and wool cap over his or her head. Whimpering, he or she shuddered and, beginning to sob, seemed to be trying to sway his or her head from side to side, trying to wiggle free.

She reached out a tentative hand to touch the figure's shoulder:

"What are you saying? I can't understand what you're saying."

As if responding to her voice, the figure seemed to try to lift its face away from the dash and toward her, but could not.

"Is your neck broken?"

All at once, the figured stopped squirming and went silent and still.

Alarmed and deeply afraid, she began to wail:

"Are you dead? Are you dead?"

Thinking at last to turn off the music, she then shook the person's shoulder, once, and then harder and harder until the head was swaying side to side, the coroner surmised, not unlike a boxer's speed bag. In shock, she would claim later, in considerable pain and not in her right mind, she pushed the stick into P, reached for the key still in the ignition, and turned it. The engine caught, and she pulled the stick down to D. When she pressed the accelerator, the car lurched to the left, the front-end evidently having sustained damage in the crash into the curb. Fighting the pitch to the left, she turned the car to face the proper direction, and wobbled for home.

II.

HER HOUSE WAS A MODEST, two-bedroom ranch with a double, attached garage and unfinished basement, located in a modest neighborhood less than a mile from the house she grew up in. A starter home, made possible by her parents who supplied the down payment, and it was very like the houses on her block and the blocks surrounding. The façade was of red brick, offset with beige siding around the recessed entranceway and the exterior walls not facing the street; the heated garage, comprising a third of the house, was set-forward on the right and a paved sidewalk led from the driveway to the front door. The front yard was modestly landscaped, with a maple close to the street, a few junipers along the sidewalk, a strip of flower garden running alongside the driveway. The rest of the front, sides, and back was lawn, all securely enclosed by a four-foot chain link fence.

As to the inside of the house, I came to know it well. On a number of occasions, after the police had unsealed it, her parents allowed me the run of the place and by the time I decided it was time to leave Cleveland, I had studied the layout and contents of each room as if I were a detective, as if looking closely and carefully at everything connected to her and the accident would somehow tell me everything I wanted to know, enough, at least, for the book I thought I might write about the case. But if even the simplest facts cannot be known—you listen to enough testimony and different versions of events and you realize that you can only take your best guess about the who, what, where, and when—then how much more problematic the why? And if the why remains mysterious despite all the ghostwriting you care to do, then how much more elusive still the meaning of a thing?

But everyone knows this. It's why we like cop shows and football.

Or maybe it's this: if you shine a light on a thing, or a thousand lights, the more you try to illuminate, the deeper become the shadows?

Whatever the case, she turned her car around and zigzagged home. The route probably took her nine minutes or so—I drove it myself a couple of times to see how long it might take from the front of the school to the house—and nobody saw her. What the odds are of nobody coming along while she was stalled, or nobody looking out their windows upon hearing the crash, or nobody passing her as she limped home at around 2:30 a.m., I cannot say. But she made it and, turning into her driveway, pressed the button on the rearview mirror that activated the garage door. She drove into the garage, put the car in park, and switched off the ignition.

She claims not to know how long she sat in her car, yet certainly long enough for the auto-timer to shut off the overhead lights in the garage. In the dark, then, a stranger lodged in her windscreen, not knowing whether he or she was dead or unconscious, she at last tried to open her door but had some difficulty as the shopping cart had evidently banged the roof hard enough to torque the metal over the doorframe. With some effort, she forced it open, climbed from the car, and staggered to the door leading into the kitchen, pausing long enough to push the button to close the garage door. Once inside, she sat down at the small table, and wept. Again, we don't know for how long she sat, but she eventually stirred herself once more and, picking up the phone, dialed a friend.

I'll call him "Jeremy."

When, after the requisite number of rings, his answering machine picked up, she hung up and dialed his cell. When his voicemail activated, she broke the connection, sent a text—AH CM RFN—and redialed his landline. This time, when the machine picked up, she demanded that he answer, alternately howling and sobbing, all the while attempting to explain why he needed to be there. (I can report that his machine, being subpar, continued to record even after he answered and that he forgot, or so he claimed, to delete the message; the recording was duly entered into evidence, but by the time both the prosecutor and the defense attorney finished explaining what the jury was hearing, it amounted to little at trial.) At last, she succeeded in rousing him from his slumber:

"Hello? What? Who is this?"

"It's me. You have to come over right away."

"I have to come over right away?"

"I ran someone over."

"What? Why are you yelling at me?"

"I ran someone over. I think they're dead."

"You ran someone over?"

"They're stuck in the window."

"They're stuck in a window? What? Wait: you ran over two people?"

It went on like this for a while, and I suppose it sounds comical in the telling, but the sheer terror and gasping in her voice gave one quite a different feeling, hearing it in the courtroom. She was clearly hysterical, and deeply, deeply aggrieved, and he had clearly been deeply asleep but was doing his best to fight his way to consciousness and understanding.

Eventually, he seemed to grasp some measure of what she was saying and said he would be right over. True to his word, he was there in about twelve minutes. He entered the house through the front door—she had given him a spare key in case she needed him to pick up her mail and water her plants—and heard her crying in the kitchen.

She was, he told the court, a bloody, panic-stricken mess.

There were countless cuts on her face, and she was trembling and bawling, and if she had been difficult to understand on the phone, she was little better in person. By times, sobs convulsed her entire frame, and there were shards of glass embedded in the right side of her face. The region around her eye was particularly gory, with a long, bluish sliver protruding from her eyelid causing her to blink and blink while blood slithered from the wound, gummed her eyelashes, and then trickled down her cheek and jaw, soaking into her long black coat. There was a considerable gash in her eyebrow adding to the stream, and more glass stuck in her forehead and temple.

Jeremy nearly collapsed to the floor when he saw how torn up she was, but he grasped the back of her chair, steadied himself, and looked upon her with a mix of revulsion and concern:

"What happened?"

I met him several times and listened carefully to his testimony, and if he was, back then, perhaps a bit soft—he was six-one or six-two and no doubt two-sixty or two-seventy—he was loyal to her and, in those first moments in her kitchen, her face pulpy and beginning to swell and show bruises, he decided—without knowing it fully at the time, he later told me—that he was there for her, whatever had happened and whatever would happen. Right or wrong, as the expression goes, he had her back.

When he insisted that she go immediately to the hospital, she yelled at him to be quiet and to listen to her. With some coaching, he located the first-aid kit her mother had purchased for her, a pair of tweezers, several clean facecloths and hand towels, and then filled a stainless mixing bowl with hot water and a pump or two of antibacterial soap. Thus armed, he began to pull the embedded glass from her skin, gently tugging at each piece with the tweezers, and then even more gently daubing the cuts and gouges with a damp facecloth.

"You're going to be all scarred up."

"Keep going."

"You need to see a doctor."

"I'll scream."

He looked devastated:

"But your beautiful face."

"Jeremy, you will do it, or I will do it myself."

As I say, he was no match for her, especially under such upsetting circumstances, and he conceded and attended to the dozens of cuts and slices as carefully as he could while she continued to weep and, by times, to exclaim in physical or emotional pain. Whenever she cried out, he would flinch as if struck and wait for her to calm down before resuming. After dealing with some of the larger gashes, cleaning them and applying an antibiotic cream and band-aids, he felt steady enough to deal with the shard protruding from her eyelid. The splinter, as he discovered, had penetrated the lid and was minutely slicing, with each blink, deeper and deeper into the eyeball, and the area from the iris to the corner was swollen and turning a jaundiced crimson. Grasping the now-slippery glass with the tweezers as firmly as he could, he tugged on the sliver. With each tug, she cried out in pain and blinked furiously, the eyeball now beginning to ooze blood and a clear fluid. Knocking his hand away, her fingers searched for the glass, located it, and pulled it free. By this time the abraded area had become so puffy and turgid that it obscured much of the iris and pupil and she could no longer see from her right eye. She controlled her blinking long enough for him to clean the eyelid and place a circular bandage over the wound. In a few minutes more, he had finished removing the remaining bits of embedded glass, and the right side of her face was a patchwork of glistening scratches, puncture marks, and band-aids.

As he cleaned away the debris and collected the bloody facecloths and put them to soak in the kitchen sink, she slumped in her chair, hanging her head over the backrest, and wept anew:

"You have to go to the garage."

Suddenly terrified, he busied himself at the sink.

She stared at him from her one good eye:

"They're out there."

"I don't understand."

"You do so."

At that point, he told the jury, he felt as if he were going to be sick; and he knew, too, that from that point on, he had gone from helping a former girlfriend to being part of whatever had happened:

"The people you hit are in the garage?"

Howling, she gestured with both hands at the doorway:

"Go see."

Slowly—he told the court he felt as if he were walking on the bottom of a darkened pool—he stepped to the door and pushed it open until he could see the front of the car:

"Good lord!"

Even in the half-light spilling through the doorway he could make out a figure protruding from the windscreen, the knees and shins resting on the hood, the shoulders and head buried in the interior.

"What have you done?"

Enraged, she staggered to his side:

"Shut up. Shut up. Shut up."

When he began to reach for the light switch, she clawed at his arm:

"No. There's a flashlight on the workbench."

Once he located the flashlight, he turned back toward the car and stood away from the driver's side, his gaze fixated on the torso and legs protruding from the windscreen. The shapeless form was wrapped, he could see, in several layers, the outermost an old and very soiled pea coat; equally filthy jeans covered the legs, and he or she had on a pair of steel-toed Dickies, tattered and worn-soled. Red-topped wool socks protruded from the snow-soaked boots.

Reluctantly, Jeremy approached the driver's side window and aimed the flashlight through the window. The figure hung face-first against the dash, the deflated airbag still clinging to its features. The shoulders and upper arms appeared perfectly still, and if the body was breathing, he could not tell. Aghast, he pressed his forehead against the cool window, closing his eyes, willing, he told me later, the body to disappear, hoping, he said, that this was not happening, that he was having some sort of waking nightmare which would suddenly end and all would be as it had been before, that he was, in fact, standing at her front door about to knock, picking her up for their first date.

Quietly, she had stepped to his side, and finding him leaning against the window, eyes closed, she gently shook his arm. Suddenly exhausted, he had to press both hands against the window to ease his forehead from the glass. Still hunched over low enough to see into the car, he tapped the flashlight on the window, but the figure did not stir.

Without waiting to be urged to do so, he lifted the door handle, and pulled the door open. Gingerly, he eased himself into the driver's seat, trying not to make the car rock too much as it took his weight. Once settled, he rotated toward the body and, leaning over, peeled the by-now blood-soaked airbag away and shined the light on the inverted face. Like hers, it was bloody and shredded by glass—numerous shards glinted in the light—but also mangled and swollen by the impact. So torn up and gory was it, that he could not tell the gender. Leaning over further, he tugged the blood-soaked hoodie away and pulled off the even heavier and dripping wool cap. A mess of long, lank hair and blood poured out. If the face was a mess, the forehead and top of the head were even worse. The skull was clearly shattered and the scalp was torn away, here and there, in ghastly, flopping patches.

By now, Jeremy's hands were covered in blood, and as he watched, blood dripped from the ragged scalp and pooled with the blood, glass, and bits of skin and clumps of hair already on the floor mat. He began to weep and, all at once, clambered from the car. She caught him in her arms and held him until the tears subsided. Somehow, she had a rag and used it to wipe the blood from his hands. After a time, he was able to get himself together:

"I think he's—"

"It's a he?"

"I'm not sure—the face is such a mess, and under the blood there's dirt and sores. . . . But I think he's still alive."

"What?"

"I think that if blood is dripping, then the heart is still pumping."

"Couldn't it be that the blood is pooling, because he's upside down, and it's just leaking out?"

"I don't know. Maybe. We have to call someone."

"No."

"If he's alive, we have to."

"No."

"Then he'll die. In your garage."

"He's already dead. Look. You can see he's not breathing."

"I tell you we have to call someone. Otherwise, it's murder."

She ran from the garage into the house and slammed the door behind her.

From the testimony in court, and from my interviews with them, I know that they spent the rest of the night arguing about what to do. He was adamant, but she more so, and if she never quite succeeded in persuading him to accept that the person was already dead and that there was nothing they could do, she wore him down into a sort of stalemate. At sunrise, sick at heart and emotionally and physically drained, he told her that he had to leave, that he had to go home and change and get ready for work. She demanded that he call in sick and stay with her, and that he call the title company where she worked and tell them that she was unwell and would not be in that day or, very likely, the next.

Eventually, he left—he was late for work—and she went to bed, all but burying herself in the numerous, brightly-colored throw pillows she had collected or been given over the years.

III.

THE PILLOWS ON HER BED: I counted nine, each one distinct in size, color, and finish. A few were square, others rectangular, most motley, yet elegant, and only one a monochrome, a sort of mustardy gold with a durable, hardy nap. Collectively, they seemed to go together, at least to my eye, as if some care had been given to their inclusion in the casual, pyramidical heap.

We think, don't we, that we know someone a little better after we have been to their home, that the deeper we penetrate into the interior, the deeper the glimpse we have into their lives? As if to move from room to room were to glimpse more and more of what matters most to them, to glimpse a little deeper into their hearts and souls? a little deeper into their minds? perhaps even into their unconscious?

What, then, to make of nine assorted pillows?

Beyond driving home with a body embedded in the windshield of her car, the only other even marginally remarkable thing about her life was those pillows. I am not ashamed to admit that I went through all her things. I went from room to room, looking in drawers and closets. I took notes, and read and re-read them to make sure I had my words in the proper order, so they would make sense when I consulted them later. I looked at her check book and bank and credit card statements. I looked in her medicine cabinet, in her jewelry case, her tub, and I can tell you that as far as I could see she lived a perfectly normal life. A perfectly average American life. No kinks, nothing hinky, nothing—even in hindsight—to predict the events of that week.

So, nine colorful throws—make of them what you will.

Maybe I tried too hard—am still trying too hard—to understand why she did what she did. Perhaps there's no mystery here, nothing too difficult to understand: she didn't want to get into trouble, and she needed time to think her way out of a terrible situation. A perfectly ordinary response to a most unfortunate accident. A hit-and-run with a twist, that's all (though her lawyer didn't see it that way; and she, in turn, did not see matters the way her lawyer did). Whatever the case, she went to bed, buried herself in pillows, and slept and slept.

When she woke, it was after four in the afternoon and already winter-dark outside. She made herself a pot of coffee and sat at the kitchen table, waiting for Jeremy to return. In court, she said that she did not open the door to the garage; she never once looked in at what she took to be a corpse stuck in the front window of her car. Instead, she insisted, she sat in a kind of stupor, a vacancy, not thinking or unable to think, wrapped in a warm terry towel bathrobe Jeremy had given her for a present, one leg over the other, elbow on the table, chin in the palm of her hand, staring, coffee going cold, untouched. She reported that she never even turned up the thermostat, despite the storm brewing outside.

Over the course of the day, the weather had turned, becoming much colder, a front of howling Arctic air from Canada sweeping over the lake, collecting energy and moisture to turn into heavy, churning snow. Icy winds buffeted the house and the snow began to pile up. Sometime after 8:00 p.m., Jeremy knocked on the front door and let himself in, a blast of cold reaching through the living room, via the open floor plan, and into the kitchen. She told me that the frozen draft around her exposed ankles snapped her from her torpor and she looked up at her friend through her one good eye, her right eye having swollen and crusted shut while she slept.

"You look terrible. I really wish you'd let me take you to a doctor."

"No."

"There might be more glass stuck in your eye. You'll go blind."

In a few moments, they once more arrived at an uneasy stalemate and she asked if he would look into the garage.

"Why? What's happened?"

"Nothing. I don't know. I haven't looked."

"All day? You never looked once?"

He told the court that he then cursed and suggested, under his breath, that the crash must have done some damage to her head, but if she heard him she did not let on. Not wanting to, but not knowing what else to do, he picked up the flashlight from the table and opened the door to the garage.

It hit them both at the same time:

"What is that smell?"

It was, they both acknowledged, awful. A terrible, palpable stench, and it filled the kitchen.

She whispered:

"The body's starting to rot."

"In one day?"

"How long does it take?"

Grabbing a tea towel from beside the sink, he covered his face and went into the garage. He flicked the light over the body, trying not to retch from the stink that penetrated through the damp cloth. He called back:

"It doesn't smell like something rotting."

She was standing in the doorway, holding the collar of her robe over her face:

"What does it smell like?"

"Shit."

He quickly crossed from the car to the door and, forcing them both into the kitchen, slammed it shut.

She said that that meant he was dead for sure.

"He shit himself so that means he's dead?"

"Isn't the last thing that happens before you die is that you shit yourself?"

"Maybe if you're hanged, but not in an accident."

"People in car crashes don't shit themselves?"

"What do I know what people in car crashes do?"

"So you don't know."

He said he was going home.

She told him that they had to do something about the smell, or someone would notice.

When I interviewed him after his trial, Jeremy told me that after this point nothing made sense anymore, and that he soon did not have the heart to argue with her about anything. She said maybe the meter guy; he said they didn't do that anymore, it was all done remotely by computer. She said maybe her dad would come by to snow-blow the driveway and sidewalks; he said to call him and tell him not to bring over the snow-blower, that Jeremy was going to shovel. She said it would make her entire house smell; he said to keep the door closed. She said she couldn't have a shit smell in her garage; he wanted to know what he was supposed to do about that? Seizing her chance, she told him that he had to clean it up.

"What? No damn way."

"Somebody has to."

"This is your mess. You do it."

"I'd be sick. I couldn't do it. You have to."

He gave in, and their discussion turned to how best to proceed, Jeremy insisting that there was no best way, that all of this was madness, worse than criminal, depraved, and how could it be that he, a grown man (evidently not in his right mind), found himself in someone else's garage, somehow responsible for cleaning the shit off what might very well be a dead person? After assuring her that there was no way he was going to wipe a corpse's ass, they settled on hooking up the garden hose to the big sink in the mud- and laundry room behind the kitchen, and running the hose, with the spray nozzle attached, into the garage.

After retrieving the garden hose caddy from the far corner of the garage, he carried it into the mudroom, hefting the heavy hose and plastic contraption into the sink and unwinding enough of the hose to reach the faucet. Unfortunately, as he discovered, the coupling was too big for the end of the faucet—which wasn't designed, at any rate, to have something screwed onto it other than the aerator—and he had to dig around on the workbench against the back wall of the garage to find a roll of duct tape. Back in the mudroom, he forced the end of the hose over the aerator, stopping after it had traveled several inches over the tall, gooseneck spout. Taking the duct tape, he wrapped it several times around the end of the hose and cold steel until he thought the seal could take the back pressure without sliding or popping off; taking hold of the spray nozzle end, he began to unwind the hose, snaking from the mudroom, around the kitchen table and chairs, and out into the garage.

"Now what?"

She handed him a pair of yellow rubber kitchen gloves:

"You'll have to pull his pants down."

"This is a nightmare."

From the doorway, she called to him that he would have to begin with the boots.

For a long time, he stood, repelled at what he had to do, and still uncertain about how best to proceed. At last, he made up his mind and, breathing through his mouth, he approached the body and began, rather gingerly, to hike up the coat and hoodie and two—as it turned out—shirts. With considerable twisting and tugging, he managed to work the shirts free from the jeans and to bunch the shirts and outer-garments up around the beginning of the ribcage.

The smell, he told the court, was incredible. Why one shit should smell so bad, he didn't know, but it did.

Next, he unbuttoned the jeans and forced down the zipper.

He said that, at this point, his face was unbearably close to the body, and that the body had an unwashed pong of its own.

Going around to stand almost behind the person, he tugged on the jeans and long underwear, working them as if he were grappling with a lively steering wheel on a bumpy road. After a minute or two of wrestling with the soggy, reeking garments, he had the buttocks exposed. His legs all but giving out, he staggered but managed to steady himself against the car:

"It's a woman."

When the prosecutor asked him if, at that moment, the nature of the assault and kidnapping changed, Jeremy replied that discovering the person to be a woman probably made it all that much worse, though he conceded that events had gotten so far out of hand he didn't know if anything could make it worse than it already was.

"What do you mean it's a woman?"

"What do I mean? See for yourself. It's a woman."

He told me that he wanted to run, to throw up, pass out, scream, smash his skull against the car, to open the big door and call to the neighbors, to lie down in the deepening snow and die. Yet somehow, he fought off panic and dread, and re-set himself to the task at hand. Turning back to the body, he decided to take off the boots and to throw them in the nearby garbage can. He then worked the pants and underwear down over the legs and threw them in the trash as well, leaving only the clammy, greasy wool socks. Taking a plastic grocery bag from his pocket, he steeled himself and, pulling the bag over his hand like a mitten, reached between the cheeks, scooping most of the dry, compacted turd into his hand as if he were picking up dog waste from the sidewalk. Gripping the excrement, he used his other hand to pull the bag around it and then tied the handles into a double-knot and tossed it after the jeans and long underwear.

Once again fighting off the urge to vomit, he picked up the

spray nozzle and considered how to wash away the rest of the ordure. He walked to the back of the car, dragging the hose with him, and stepped up on the narrow bumper. He had a perfect angle:

"Turn on the water."

"It'll spray all over the wall and work bench."

By this point, he recalled, he was trembling so badly that he could barely hold onto the nozzle. Climbing down from the bumper's narrow ledge, he looked around the garage for something to block the spray. Finding a nylon tarp and stepladder, he clumsily tacked—despite her objections—the tarp to the ceiling so that it hung down to the headlights, and he then returned to the back ledge.

"Turn on the water."

She disappeared from the doorway and a moment later the hose jumped as it filled. Taking aim, he squeezed the nozzle. The water erupted with considerable pressure and he scoured the area as well as he could, the deflected spray and bits of waste tap-tapping against the tarp and pooling on the floor. When he'd had enough, he released the trigger and let the hose slither through his hand until the nozzle hit the floor. Tumbling awkwardly from the bumper, he reeled toward the kitchen, stopping only long enough to slip off his wet shoes on the mat in front of the door. He collided with the table and collapsed onto the nearest chair.

"You can't leave her like that."

He stared at her stupidly:

"What?"

"You can't leave her like that."

"Like what? Dead?"

"Uncovered."

She handed him a pair of sweat pants. They read *Cleveland State* across the seat.

"I'm not going out there again. No way."

"Just slip these on her."

Furious, staggering to his feet, he towered over her:

"How long is this going to go on?"

She thrust the sweat pants into his hands.

When he finished cleaning up the mess, hosing down the tarp and sweeping the water to the drain and the bits of debris into a dustpan and emptying the contents in the trash which he then closed with a tie and carried to the curb, he climbed into his car and never returned to her house.

IV.

AFTER HE HAD CLEANED UP the woman in the window and wrestled her into the sweats, Jeremy departed and the young woman, in keeping with her previous conduct, had gone to bed, burying herself once more in the assorted pillows. As before, she slept and slept, awakening the next morning well after 10:00 a.m. That day, and the next, she claimed in court, passed, but she has a rather imperfect memory of what, exactly, she did in that time. She did not go into the garage, she reported, and she did not make herself any food, and she seems to have spent the time sleeping or sitting at the kitchen table, detached and inert, staring out the window at the storm.

The storm, meanwhile, had settled over the city. The winds from the north were bitter and heavy with snow and conditions outside had become treacherous, evenly deadly, with officials warning people to stay inside and the police doing sweeps for the homeless in order to take them to shelters. People were asked to check in on the elderly. The temperature didn't climb above minus thirty during the day, and crews worked around the clock trying to clear the main arteries, hauling the snow to empty lots and municipal fields all over the city.

On the second night, just after 9:00 p.m., she stirred herself and decided that she needed cream for her coffee and a pack of cigarettes (though she hadn't really smoked since college). A few blocks away was a local gas station and mini-mart. She proceeded, she explained, as if she were some sort of machine, an automaton, dressing herself in warm clothing, including a new winter coat that her mother had picked up for her, and a hat, scarf, and gloves. She slipped on her big winter boots, found her car keys on the hook near the door to the garage where she always left them, and went into the garage.

She claimed that, by this point, she did not know that there was a body embedded in her Priam. She did not see a body when she went to the car; she did not see a body when she climbed into the driver's seat and fired-up the engine.

The body, we know, had by then slithered further inside the car. Perhaps the extra weight of the water-soaked coat and hoodie had dragged her downward, or perhaps all the commotion had caused more of the window to fragment, thereby enlarging the opening. Perhaps both. Whatever the case, the crown of her head now rested on the floor mat amid the gummy slicks of hair and blood and bits of shattered glass. Her neck, taking the weight, was oddly and abruptly bent, her chin pressing against the top of the sternum. Now, her torso was fully inside the car, with her hips and legs projecting outside the windscreen, almost as if a diver closing toward the pike or jackknife position.

Her claim not to know there was a body in the car beside her certainly taxes credulity, but her lawyer hammered away at the point as evidence of a dissociative state following a significantly traumatic experience—such as losing control of one's car and striking another person—wherein one endures, in the course of the calamity, a stunning strike to the head—as occurs frequently in car crashes where the front airbags deploy but the automobile does not have head-level side-impact airbags; he provided statistics and CDC reports and offered PowerPoint slides and charts to illustrate and reinforce what he called the facts—plainly in evidence—of the matter.

Whatever view one takes, we do know that she climbed into

her car, put on the seatbelt, turned on the car, adjusted the rear-view mirror, activated the built-in seat-warmer, switched on the satellite radio, pressed the button to open the garage door, and put the transmission into reverse. By then, over a foot of snow had fallen, and the clouds were still thick and heavy with snow driven by bitter, swirling winds. She took her foot off the break and gunned the engine, the car slewing backwards down the driveway and into the unplowed and deeply rutted street. The snow was so thick that the car immediately became hung-up, the heavy powder rising to the undercarriage and higher on the sides where the weight of the car had not compressed it. About a third of the way into the street, she yanked the stick into drive and lurched to the left, the front wheels spinning uselessly in the thick snow. As her father had taught her, she gave the engine more gas and as the car strained forward she pressed on the brake, holding the car at its slight apogee. She then popped the stick into reverse, let the car fall back, hitting the gas at the same time, the all-season radials struggling for purchase. In this manner she rocked forwards and backwards until she gathered enough momentum to reach the ruts in the middle of the street. Once clear of the higher snow, she slipped into drive and began to wobble, the front end sheering this way then that, in the direction of the mini-mart. In the course of her drive, she passed several other vehicles and one even honked but kept going—perhaps they were afraid of getting stuck if they slowed down. From the slow, snow-laden neighborhood streets she made it onto the wider and somewhat plowed streets of the commercial area—the snowplows had pushed the snow to the middle of the streets, creating high, cement-like barricades—and managed to steer around a minivan either stalled or stuck in one of the periodic, wind-driven drifts. Depressing the signal to indicate a left-hand turn, she hammered the accelerator to the floor and shot through a gap in the mid-road snow-wall—without being able to see, perhaps, if there was oncoming traffic—and into the parking lot of the gas station. She turned off the engine and climbed from the car.

There were a couple of kids standing in front of the mini-mart, evidently enjoying the snow and the spectacle of cars slip-sliding towards their various destinations. They wore Cavaliers caps and the sort of oversized jackets favored by snowboarders. Trading looks, they watched her climb from her car:

"Dude [and I repeat this word not because I love it—quite the contrary—but because that's what he said, according to his own testimony], there's someone sticking out of your car."

He and his buddy then turned toward one another and traded jovial elbows and shoves.

The other said:

"Yeah, and it says *Cleveland State* on the ass."

At that they both cracked-up.

She paid them no attention and went into the store and bought a half-pint of cream and a pack of Salem's. When she left the store, she passed them again, once more ignoring them—or not knowing they were there at all—and got in her car and darted crookedly into the street. After watching her sway out of sight, they went into the store to tell the clerk what they had seen. In turn, he nodded at them and went back to restocking the candy bars in front of the register. They went back outside and, using one of their cell phones, dialed 911 and told the emergency operator about the woman in the tiny blue car with someone stuck in the front window. After asking him to repeat that, the operator told him that their system had caller I.D. and that it was a misdemeanor to prank call 911.

Of course, the tape of this conversation was later entered into evidence and the operator, though not reprimanded, was encouraged to route all suspicious calls through her supervisor. The prosecutor, for his part, said he was sure no one could blame her for not believing the boys. After all, who would hit someone and then drive around with the body protruding from the car?

The two boys, for their part, hung up and went to one of their places to play video games.

After she got home, the car once more back in the garage, she made an instant coffee, fussed about to find some matches, opened the cigarettes, lit one, and called Jeremy.

Despite himself, he answered.

V.

HE ANSWERED THE PHONE, and they talked—the phone records indicate—for a long while, but he refused to go to her place. Later on, neither one could recall the substance of the conversation; mostly, it seems, they argued over whether or not he would go to her house. At last, he hung up and, as far as I know, has not spoken with her again; in court, she said that he had never really been her boyfriend—they had gone on a few inconsequential dates—and that she really did not find him attractive—he was too heavy and had soft hands. At most, he was a guy-friend, while she mostly hung out with her girl-friends from work or the club.

At any rate, he hung up, and a couple of days later, she was arrested.

He had not, of course, ratted her out.

After another day of being in a daze and surviving on coffee and cigarettes, she awoke the following morning, ate a proper breakfast, showered, dressed, and caught the bus to work, her right eye still an oozing, gluey mess. Her mother, not having heard from her for a few days, decided to visit her to see if all was well. Also having a key, she let herself in the front door and after finding that her daughter was not home, thought to check in the garage to see if her car was there—she was worried, with the snow still piling up and the temperatures hovering around minus twenty, about her driving in such bad weather. By this time, the body had fallen all the way through the window and the mother, alarmed by damage, tiptoed over to the car and saw a figure, wearing her daughter's sweatpants, curled up awkwardly on the floor and passenger's seat. For an instant, she thought it was her daughter, dead, stuffed in the car by some murderer, but in a frenzied groping at the body discovered it was not.

In turn, as she explained to the police, she thought that a homeless person had, in the process of looking for someplace warm to sleep, broken into the garage and, finding the door to the kitchen locked, had smashed the car window both out of anger and as a means to access the additional shelter of the vehicle. Upon reaching this conclusion, she dialed 911.

In this way, the body came to light.

Officially Jane Doe No. 67, for that year, the City of Cleveland.

For a time, there was some confusion over what had happened. At first, the police thought that perhaps the mother was correct, but they had to revise that opinion once the coroner arrived and determined that the woman had suffered catastrophic head and neck injuries.

The coroner also determined that she had been dead for less than twenty-four hours.

Had she done this to herself? That is, had she, in a fit of desperation or madness—perhaps she was schizophrenic, as the homeless often were, anyway?—tried to break into the car by using her head as a battering ram? Had she been trying to kill herself? But how, then, to explain the damage to the roof and front end of the car? And, if she were looking for shelter, the garage was heated, so she could have lain down on the floor and perhaps been warm enough. And, where were her shoes or boots, and how did she come to have on one piece of the resident's clothing? No, there seemed to have been some sort of accident, and the detective in charge at the scene ordered that the young woman, then at work, be taken into custody.

She was arrested at the title company and the mother, understandably distraught, said afterwards that if she had thought for one moment that her daughter had been in an accident she would not have called the police. She would have called her husband. Nevertheless, once she heard that her daughter was to be arrested, she did call her husband, and he got out the yellow pages and found a lawyer to meet his daughter at the police station.

As luck would have it, they found a good lawyer. A diligent reader of newspapers and all sorts of government and automobile and insurance industry reports about accidents and settlements, he was among the first lawyers in the country to notice that a number of Priams had been involved in an unusual number of unusual accidents. The model, it appears, had a strange tendency to accelerate on its own. From a certain point of view it was the perfect car: it crashed itself into all sorts of things, including people.

At trial, he argued that the car had, just then, suddenly accelerated and that the driver had no control over the vehicle. Sadly, at that moment, Jane Doe had begun to cross at the sidewalk in front of U.S. Grant High. Through no fault of the driver, a terrible thing occurred. At the point of impact, he explained, the front airbags deployed but the momentum of the uncontrollably accelerating automobile caused it to spin out of control and when it hit the curb the driver's head was driven sideways and then back in the other direction, colliding with the upper door frame. She sustained, he reported, an appalling concussion that thereafter adversely affected her cognitive reasoning skills. He produced a doctor's report to that effect.

The car hit the woman, and the driver, having been traumatized by the event, was not, subsequent to the event, in her right mind. She was, in a word, not guilty. In fact, she was as much a victim as the homeless person.

His strategy worked—the prosecutor did his best, but had a difficult time accounting for why she had kept the body in her garage and then had gone for a drive, during the worst blizzard of the year, for a half-pint of cream and a pack of cigarettes. Though he did not say it aloud, I sensed that he probably thought that she was either a sociopath or that she very likely had been injured in the crash. He had no other evidence for the former, and her lawyer provided all the evidence the jury needed for the latter.

Subsequent to the criminal trial, the same lawyer and his partners filed suit against the automobile manufacturer, and they won a considerable judgment. The young woman used some of her money to take a holiday in Cabo.

Jeremy, not enduring a blow to the head at any point during that week, was tried separately and convicted of kidnapping, assault, and manslaughter. When I interviewed him in prison some months after the trial, he had lost a lot of weight and his hands were coarse, nicked, and stained—he told me that he had discovered weight-lifting and was working in the prison's auto shop, learning a new trade for when he was released. When I asked him what he thought, now, about his friend, he told me that although he never wanted to see her again, he did wish her well. What was done was done, and all he wanted to do was serve his time and get on with his life.

For me, there will be no book—there was some talk of the driver and her lawyer writing a book about her ordeal—but my ability to put words in order, since leaving Ramstein, has begun to re-degrade, the words I want popping around like bingo balls inside my skull, the words on the page scuttling here and there like ants defending a colony under attack. When I speak, I sound like I'm drunk.

Two more details:

First, when I asked her, after the trial, if she agreed with her lawyer's arguments about why she had left the woman embedded in the window, she shook her head:

"No. He didn't get it right. I did hit my head—they found my hair and traces of my blood on the doorframe—but that wasn't it. I just wanted people to like me. Nobody likes someone who kills a homeless person."

Second, she told me—now that all was said and done—that she had lied to the police, and to her lawyer, and to the court. On the night before her drive to the mini-mart, she had gone into the garage. She had gone because she could hear the woman in the window talking. She had listened at the door for a time and then, picking up one of the kitchen chairs, had gone out to sit by the passenger's side of the car. As she listened, without speaking, she heard the woman say that she had been born in St. Louis, and that she had lived in Detroit for a time where she had done all right. She had had a job and a couple of kids, but for some reason things began to go out of focus and she lost her job, and not long after that, her kids, and while things sometimes came back into focus, mostly they didn't. On more than one occasion, as our young woman listened, the dying woman said her name, and said that she was afraid to die and that she did not know where she was or why she was so cold and in such pain, her head pounding and pounding, but still she did not want to die and if her children were lost to her, she was sad to think that they might be sad to hear that she had died.

Stones

STARLIGHT, DIFFUSED by swirling snow, fell through the curtainless window, an icy rectangle laid over the plank floor, the worn throw rug, and up and over the simple wooden table and chair set in the corner. Hanging from the back of the chair was a thick workman's jacket, its dull tan color glowing bronze in the pale light. Folded neatly on the seat of the chair were lined wool pants, a heavy wool sweater, a plaid work shirt, long cotton underwear, and a pair of patched wool socks. Work boots, carefully aligned, sat at the foot of the chair. A box, tied with twine, sat beside the boots. The rest of the room was dark. Darragh, lying beneath several blankets, stared at the table and chair and his work clothes. He thought that if he stood in the patch of weak light, he would be able to see the plume of his breath.

He had heard his father, Owen, rise heavily from the bed in the next room, had heard the creak of the bed and the floor as the old man set his weight on the boards. He had heard his father's slow steps across the floor toward his chair and clothes and boots, the shuffling of his dressing, the squeak of the chair as he settled his massive body onto the plain wood chair as he pulled on and tied his work boots. He had then heard Owen take the last few heavy steps, his boots solid on the floor, to the door. He had heard the old man's deep wheeze as he stepped from his room into the hall leading to the kitchen. This morning, instead of knocking on Darragh's door to call him to work as he always did, Owen had kept going, and did not stop in the kitchen to add more wood to the stove, did not stop to make tea. There was no clang of iron or wood on iron, no running of water and the setting of the kettle on the stove. His father had kept going, through the kitchen and out the back door into the cold and falling snow. After that, he could not hear where the old man had gone, whether he had gone to the barn to feed the cattle and horses or to the shed to work on the plow he was readying for spring.

An hour later, perhaps near six, he heard his mother rise, and though nearly as tall as Owen, Siobhan moved without making the floor sigh or creak. He could hear only the occasional rustle and step. Her door opened and closed, and she made her way to the kitchen, stoked the fire and set the kettle. Reluctantly, Darragh slid from beneath the covers and swung his legs out and set his feet on the boards.

The cold wrapped around him, and sitting up he was able to see out the window to the yard. Thick, lazy snow drifted downwards, moving in slow swirls, catching and re-catching the light, giving the yard and trees and barn and fields beyond a pale blue cast.

Darragh shivered, but did not rise. He stared out the window, but could see no tracks leading to the barn. At last, brought back to himself by the sounds of his mother preparing breakfast, he heaved himself from the bed and stepped to the chair and his clothes. Dressed, he felt no warmer. He opened his door, squinting against the light from the kitchen, and looked down the hall. The downward doorframe to the kitchen bisected Siobhan, her back and shoulders and arms to the elbows visible, her face and front and lower arms and hands out of view as she leaned over her pans. She wore, as she always did, a shapeless dress, with a colorless, well-worn apron.

When he stepped into the kitchen, his mother looked over to him, her eyes expectant.

He sat down and she placed a steaming cup of tea on the table before him and nudged the sugar bowl and spoon forward. He nodded his appreciation and slowly measured out two spoonfuls of sugar and deliberately swirled the spoon in the tea. Siobhan, still gazing at him, turned away, returning to the sausage and potatoes frying in a large cast iron pan. Darragh sipped the scalding tea and set the cup down, keeping his hands around the tiny mug for its bit of heat. He did not look at his mother, but kept his head down, staring at the amber liquid and its curls of steam.

When Siobhan set a full plate of sausage, potatoes, and eggs in front of her son, she looked once more at him, but he would not look up. She turned away, collecting the pan and utensils and poured a little soapy water from the sink into the pan.

As Darragh ate, he kept his eyes on his plate, but now and again he looked up at the black and white photograph of Hugh, his brother, who had died on his first day at the war. It hung on the wall above the table, Hugh in uniform, grinning, his cap at a jaunty angle, his cheeks high and light, his face young and thin. He had been nineteen when he signed up, and twenty when he had been deployed with the Seaforth Highlanders in North Africa. On his first day ashore, the Highlanders attached to Montgomery's Eighth, he had crouched beside a wall during a mortar attack and the wall had fallen and sheared off his legs and crushed his chest and he had been buried in Sicily. Of all his brothers and sisters, Darragh felt the greatest affection for Hugh, and he grieved still at the way he had died. He hoped that it had happened all at once, and that his youngest brother had felt no pain and did not glimpse his legs lying apart from him, the blood rushing onto the sand or rock. He hoped that Hugh had been knocked unconscious, and that he had not lain there gasping for breath, knowing only agony and creeping darkness.

He felt his mother's hand settle gently on his arm and he looked away from the photograph and turned toward her. Her eyes still held the same expectant look, mingled now, he could see, with thoughts of Hugh. He had been everyone's favorite, always smiling, just a little sly, the baby of the family, fifteen years younger than Darragh. Siobhan looked away from the image, and then at Darragh.

Darragh shrugged, and said:

"It's this ground."

"I know."

She shook her head:

"I know it as well as anyone. If I had the making of this world. . . ."

Darragh nodded, without looking at her:

"I know."

Siobhan seemed relieved and she turned to the stove and reached for the kettle. She poured more tea into his cup and reset the kettle:

"If any of us had the making of the world, well, then."

She smiled a weak smile and touched his hair, almost all grey.

Darragh glanced out the window above the sink. Snow continued to fall, and the wind seemed to be picking up. Snow pelted the window and deeper in the yard he thought he could see it gather in gusts, rushing downward or swirling upward or skittering along the iron-hard drifts running between the barn and the house. He took a deep breath:

"I heard poppa go outside."

She nodded, and turned away, her wide shoulders falling. She eased herself onto the chair opposite Darragh and stared out the window.

"I heard poppa go outside. But I don't see a light in the barn."

Siobhan turned to look at her son, her face showing fatigue and sadness. He waited, but when she did not speak, he stood, taking a last gulp of tea:

"Breakfast was fine. I'm glad for it."

He washed up at the sink and headed back to his room.

He pushed open the door, but stood for a moment. The same cold rectangle of light fell across the floor and chair and table, and he stared at his coat on the back of the chair and the box sitting on the floor. Then, with a couple of steps, he reached the table and swung his heavy coat over his arms and shoulders in one motion and then tugged on the fronts to settle it around his neck. He pulled his wool cap and leather gloves from either pocket, put them on, and checked to make sure his keys were still in the right side pocket. He then bent and jabbed his thick fingers underneath the securely fastened twine and picked up the box, packed with a few extra shirts, pants, socks, and underclothes. He straightened, turned, and walked from his room, closing the door behind him.

His mother was no longer in the kitchen, but he had not expected her to be. He kept walking and pushed open the backdoor, the harsh, freezing wind cutting through even his thick jacket. He could feel snow sting his face. He looked down. His father's tracks, though beginning to fill, were still visible, but they did not head toward the barn or the shed.

Darragh muttered:

"What now?"

And repeated a phrase his father used when angry:

"Jumped up Jesus Christ."

He walked slowly to the old Ford, leaning into the swirling snow, his shoulders up and chin down, trying to protect his neck and face. When he arrived at the truck, he heaved on the door and lifted himself into the cab, setting the box beside him. He slammed the door closed and, shivering already, put the key in the ignition. The engine stuttered, but caught, and he turned the fan and heater onto full. He sat for a few moments, and then swung open the door and stepped out, reaching into the back for the broom. He began sweeping the snow from the windows and hood, and the loosened snow swirled around him, settling on his cap and jacket and back on the hood and windows. At last satisfied that he had done what he could, he replaced the broom and looked back at the house.

His mother stood at the kitchen window, but through the snow he could not read her expression. He waved, and she waved back. As he walked back toward the cab, he watched her and she continued to wave.

From out of the moiling snow and darkness, Darragh heard a faint, but sharp concussion. Stopping short, he tried to locate and recognize the sound. The wind puffed around him, and it was all he could hear. Then, the concussion sounded again. It seemed to come from the fields beyond the barn. It sounded again, louder, cutting through the wind and snow, sharp, harsh, solid. He could not place it. It sounded perhaps like a hammer on something hard, but that was not it.

Darragh held his breath.

The strike again, but from far away, from somewhere out in the dark, snow-deadened fields. When the concussion sounded again, Darragh realized what it was. Aghast, he could not move his feet, but turned his shoulders and looked back at the house. His mother was no longer at the window.

When the clap rang again, Darragh heard it and felt it in his hands.

The backdoor of the house banged open, and Siobhan, bundled in her winter coat and scarf and men's wool hat stood on the step, her arm holding the door. She called out:

"Darragh, what's wrong?"

The concussion came again, and then again, and Siobhan turned to face the fields.

When it rang out once more, Darragh felt it in his hands and wrists, could feel the force of the striking, could feel painful vibrations in his palms and the bones of his forearms. When it sounded again, the jolt ran higher, over his elbows and into his shoulders. Once more, and he felt it in his chest. All at once, his mother was beside him, wrapping her arms around his closest arm:

"What is that?"

She sounded afraid.

He looked at her, but could not speak. The pounding came again and again, each strike distinct, piercing the wind and snow, painfully sharp in their ears. Siobhan began to shake her head in disbelief. Clinging to her son, he a head taller, immense, she tall, shapeless, the wind and snow gusting around and through them. Then the concussions abruptly stopped. Siobhan kept shaking her head, side to side, side to side, her eyes wide and disbelieving. When it sounded again, they both recoiled as if struck with something solid.

Coming back to herself, Siobhan pulled her arms from Darragh and pushed him toward the cab of the truck:

"You go, Darragh."

He shook his head.

The concussions kept coming, but slower and slower, and then fainter and fainter.

"You go, Darragh!"

He shook his head again, and looked down at the snow. He thought he could drive his boot through the snow and frozen, peaty ground. He thought he could drive his fist through the ground and find a stone, a stone waiting, through water and frost and ice and sun, to work its way to the surface. With his other hand, he could reach into the soil and find another, rounded, heavy, hard. Those two and a hundred or a thousand more.

Siobhan was pushing on him, urging him toward the cab. The concussions had stopped altogether. He said:

"You won't be fine. So don't say you will."

"It doesn't matter."

"I could go out there."

She stopped pushing and looked up at him:

"Why?"

With that, Siobhan stepped around her son and pulled open the truck door and waited until he had climbed inside to slam it shut, the wind churning still, the snow and ice swept aloft or plunging toward the earth.

Robbie

ONE OF THE THINGS I liked about Robbie was that he talked even less than I did. If the foreman gave him instructions, or somebody asked him to lend a hand, he usually just nodded and did what he was told. If someone said something funny, he would grin, but he never joined in the jokes. For lunch, he usually ate by himself, sitting high on the fence gazing down at the cattle or hogs in the pens, munching on his sandwich, sipping his Coke, keeping his own counsel, staying apart from the others in the tiny break room.

Most people are like wolves—I won't say dogs—and when they get together, instead of biting at one another's cheeks and sniffing, they talk. They have nothing to say, nothing that needs to be said, but they talk anyway, their way of fitting in, performing the rituals, finding their place in the hierarchy.

I heard Doyle, one of the meatcutters, say that he thought the Joker, or so he and some of the others called Robbie, was a fucking retard who didn't even know how to talk, but I kept my mouth shut while a couple of others in the cutting room joined in.

"That boy's a halfwit, I'm telling ya."

Slazak, the head meatcutter, said:

"He ain't so bad. He does his job. More than I can say for you."

"What, clean-up? You have to be stupid to stand that."

One of the young women said she thought he'd be cute if it weren't for the scars and how shy he was. Although I had never asked him, you didn't need to be Sherlock Holmes to figure out what had happened to cause the scars and toothlessness. As a kid, Robbie must have been snowmobiling and had suffered the classic, sometimes killing accident: he had driven through a barbed-wire fence, the upper strand catching him across the mouth, ripping out the front teeth top and bottom and slicing and tearing open his cheeks most of the way to the back of the jaw. He'd been lucky not to be decapitated, and although he had a plate for his uppers, he perhaps couldn't afford or didn't think he needed one on the bottom, and his lower lip sagged inward.

"Watch it, Jodie. I doubt he's eighteen."

"Show the Joker yer tits and see what he says! Now I think about it, how about you show me yer tits?"

Jodie, barely eighteen herself, was about to reply when Slazak interrupted:

"Knock it off, Doyle."

One of the other things I liked about Robbie was that, just as Slazak said, he did his job. He kept his head down and worked steadily. Like me, he showed up just before midday, and we worked on the kill floor, or in the cutting room running the grinder or silent cutter or patty machine, or wherever they needed us. After everybody left at four, we divided the clean-up between us, Robbie usually taking the kill floor and pressure washing the cutting boards and equipment that I would disassemble and dolly or roll back to the kill floor to be cleaned. In the meantime, I would use a scrapper and pressure washer to clean the floors and walls in the cutting room and coolers, and then mop the lunch area and office. Robbie always showed up early, and he didn't hang fire when he was supposed to be moving sides out of the chill cooler and into the cutting room cooler or loading the delivery truck. He didn't sneak product out the side door and into his vehicle when the owner, Mr. Vickers, always too busy working to run the place, wasn't looking. He didn't hassle the women, and if we were working together and it was time for a break, he always passed me a cigarette as we went out the backdoor by the unloading chutes.

When I thanked him, he would just nod.

Far as I know, I was pretty much the only one who bothered with him and after we finished the clean-up I would sometimes dig a six-pack out of the cooler in the back of my truck and hand him one and we sat on the tailgate, smoking and drinking beer, looking across the highway at the trees mostly blocking our view of the river. Sometimes, we would catch a glimpse of a drift boat or canoe or some kids on inner tubes lazing away a late summer afternoon.

One time I asked him:

"You ever go fishing?"

He shook his head.

"Floating?"

He nodded:

"I been a few times. You know, with some friends and some girls."

"Nice."

He shrugged, and most days after a couple he would say thanks for the beers and climb into his truck, a late model Chevy which he kept immaculately clean, and head, I supposed, for his tiny apartment in town. I didn't know much about him, and as I only worked summers, I didn't see him for months at a time and even when I was around I rarely saw him in town.

Mostly we worked on the kill floor, and since he went back to clean-up fulltime—a shit job if there ever was one—while I was back in Brunswick, I tried to take more than my share of the crappy jobs, like emptying the paunches into barrels and hauling the barrels to the dump to spill off the back of the trailer, the half-digested contents and muck inevitably splashing back onto your face and arms and hair. Or like digging the immense blood clots and hair and hog toenails from the collection pit in the floor at end of the line, just before the big chill cooler door, or hauling the offal barrels into the hot, super-stinking offal room where they waited to be picked up by the truck from the rendering plant in Missoula. On beef days, we took turns running the stock into the knocking box and stunning them or running the splitting saw and washing and shrouding the sides before pushing them into the chill cooler to begin setting up and ageing. On hog days, we did the same, sometimes working the splitting saw or dumping the still twitching carcasses into the scalding tank and dehairer, blow-torching the areas the metal-tooth'd paddles couldn't quite reach. There's nothing like the smell of burning jowl- or ass-hair, nothing like the noise of the dehairer as it spins a carcass, the blow-torch adding a roaring, blue- and orange-flamed whoosh to the clanking and clanging and stink.

One day, late in the summer, while I was washing the bone dust from the spine of a steer I had just split, I felt a tap on my leg. I looked down from the hydraulic platform and saw Robbie holding the old, greasy, and thoroughly beat-up and duct-taped .22 we used for stunning. He was looking up at me and motioned that I should follow him. I hooked the hose back on its ring and climbed down. Weaving our way around the skinner and the gutter, and past Stovall as he was cutting the bung on a heifer he had stuck and hung by the achilles on a spreader, I shadowed Robbie out the back door. He stopped immediately at the head of the knocking box and gestured at the animal inside.

It was an immense and immensely muscled bull, an old guy, as docile as an old dog, and he was so thick that his shoulders were pressing on the one side against the fence of the nearest holding pen and on the other against the knocking box door. And, he was so long that Robbie hadn't been able to close the gate behind him, and his back haunch twisted back into the narrow passageway leading up to the box. Blood was running down the old bull's forehead and around his eyes and down his muzzle and flowed in a stream from either nostril. He was so tall that he looked us in the eye, and he stared placidly, unalarmed and tranquil, a long and happy life behind him and no sense of his immediate fate.

Destined for hamburger, he was so large and so muscly that even boned-out and cut into strips, the meat would bind the grinder and cause it to overheat and smoke, and we'd be forever taking off the cap, plate, and knife and unclogging the worm.

I looked at Robbie and he half-grinned and shrugged:

"I shot him three times."

I looked back at the bull's forehead, and sure enough, there were three holes tightly together, each singed black and running with blood. In order not to introduce lead into a carcass, we used .22 longs with plastic tips, and evidently the old boy's hide was so heavy, and his brainpan so thick, that the bullets wouldn't penetrate or at least drive a splinter of bone into the brain. Still, he must have had a headache, yet it didn't seem to bother him or he could have walk-pushed his way through the metal frame at the head of the knocking box and back into the alley leading to the pens and unloading chutes. He was big enough, if he wanted to or we pissed him off enough, to break free and go for a walk on 93, north through town and toward Stevensville or south toward Victor, or to head through the trees on the other side of the highway and wade across the Bitterroot. Or, he had the option of heading west, past the big houses on the acreages and up into the mountains.

I reached for the beat-up, stubby rifle, and Robbie dug into the box of bullets on the small shelf against the cinderblock wall. He passed me a round and I chambered it and climbed up the metal fence, trying to get high enough to shoot downward into the bull's head. Poking the barrel against one of the holes already there—the bull half-snorting and shaking his head as if to dislodge a fly—I pulled the trigger. The bullet followed the route of its predecessor and the bull looked up at me, blinking. More blood ran from the spot and from his nostrils, but he hadn't dropped. He flicked his thick white and gray tongue up one nostril and then the other.

I looked at Robbie, and he looked at me.

"That didn't work."

Robbie grinned.

"Tell you what, Robbie. You climb in there and strangle that bastard."

He grinned wider, but also shook his head.

Just then Stovall banged through the door from the kill floor:

"Joker, what in the hell are you guys doing? Give me something."

Robbie had stepped a little behind me, and I gestured at the bull with the rifle:

"A big ol' bull. We shot him four times, but he won't drop."

"Fuckin' idiots. Get the shotgun, and drop that fucker and let's go. Yer wasting time."

Robbie darted past us, heading for the compressor room where we stored the 20-guage and the round-ball slugs. By the time he returned, Stovall had already gone back inside, and Robbie looked at me and then handed over the shotgun and a shell.

"Did you bring the earmuffs?"

He looked uncertain for a moment and then shook his head.

"Fuck it. Stovall'll kill us if we don't drop this guy."

I climbed up high on the fence, high enough to accommodate the long barrel of the shotgun, opened the break-action and chambered the slug. Closing the gun, I climbed to the penultimate rail and aimed down at the top of the bull's forehead and pulled the trigger. The big bull dropped instantly, the ball having smashed through the tough hide and thick bone.

Robbie said something I couldn't hear due to the ringing in my ears—the concussion had rebounded off the wall and thereby hit me twice—and rushed inside and pulled open the gate of the knocking box, but the bull was too immense to fall through the opening so Stovall could stick it and begin skinning and breaking it down. I watched Robbie attempt to pull the bull's massive head in by the ears, without luck.

I said something to him, but I couldn't hear myself. I climbed down and set the shotgun against the wall, and then climbed back up and over the fence and dropped down onto the back of the bull. Through the opening I could see Stovall, and he was clearly pissed and yelling something at Robbie that I couldn't make out. When he looked up at me, still yelling, I flipped him the bird:

"Can't hear you, asshole."

I don't care for people cursing, especially at me. He yelled louder:

"Get that fucking thing in here."

"Good idea. Never thought of that."

Robbie looked alarmed, as well he should have: he needed the job a lot more than I did, and he had to work with Stovall and the others, who treated him indifferently if not poorly, and I could pretty much get away with whatever I wanted. For whatever reason, Mr. Vickers liked me, and I'd been working summers for him since middle school.

My ears were ringing and my head aching and the hanging smoke from the shot was burning my eyes. Pressing my back against the fence, I dug the heels of my rubber boots into the back of the bull and tried to rock the massive bulk down the inclined floor of the knocking box while Robbie wrestled with the head, trying to get it unstuck from the outside of the opening. I pushed and Robbie pulled, but we couldn't get the ton or more of the old bull to roll into the kill floor.

Stovall, rather than trying to help, stood back with his hands on his hips:

"You guys are useless."

At that, I slid down the side of the bull and ducked under

the knocking box door. I wanted to tell Stovall to stop bellowing at Robbie and me, but I gestured instead at the second winch hanging on the rail:

"Tie a chain around his neck and use the come-along."

By this point, the others were looking up from their work.

"Let's see it."

Pulling on the chain for what seemed like ten minutes—the second winch was mechanical, not electric—I at last had enough to wrap around the bull's neck. I passed the hook-end to Robbie and after a struggle he managed to lift the head enough to loop the chain around the massive neck. He snagged the hook around the chain and even as I started pulling on the reverse loop, I motioned to Robbie:

"Get behind the head and try to force it through. If we don't clear the doorframe, he'll just be jammed there."

Sure enough, the winch lifted the head and shoulders, but almost straight up despite my pulling on the taut links with what weight I could, the chain rasping against the cinderblock, the near shoulder jamming against the underside of the opening, the bull's dead eyes bulging as the chain bit in, the noose tightening and tightening. I backed away some of the chain, and Robbie and I grabbed the foreleg, trying to pull the semi-suspended front end through the opening. No luck. I then lowered the chain and hook on the power winch and tied it around one of the back legs, but the bull was so long that the hoof wouldn't come forward enough to fit through the doorway. By this point, the line ahead of us was empty, and the others were standing around, looking at us, offering advice, laughing at our antics. Even the government inspector had suggestions.

We wrestled unsuccessfully with the huge bull until Mr. Vickers came through the swinging doors leading from the hallway to the kill floor. With a single glance he took in the situation, and in less than five minutes, after barking at Stovall and pushing him and the others into action, the big bull slid onto the floor and Stovall stuck him—the blood already clotting and reluctant to drain—and used the largest spreader to hang him from the heels.

Mr. Vickers pulled Robbie and me aside:

"You boys know you're supposed to save those big fellas until last, so if it gets stuck it don't hold up the line? If needs be, one person can handle it from there, and that way I'm not paying everyone to stand around."

We both nodded our apologies.

Exhausted, we got back to work, and it seemed as if every machine in the place had been used, from the tenderizer to the sausage machine, and there was a mess at every station, and we didn't finish clean-up until almost 10:00.

The next day, Wednesday, Robbie didn't show up for work and I was there until past midnight. When he didn't show up on Thursday, Mr. Vickers evidently went to find him, but came back empty-handed. He called me into the office and asked if I knew what had happened to Robbie? I didn't, and he asked me if I would go over to Robbie's apartment and see if he would come to the door and talk to me. He gave me the address and directions, and I took off my helmet and apron, frock coat and boots, slipped on my runners and drove over to a cedar-shake and peeling green-paint four-plex behind the strip mall and truck stop on 93. Robbie's truck wasn't there, but I knocked on his door, anyway. There was no answer and I couldn't hear anyone inside. Walking back to my truck, I moved it to where I thought he could see it if he looked out the windows overlooking the weedy, potholed parking lot. I honked, and then went back and knocked on the door again.

I heard from Jodie that when Stovall, who had also missed work on Wednesday, showed up on Thursday morning driving Robbie's truck, Mr. Vickers had told him to get his helmet and knives and any personal belongings and to get out. He would mail him his last paycheck.

I never saw Robbie again, and I never heard where he had gone when he left town, yet I managed over the next days to piece together a little of what had happened. When Robbie and I had finally finished on Tuesday night, he had stopped by Eddie's, a place favored by hunters, militia-wannabes, and truckers. Some said he was at the bar with Stovall and Doyle and their buddies, but I don't think so. I think he stopped for a hamburger and a beer, if the barkeep would let him have one. At some point, while Robbie was minding his own business, not saying a word, Stovall and Doyle must have gone over to him and then become all mock-friendly and back-slapping, saying, Thanks for picking up the tab, Joker. That's a good boy, Joker. There was no way Robbie would give in to that, and when he shook his head no, as he must have, they and their crew had crowded around and run him outside. A skinny kid of sixteen when his little old father had first brought him to the plant to ask if there was any work, he had bulked-up some but was no match for four or five fully grown men. In a dark pocket of the parking lot, they had beat and stomped him into the gravel, and a sharp one among them, very likely Doyle, had taken Robbie's keys and plucked the title from the glove box. Putting a pen in his hand, they had then moved it across the place you sign when you're selling a vehicle, and that was that. No charges; I doubt anyone even called the cops.

On Friday, I thought to wait at 4:00 by Doyle's car, one of the long, heavy s-hooks in hand, ready to kneecap him for what they had done to Robbie. I thought maybe I would have to hurt him badly, or he would do for me.

Gone to Ground

I.

THEY MOVED QUIETLY, avoiding the endless switchbacks up and down the steep pitch, wary of landmines and patrols, dropping their night vision into place when the cloud cover obscured the stars. The air was thin and cold and Cal could hear the labored breathing of the others as they climbed without break, struggling for footing when the terrain became particularly sheer or strewn with sand and scree.

When Barrett fell back from point, signaling that he had to piss, the LT motioned for Cal to take the lead and he pushed ahead, his heart pounding, lungs rasping, remembering that the first time they had had to climb a mountain and then bushwhack across it before dropping down to their target he had had a blistering headache and kept retching—as silently as possible—even though his guts were long empty. His hands had become so swollen that he could barely close them, and he couldn't remember the name or the number of the mountain or the target. Then, as now, there was no turning back: the target and extraction point were ahead and unless one of them started blacking out or their lungs filled with fluids the LT would not call for an evac: the target would learn of the intrusion, and slip away and it could be months or even years before they found him again, if at all. Now, the altitude didn't bother him.

They had been climbing since just after sunset, and had, at

least according to the altimeter in his watch, about another fifteen hundred feet to ascend before turning and circling to the west and then north in order to arrive above the village and then descend into it, on the hunt, just before dawn.

As he brushed past, Cal recalled Barrett's aside from a few briefings ago:

"Village? Three huts and a cave? It's five thousand years ago in this country. And you see how they treat their women? Worst people on the planet. The only ones who come close are the Pukeistanis—acid in the face, cutting off noses and heads, marrying little girls to ancient creeps."

Cal had nodded to himself—it was difficult to like the Hajis—but then M&M had said:

"I know, right? It's like locking your sister in a room with football players and hoping she'll be all right."

Barrett had muttered that he didn't find M&M all that funny, but he laughed, anyway.

Cal heard the LT whisper for a halt and he dropped to one knee to allow the rest to close on his position. Once gathered, the LT double-checked his watch against theirs, took a GPS reading, and verified it on a topo. He shook his head:

"We're moving too damn slow. We're at least half an hour behind."

The way ahead looked to be even steeper than the terrain they had been covering.

"I'd just as soon not get stuck out here in the daylight."

The LT looked from one to another, and the three nodded in turn. He passed around a Ziploc filled with jerky:

"Cal on point. Keep hydrating, and keep on the look-out for bad guys."

By the time they had reached their marker to begin traversing to the west, they were almost back on schedule. Climbing above a path that ran both east and west from a short switchback, they spread out, Cal in the lead, moving quickly, trying not to dislodge rocks and send them tumbling and echoing downslope. They had nearly a four mile hike around the mountain until they arrived above the village, and Cal set a blistering pace: better to have lots of time to scout the descent than to be rushing as they closed on the target. Keeping the trail about twenty yards below him, he zigzagged up and down as the terrain necessitated, skirting boulders and climbing above abrupt ledges and fields of clanking talus. They were well above twelve thousand feet, but his legs felt strong and elastic, and he enjoyed the scrambling. Gaining back lost time, and then some, they pressed on without stopping until they were forced to slow as the slope became more and more sheer. Holding his position, Cal waited for the LT:

"Try to climb above this face, or drop to the trail?"

They lowered their night vision into place. The crag seemed to rise five hundred feet or more, and the path below turned into a wide ledge that bent around the base of the jagged, weathered escarpment. They knelt for several minutes, listening intently, but neither heard anything beyond the wind and the occasional clack of shifting stone.

The LT signaled for Cal to cut down to the path:

"Let's keep moving."

Slipping and sidestepping his way down the steep drop, Cal reached the track and moved as silently as possible, staying as near to the scarp as possible. As he rounded the corner, he almost bumped into two men. Automatically, he dropped to one knee, simultaneously raising his rifle. The men, as shocked as Cal, stopped abruptly. Seeing no weapons at the ready, Cal hesitated.

In that instant, he realized his error. He heard the LT curse softly.

Even as the men began to raise their hands, Barrett swept past the LT and Cal and struck the nearest man in the neck with the heel of his hand. The man crumpled and, without losing a step, Barrett stepped over the falling man and struck the other in the temple with his fist. The second man staggered backwards, almost losing the trail, and Barrett swung around behind him, his right arm around the neck, and choked him into unconsciousness.

In a few seconds more, M&M had zip-tied their arms behind their backs and gagged them with tape. When the first man began to stir and moan, Barrett let him lift his head from the rock and then stomped it back into the ground. Blood trickled from the man's nose and mouth, but he did not move.

The Rangers looked from one to another, and Cal looked down.

They all knew what had happened only a few weeks ago to a SEAL team operating on the Pakistani border. They had run into three men and, not knowing whether they were Taliban or simply villagers, had given them the benefit of the doubt and let them go. The freed men immediately returned with their buddies and had blown away all the SEALs save one who had been thrown into a crevice by an RPG and hidden by debris. Since the reports came back, the LT's squad had hedged around the question and, in not so many words, had made their call.

M&M whispered what they all were thinking:

"Now what?"

They looked down at the two men at their feet. One was older, perhaps in his fifties, his long beard mostly gray; the other could have been his son, a younger man in his twenties or thirties. They were carrying AKs, but lots of Afghanis carried AKs, especially in the mountains, and they could be from the clans or Taliban or Al-Qaeda. The squad, like the SEALS before them, had no way to tell.

Cal looked from his boots to the sky. The stars were bright and clean, distinct, blue, and only began to waver as he stared. Occasional, tattered clouds ribboned past, pushed by the icy winds aloft. He lowered his gaze to the horizon, and saw ridgeline after ridgeline, mountain peak after mountain peak reaching all the way across the frontier and into Pakistan. Below them, the valley was narrow and remote and lost in black shadows. He supposed the terrain was stark and beautiful, but it was also stark and ugly, treeless and parched, and sand and chips of rock seemed always to be pitting against his clothes and helmet and face.

A country where rivers evaporated before they reached the sea. What was the good of a country without rivers?

The LT cursed again, and nodded.

Cal gasped, not realizing he had been holding his breath.

Barrett double-checked his carbine. Distracted, Cal likewise began to elevate the nose of his weapon. The LT reached out and put his hand on the short barrel and gently eased it back down:

"RHIP."

M&M said:

"We could double-zip and -tape them, and tuck them behind these boulders. We'd be long gone before anybody found them or they could wiggle free."

Barrett, looking grim, shook his head:

"Do you want to take that chance?"

"Do you want—"

The LT cut them short:

"We have a target."

Cal, even though the temperature was near freezing, was sweating profusely, blood pounding in his chest and ears.

The LT bent and grabbed the older man by the back of his heavy vest and lifted him until he was on his knees at the edge of the path, semi-conscious, hovering over the steep incline. With his push-knife, he cut the zip-tie and gagging-tape, and put them in a vest pocket. Barrett grabbed the other and wrestled him into the same position, likewise cutting away and pocketing the tie and tape. They grasped the swaying men by the collars and held their weapons several inches away from the back of the men's turbaned heads. Exchanging a glance, they both looked back to the Afghanis, and pulled the triggers.

In the flash of light, out of the corner of his eye, even as he was conscious of the two bodies falling and tumbling down the pitch, Cal had heard or seen something:

A gasp. A face. Something round and white, fifteen or twenty yards to the west, below the path, behind a rock.

Somehow, the LT had sensed it, too, and he hissed:

"DT!"

And waved Cal after the apparition, but Cal was already in motion. He was the best shot with a rifle, and while they all had their nicknames—LT, M&M for Martinez-Moreno, Tyler Durden for Barrett—he disliked his intensely and the squad tried not to use it: DT, double-tap, one in the chest, one in the head, as he had been trained.

Running as fast as he could along the trail, he tried to listen above the sound of his own breathing, bouncing gear, and pounding footsteps for the direction and speed of the other. As he ran, the path widened, and the slope below became less precipitous, and for a moment he could hear but not see someone fleeing ahead, seemingly leaping and skimming down the incline. Slowing every ten or fifteen yards to lift the night scope atop his rifle to his eye, he scanned the terrain below and ahead of him but he could not find a target among the shifting, ravine-cut and stony grade.

Whoever it was, he clearly knew the land and was comfortable on it, flying down the mountain ahead of Cal. Though he couldn't be sure, they had probably dropped several hundred feet in a few minutes, and Cal, by times, was having difficulty maintaining his footing on the loose rock and steep incline and several times his feet shot out from under him and he dropped several yards as if on a luge.

All at once, a face appeared above an outcropping thirty yards down the pitch, and without hesitating, Cal dropped to one knee, braced, and squeezed off a round. Through the scope, he could see the top of the target's head erupt into a fine mist, and then it disappeared behind the rock. Scrambling as quickly as he could down the rough, flinty grade, he reached the boulder and swung around it, rifle at the ready.

A kid, a boy, maybe twelve or thirteen, the top of his head split open as if by an axe.

He knelt beside the boy and checked for a pulse even though he knew he would find none. Save for beads of sweat and sandy grit, the boy's face was clear, untouched by blood or bits of scalp or gray matter as he had crumpled to the ground. Cal stood, and rocked back and forth on his heels, his chin on his chest, panting for air after the long descent and dissipation of adrenaline.

Son, father, and grandfather? Who could say.

As on other missions, he could hear M&M talking to himself, always doing his voices, an expert mimic, as he double- and triple-checked his gear while they waited for the bird:

"Are you an assassin? I'm a soldier. You're neither. You're just the next in line."

Cal could smell the kid's blood, and he turned away, skirting the rock and gazing upslope to see if the way was clear. As he looked up the gradient, scanning through the short optic on his carbine, he could not see the others. Maybe, while he was chasing after the boy, they had double-timed it above him, proceeding toward the primary. He would have to catch up, if he could, or otherwise hunker down in a defensible position, activate his emergency transponder—but only after he was reasonably sure the mission had played out—and wait for extraction.

During the mission briefing, the CO and IO had stressed the importance of locating and eradicating the target, and it had been clear that the bosses would rather send the SEALs or SOC Marines than the Rangers, but the other units, including the Airborne, had targets of their own and were scattered across the frontier. The Haji, whoever he was, was high on the list, an

H-VT, and the Rangers would have to do, but that meant the LT and the others would have to press on without Cal if he could not rejoin them well before dawn. The underlying message at the briefings was always the same: don't screw up. And the truth was, raids and predator strikes worked. They eroded the command structure and spooked the Hajis into keeping a relatively low profile.

As he climbed toward the path, he thought he heard, on the swirling breeze, a skittering of rock well below and toward the east. He pulled up and listened as hard as he could.

The LT, Barrett, and M&M had no reason to have gone in that direction even if they had suspected or detected hostiles or other unknowns. If that was the case, or if they had detected someone above them, then the mission was compromised and the LT would have sent Barrett to scoop up Cal before they beat a retreat to the original drop-off. No way the LT would have them chasing all over the place in the dark when it was clear that there was too much traffic to reach the primary.

A goat? Someone who had heard the bodies falling, and was coming to investigate? A fourth with the two men and the kid? Another child? There was no way to know, but if the others were bearing down on the target, then Cal had to try and intercept whoever it was before they could reach a radio or otherwise sound the alarm.

He glanced at his watch: nearly 4:00. He rescanned the rise above him through his night scope. No Barrett. Were they lying low to avoid detection until they could withdraw? He had no way of knowing, and no way of finding out, short of physically locating his team. They had strict orders: do not break radio silence. The Hajis were listening, and breaking radio silence was as good as terminating the mission.

As quietly as he could, he pivoted back downslope, and began moving as quickly as he could in the direction of the sound.

The image of the boy with the split-open head hovered before him as he traversed the grade. In a country where there was always war, why didn't they tell their kids that when in doubt, go to ground? Cal didn't know whether the Koran retold the story of Lot's wife, but he imagined that most cultures had similar tales: don't look back. Never look back. Run as fast as you can, or better, find a hole or a cave and drop into it, and even if the odds were always against you, at least you had a chance if you buried yourself alive. But never look back.

What if it was another child ahead of him?

He often thought about one particularly emphatic officer at Merrill telling them that they shouldn't allow one decision to make others inevitable, but needed, in all situations, to assess and re-assess. On the other hand, sometimes you had to make a call and stick with it. When pressed, the officer had explained to them that, whatever else he knew, he knew that they lived in a fallen world, and that even a smart Ranger was going to be wrong most of the time:

"Let me make this simple for you. In the end, you have only two jobs: do whatever you can to complete the mission, and do whatever you can to protect the lives of your squad."

As he slipped and staggered down the side of the mountain, Cal decided this was neither the place nor the time to parse words, and he wasn't sure that, as a 2.8 in three semesters of farm management at MSU-Billings, he was a smart Ranger. Several minutes had passed since he had heard the sound, and he slowed his descent and stopped, listening as intently as he could. The icy wind at his back had increased, and he couldn't hear anything other than the wind and the usual shifting and clacking of stone. Bringing down his night vision, he held his position and scanned the steep, jagged terrain below and to the east. Nothing. No one or no thing moving. He waited several minutes, rising from a kneeling position to gain as much field of vision as he could. Nothing. No sounds, nothing moving. Maybe he had only heard the groaning of the rocks, or maybe his mind had manufactured the sound. He was about to give up and begin the long process of retracing his steps back in the direction of the insertion point—and therefore away from the target village—when, several hundred yards downslope, a tiny figure bolted into view in a draw, moving fast and almost straight down the precipitous terrain. Although it was dark, and the figure was running and disappearing in the shadows and depths of the gully, Cal could see that it was certainly another child, this one even smaller than the other.

In the last moment of visibility, the target too far away, he squeezed off a round, just missing. Leading into the absolute black, the scope unable to grab any light, his mind racing, calculating the Kentucky windage and the target's speed, he fired again but did not hear the hollow thump of contact. Rising to his feet, he ran for the draw, leapt over the lip, and dropped into the darkness, falling several yards before landing hard on his heels and falling heavily onto his side.

For a moment, he could not catch his breath, yet staggered to his feet and shuffled forward, attempting to close on the fleeing child. As his lungs began to work again, he surged ahead, slowing periodically to listen and scan with the scope. He followed the draw for close to forty minutes, but made no contact. It was already after 6:00, and the horizon to the east was showing a thin line of purple. He couldn't be in the open much longer. At the same time, if the LT, Barrett, and M&M had reached their marker, they would doubtlessly be in ready position above the village, preparing to begin the assault. M&M would stay high, providing cover and picking off unfriendlies as they appeared in the open, while the LT and Barrett would storm the hut, taking out the target and any other resisters. Cal doubted whether, at his present distance, he would hear gunfire or explosions unless the Hajis put up a strong fight or had the village wired and booby-trapped.

Pressing on, he at last reached the end of the draw and

looked out over a small plateau. Several hundred yards away was a dwelling, smoke rising from its chimney, and a goat pen extending around the back half of the mud and stone hut. As he scanned the treeless, bouldered table, he detected no movement, and there appeared to be no alarm in the dwelling. The goats seemed to be doing what goats do. Had the child—certainly not a girl?—gone to ground? Had Cal run past him in the dark? Had he, impossibly, hit him with the shot in the dark, but not stumbled across the body? Was he behind him, sneaking up, ready to cut his throat?

As he scanned the tableland, the horizon turning from purple to rose, the child once more popped out from behind an outcropping of stone, like a grouse taking wing, flying toward the shelter. Instinctively firing a round, he saw the figure spin wildly, stagger, regroup, and run. He fired again, and then once more.

If he could drop the boy—judging by his size, he had to be no more than ten or eleven—before he could alert those in the house, then he could maintain a watch until he thought the LT and the others were hightailing for the extraction point.

The second shot had hit the kid in the back, but he had cried out before the third shot struck the back of his head, exploding it. A pale yellow light spilled from the dwelling as someone opened a door. Pulling tight the straps on his small backpack, and changing out the magazine, Cal went to full auto as he charged, with all of his remaining strength, toward the structure.

II.

AS HE RAN, he switched his rifle to his left hand, and snapped a M67 from a clip on his vest with his right. He flipped off the safety clasp and pulled the pin, keeping the spoon hard against the cold metal casing. Nearing the corner of the pen enclosing the back of the hut, he let the spoon fly and, turning sharply to his left, sprinted parallel to the wooden fence. Passing in front of a window, eight or ten feet away, he tossed the grenade side-hand through the oilskin pane and raced toward the front corner of the hut. The frag exploded almost immediately, the sand-blasted walls seeming to bulge outward like a chest expanding with air, and he could hear shrapnel zinging from the pane-less window behind him. As he rounded the corner to the front of the structure, he changed the carbine back to his right hand and brought it to ready. Skidding to a stop in front of a rough-board door, he steadied himself to kick it down.

From the other side of the entry fire erupted, the hollow clack of an AK, raking Cal in a downward slant across his chest and armor. Each round struck like a hammer, pushing him back on his heels, and as he was falling away, a round snapped past his groin plate and buried in his hip.

He cursed as he was knocked back again, this time to the ground, and even though he could not see well due to the alternating breakers of pain and nausea, he struggled to twist toward the entry and return fire. Whoever was on the other side had continued to squeeze off rounds, but seemed no longer able to see Cal through the spaces between the boards. The bullets whined overhead, and Cal, his arms and carbine almost twisted into a knot, unleashed a burst through the center of the door.

The fire from the other side stopped at once.

Squeezing the sweat and tears from his eyes, he lay back for a moment, trying to catch his breath and control the burning pain and rising fear. Dizzy, bright white and blue spots bursting in his field of vision, he turned onto his stomach. He retched as he pushed himself to his knees, and his legs shook and almost buckled as he forced himself to stand. He could hear the sounds of movement inside the hut, and he stagger-hopped away as quickly as he could, holding his rifle by the end of the barrel and using it as a poor crutch. The jolt of each step sent shock waves up and down his right side, and even in the half-light he could see that his desert fatigues were soaked at the hip and that the blood stain was spreading down his thigh. Forcing himself to take the pain, he limped for ten or fifteen yards, finding shelter behind some boulders. Pressing his back to the rough stone and taking the weight on his good leg, he slid slowly into a sitting position and tried not to cry out when he hit the ground.

Glancing back around the rocks every few seconds to make sure he was not being pursued, he poured water from his camelback over his hands and then tore open a packet of disinfectant and squirted the cool, alcohol-smelling gel onto both palms. Having cleaned his hands as well as he could, he tore away the fabric over the wound and probed the oozing hole with a finger, almost passing out. The bullet had struck on the inside of the hip point and shattered the immediate bone, but whether it was also lodged there or had ricocheted or traveled along the pelvis toward his spine he could not say. The pain convulsed up and down his side, rattling his teeth and, as he searched the wound, he turned his face away and brought up what little food and water had been in his stomach. Loosening his backpack, he half-slid it under his armpit and pulled out the first aid kit. He cleaned and packed and taped the injury as well as he could. He then forced down some ibuprofen with a packet of AAG and a few sips of lukewarm, sour water, trying not to puke the pills and sticky-sweet gel onto his lap.

Retching once more, but not bringing up what he had just swallowed, he listened as closely as he could for sounds coming from the hut. He could hear someone moaning, and perhaps someone whispering and trying to comfort whomever was wounded, but he thought he could also hear a man's voice. Slowly edging sideways, he peered past the rock toward the house. The door had swung in, and framed in the opening he could see a woman, small and rounded, hunched over the prone figure of a man. The old woman was touching his thickly bearded face with her fingertips, as if brushing something from his eyes. As he watched, another figure appeared beside the woman, pushing her aside, and dropping into a crouch.

Automatically, as he had been trained, and even though there were no friendlies to hear his warning, Cal yelled:

"RPG!"

He had no time to pull back as the rocket wobbled rapidly at him, one of the few killing things a body could see coming. Instead of detonating, it careened off the rock and went tumbling end over end high into the air beyond Cal's position.

The Haji knew how to load and pull the trigger, but not how to arm the grenade.

Grabbing his rifle, Cal swung it around and, finding the man, fired. Still carrying the launcher, he crumpled immediately, as did the woman beside him who had started to rise back to a sitting position.

Once more overtaken with nausea and disbelief at what he had called upon himself to do for the last several hours, he gagged and vomited down his chest and onto his lap. This was a nightmare. Killing children and old women. Children and old women mixed in with—who? Taliban? Taliban sympathizers? Al-Qaeda? Clansmen who had no more love for Al-Qaeda than for the Americans? Mountain people who wanted everyone else gone and were just trying to defend themselves, using the current weapons of war, weapons readily available in market towns on both sides of the border?

Who the hell could say?

He doubted command always knew who was on whose side, let alone who needed killing and who didn't.

What if he had just spent the last few hours destroying generations and branches of the same family? About all they seemed to own were a mud hut, a few weapons, and a handful of goats, and he had brought all of his arsenal and training down on them.

Pain and grief churned and rose together in his chest. Taking deep breaths, he tried to force them back down, to calm himself so he could think and get himself out of this place. Unconsciously, he had brought his hands together and interlaced the fingers, palms down, pushing downward slowly, as if the agony and sorrow were a ball hovering outside his body that he had to press into the ground. He shook his head, trying to concentrate.

He needed pain killers and energy if he were going to move, but he decided to wait until his stomach calmed, if it would. He slid off his pack and pulled out his comm headset—the time for silence had passed; he needed an emergency evac—and pushed the toggle. Immediately, he heard the LT's voice.

He was panting, his voice broken and raspy between gasps, clearly on the run, and Cal could hear steady, proximate gunfire.

The LT was asking for support, was under attack and climbing in an effort to keep the high ground. Both M&M and Barrett were dead, killed by Hajis commanded, no doubt, by the very one they had been sent to kill. The bad guys had been waiting, and had blown M&M away with a RPG, and Barrett had been shot in the head with something big, probably a .50 cal. The LT was calm, giving what was probably his last report, fighting a rearguard action. Cal broke in:

"Are they sending help, LT?"

"Cal?"

"Can you make it?"

Before the LT could reply, the link went dead.

III.

THE SQUAD, the men he'd been living and training and fighting with for nearly three years, was gone. He especially could not imagine the LT dead: he was too decent, too tough, too dedicated to the job and his responsibilities to be killed. And although the LT had never said a word about where he was from or about his private life—and certainly nobody had ever dared to ask him a personal question—Cal thought maybe he had heard one time, from someone, maybe Barrett, that the LT had a family somewhere, and maybe a couple of daughters.

Cal leaned against the rock and tipped his head back and stared at the sky.

And Barrett and M&M. Barrett was rough and often obscene, but he believed in what they were doing as much or more than the LT. And if he began to get wound up about the Hajis and what creeps they were, M&M would give him a little nudge:

"I know, man. These fucking people. But think of it this way: what if we'd been sent to invade New Jersey? Think how much we'd hate those inbred fuckers."

Looking back at his hip, he could see that blood had soaked through the dressing and was dripping from his fatigues onto the dusty ground.

He hoped the Hajis would leave the bodies of his team alone, but some had a history of mutilating corpses, including chopping off heads, and posting the videos on the web. They always carried a camera or a phone, and one of them always seemed to pack a sword or ceremonial knife. Rangers or another 373 team would do their best to recover the bodies and bring them home, but they might all be in pieces, unrecognizable, gnawed on by dogs and whatever else. The thought of the LT, Barrett, and M&M hacked to pieces made him feel wretched, a biliousness rising and cascading through him once more.

Taking slow, deep breaths in an effort to still the nausea and the pounding in his head, he hoped, as well, that the growing ache and watery heaviness in his guts wasn't because his intestines were draining into his abdomen. Maybe the bullet had fragmented—or had shattered bone into slivers—and shredded his insides.

He activated his emergency transponder and called through the headset for an evac: he was alone and wounded and in danger of going into shock. Send the cavalry.

Painfully shifting around the boulders on his palms, he stopped when he was facing the hut—just in case there was another Haji hiding in there, somewhere, trying to figure out how to arm an RPG or to chamber a round in an AK.

The morning was calm, and the light intense, and he could see the bodies and the gathering flies as if they were only a few feet, instead of a few yards, away. And even though there seemed to be no breeze, dust and sand swirled in the air, and apart from a few of the low, thorny bushes he had seen elsewhere on the mountain, there was very little vegetation on the tableland, and only sparse, already cropped patches of something grass-like. He couldn't see a water source. How could anybody ranch here?

The few goats were still crowded nervously into the farthest corner of the pen, save for one. He hadn't noticed it before, but it was lying in the dirt, torn-up and bloody, below the window of the hut. Evidently the frag had got it.

Who would try to live here? Try to raise a few goats on no water and no vegetation? This place made his father's ranch in northeastern Montana seem like a garden. Sure, the water tasted like sulfur, and gave the shits to any outsider who had more than one cup of coffee, and the grass was never enough and the cattle were always underweight despite extra feed, and the winters were bitter and the ranches miles and miles apart and some kids still boarded in town during the week when it came time for high school, the hundred mile roundtrip too much to drive each day, and some years it never rained, or didn't seem to, and there was never any money, not really, always a slow losing, a draining away, an emptying of something that had never been more than half-full, ever, and it felt like maybe it was still 1947 anywhere near the Breaks, but compared to this stony, parched earth, it was a place where you could believe in a living even if that living never quite seemed to arrive. But it didn't matter, anyway: he was a second son—in fact, a third child—and the ranch would never be his.

In sophomore English, just before he had dropped out, they had read a play about a king and his daughters, and although Cal could make neither head nor tail of most of it, he was a little surprised that hardscrabble ranchers knew better than kings: never divide the kingdom.

In the distance, on the breeze that had just begun to freshen as the sun warmed the rock and sand, he could hear—or thought he could hear—vehicles. Rising, in anguish, he staggered past the bodies and the hut and limped to the edge of the small plateau. Bringing up his rifle and looking through the scope, he could see three of the ubiquitous white Toyota pickups, packed with men, heading his way over a narrow, rutted track switchbacking up the mountain from the valley floor. The men in the truck-beds bristled with weapons, AKs and other light arms. No doubt they also had some rockets, and maybe a decent sniper rifle.

As quickly as he could, he hobbled back to the boulders, choked down some ibuprofen with an energy gel and water, put on his pack, and crossed the upland toward the mountain. Soon, he reached the first steep pitch and gingerly began to pick his way around rocks and sharp inclines. At intervals, a voice from somewhere would remind him that the birds were on their way, coming hot, and reassuring him that they had a GPS-lock on his emergency transponder. At others, a different voice, perhaps from someplace else, urged him to hang on. The helos were closing on his position and they were trying to re-route a drone to watch over him until they arrived. As he clambered, chewing the last of his pain pills, the voices seemed to come from further and further away. After a time, he became too tired to reply, and his tongue seemed stuck to the roof of his mouth. In all, he guessed that he had gained less than a thousand feet in the time it took the Toyotas to transverse the miles and miles of switchback and reach the hut.

He needed cover, and he needed it now, before they spotted him, if they hadn't already. Desperate, he spied a crevice, a mere split, in a patch of wind-scoured stone, protected by a small overhang of loose rock. He worked his way across a steep drop of clacking talus, afraid of falling and of giving himself away through the racket, but at last he reached the cleft. The space was neither very deep nor very wide, but he turned around and backed and wiggled his way into it, shrieks of pain shooting from his hip and guts. It was too shallow for him to stand, but if he rested his pack against the jagged rock and bent his good leg while sticking the injured one out to the side as much as possible, he could just see the slope below over the lip of the crevice. If he straightened up, he could lift his carbine over the edge and return fire. Taking the last sip of water from his camelback, he swirled what little there was in his mouth, trying to unstick his tongue, and radioed that he had found cover, but that there were about a dozen unfriendlies closing in the general direction of his position.

As he peered over the edge, he could see the men from the Toyotas ascending the steep terrain. They didn't seem to be focusing in on the tight shelter—at least not yet—but no doubt they had analyzed the carnage at the hut and were tracking him as well as they could over the rough and brittle ground. Maybe they were following blood droplets.

And it didn't matter who they were: they would find and kill him unless help arrived.

Finding little room for his bad leg, and wedged tightly in the rock, barely able to move his arms, he tried to fight the searing pain and nausea and the earth-heavy regret and sorrow churning all together in his already roiling, burning, watery guts.

He could hear Barrett's voice:

"You're fucked, pal."

Yet even through the fear and grief he could also hear one of Barrett's favorite refrains when anyone began to bitch:

"Suck it up, dumbass. What did you expect?"

What did he expect about any of it?

He had to get squared away. Settling as deeply as he could into the rock, the pain all but unbearable, he checked his carbine, scraped a shelf in the dirt and rock for his few remaining magazines, and hoped he would be conscious long enough to defend himself.

Buffalo Jump Brother

SOMETIMES, when a buddy asks a favor, you agree whether you want to or not.

One day, your buddy—call him Mackey—says to you and another buddy: "If it ever looks like it's going to happen again, I want you to kill me." You look at Arlo—he's wiry, wary, his bull-shit-detector running hot, the leader—and he nods: you know why Mackey asks what he asks, and after all that spite and ugliness, you know he means it.

Mackey had said it: "I had to marry her so I could divorce her."

A few years later, Arlo brings Mackey to Montana to see you. The old buddies getting together, the Buffalo Jump Collective, catching up, sipping whiskey, telling lies, cutting up, talking music, guitars, cigarettes. But Arlo knows, and you know—and Mackey's gotta know—that the trip West isn't just for fun, for old times, because, yes, he's done it again, and you and Arlo owe him, you made your promise, and Arlo's at the fridge at 6:00 a.m., sipping a Moose Drool, cracks one for you, and a half-hour later the three of you leave for Glacier, Going-to-the-Sun, and you pull over, and everybody knows how it has to be.

Arlo says: "Call it a hike," and Mackey looking at the clouds says he always liked Montana, says it's not like Gasoline Lake, that's for sure, his hometown in the Illinois bottoms along the

Mississippi. Oil refineries, superfund sites, depopulating towns, Church of Christ and biker bars, streams with names everybody knows but that don't appear on maps.

Later, the Rangers will say, "Where did he come from, from a plane? Christ, how far did this guy fall?" Or maybe he's falling still, your brother, your Buffalo Jump brother.

It's Not Like You Think

I LOOKED AT LUKAS out of the corner of my eye. "You stoked?" He was breathing deeply, staring down at the gorge and the turbulent, fast water.

"Am I stoked? Dude, I'm stoked." He grimaced—he wasn't a fan of dude-speak, but mimicked it perfectly—and shook his head. "Sick amped, brah."

"I'm not your brah."

He looked at me and then over at Hobie. "What about you, Hobes? You my brah?"

Lukas had met Hobie while paddling the Rio Pallaresa a couple of weeks earlier, and they had been sharing a ride and paddling the rivers around Pucón. Hobie was older, going grey, all ropey muscles and no bullshit, a former pro living on his own dime, working nine-to-five when he had to, still exploring. He was easy-going, used to the life, threadbare, his gear and boat solid but banged up. He looked from Lukas to me and then back at Lukas. "Absolutely."

Lukas nodded, distracted, as if he had not paid attention to Hobie's reply, and looked back at the gorge.

Below us was the first of four drops on the upper river. The first, known as Mezclador de Huevos—so named, no doubt, by boys—consisted of three, zigzagging steps, each of about three meters and extremely narrow, the walls on the left-hand side steep and glittering with spray and moss, the right side jagged rocks and low-hanging branches. A few hundred meters below El Mezclador was the second drop, Gabriela Mistral, a six-meter dead drop at the end of a slot canyon. The pool at the bottom was wide and deep with no rocks and no undercuts, a perfect LZ. Next, after a few hundred meters run of Class II and III rapids, was a sharp and nasty hard right turn to get set up for Éxtasis, a seven-meter drop with a clear run on the left of two pillars of rock jutting from the pool below. To the right of the outcropping, the side you absolutely did not want to hit, was a narrow chute amid saw-toothed stone, and plenty of rubble and debris at the landing. Finally, several hundred meters of easy water below Éxtasis was El Tobogán, a sluiceway barely wider than a single kayak, a playground slide of about ten meters that ended abruptly and dropped several meters into a perfectly round, churning pool known as La Lavadora. From the shape of the rock on either side and the bowl below and the power of the water, the washing machine could suck you and your boat down to the basement, cycle you toward the back wall, and drive you back to the surface only to pull you under once more. Repeat, and repeat. Yet if all went well, the same forces would spit you out into ten or fifteen meters of modest turmoil ending in a solid, blank wall of Andean basalt. A quick turn to the right, just before a scoop worn into the living stone by millennia of hydraulic action, and the river settled down into an easy ride for a kilometer or so that led to a pair of debris-choked big falls, each twenty-five meters or more, that we would portage before trying the lower river. In all, the upper river was a Mr. Toad's wild ride of about two kilometers with little time to catch your breath or to think too much or to worry about your line. You had to commit, or risk getting snagged in a strainer or burying the bow in a rock or hole and getting spun around, dumped, and very likely trashed. The lower river was a series of less impressive, yet still roiling Class IV and V drops and shelves over the course of a few kilometers, and we had arranged for one of the guide companies to pick us up at the end of the day and bring us back to the rig a sponsor had arranged for Lukas for the summer.

I looked at Lukas and Hobie.

Hobie was nodding and grinning. "Sweet."

I nodded back. "Very sweet."

Lukas ignored us and turned to look at the shelf we would launch from above the gorge and followed, once more, the water as it veered left and right, left and right, and left and right again through the three falls of el Mezclador and stared downriver, as if he could see through trees, brush, and living rock, his head swaying side to side, no doubt tracing in his mind the course of the river, mapping our descent all the way down to La Lavadora.

Evidently satisfied, he turned and looked back up river to our boats perched on the moss and spray-slick rocks above the chaos. "Beautiful day for a paddle."

It was a beautiful day. We had left the hostel at sunrise, the snow-capped cone of Villarrica emergent to the south, the mountains circling the lake steep and verdant, the air cool and damp, the town just beginning to wake up. We spent a few minutes loading our gear into the 4X4 before taking an easy drive to the Záncara, about an hour away along a remote, narrow, nearly trafficless dirt road to the east and south, winding our way through steep ravines, the mountains looming more and more the higher we climbed. When we had reached the trailhead above the put-in, Lukas pushed the nose of the Tacoma into the brush and we unloaded the boats and gear and portaged down a slick, all-but sheer trail to the river. We stowed the kayaks, paddles, and spray skirts on a ledge covered in fern and moss and glistening with mist from the tumbling river, and began to follow the trail heading downstream. As we hiked, we had stopped and looked over each of the four major drops, debating routes and hazards.

Hobie had run the upper river years before, and I listened

carefully to his advice.

"Whatever you do, don't miss your set-up and boof before Éxtasis, or it's you tumbling over a cliff and faceplanting or landing on your side or ass-backwards. If you go to the right of the outcropping, you're fucked, so don't go that way." He looked over at Lukas, and added, "Brah."

Lukas winced, but kept his attention on the river. He seemed tense, but maybe he was always that way before a paddle. I had known runners who were like that before a race, and no doubt he would loosen up once he was on the water.

After scouting the entire run, we had scrambled back up, slipping now and then on the vegetation and mud, reaching, at last, a clear space above el Mezclador.

With one last look at the river, we turned and ascended the short distance back to our boats. When we arrived at the shelf, Hobie made the shape of a gun with his right hand, pointed at a boulder leaning over the river a few meters upstream, and pulled the trigger. He climbed up to the top of the boulder and then folded himself into Sukasana to work on his breathing.

"He's getting himself centered."

"It's not so bad. You should try it sometime."

Lukas shook his head. "Hippie bullshit. No offense."

I ignored him and shimmied my spray skirt over my dry suit and tightened my lifejacket, making sure everything was safely stowed. Sitting on the deck behind the cockpit, I stretched one leg and then the other under the front deck and then dropped my bottom onto the seat. I then wiggled into a comfortable position, the balls of my feet against the braces, knees bent, legs relaxed. Snug, I grappled with the spray skirt and stretched it around the cockpit, took the paddle in both hands, arms akimbo, grip just over a shoulder-width apart, and scooted forward, dropping bow first, the back of my helmet just touching the rear deck, into a calm strip of deep water along the bank below. The water was icy cold, snow fed, and the shock of it even through my dry suit made me gasp. I edged into a thin strip of sunlight against the bank and idled, hoping to warm up and waiting for Lukas and Hobie to drop in. For luck, I tapped the top of my helmet.

A few moments later, Lukas fell from the sky, the nose of his boat stabbing into the water, his chest touching the surface, head sideways so as not to faceplant. He spun in place, the tail whirling in the air, rotating first one way and then another. Satisfied, he let the stern slap the water, dropped his inside shoulder, paddle in one hand, and Eskimo-rolled. He reappeared in a moment and took one easy stroke to swing his boat in beside me and grabbed the edge of the cockpit.

"That's brisk, baby." He shook the water from his face and helmet and chest. I pushed him out in the stream, rolled, first to the left hand, and then to the right. The four-kilometer hike had served as a warm-up, but you could never be too limber.

The sun was just climbing above the mountains, and it shone through the leaves and branches overhanging the river, dappling the rushing water, and I could smell the water and the mud on the bank and the rotting detritus of vegetation and I reached out to a nearby rock and gently pressed my hand onto a clump of moss half-submerged in the current. Water welled over my fingers, the moss soft and heavy, and when I took my hand away, the impression filled immediately with water and the moss plumped back into the shape of a cupcake top. I could hear birds, somewhere in the half forest, half jungle, and the river sounded like a strong breeze rushing through the ponderosa back home and when I half-thought of the pines I could smell the heat and resin and dust rising from the trails along the Rattlesnake on a dry August day. For a moment, I was home and I was on this unfamiliar yet familiar river. Somewhere ahead, out of sight, there was a deeper sound of water, a reverberation and crashing, water with mass and speed breaking over rocks and against the walls of the gorge, an almost machine sound, a deep throbbing of power and life and momentum, water tumbling, precipitous, pell-mell, urgent in its descent.

I put my hand into the river, but could only feel the sluggish flow along the bank and not the stronger pull of the narrow channels, rapids, and drops ahead.

With a "Yippee-ki-yay," Hobie plopped into the river a few meters upstream. Like Lukas, he swiveled his hips and rocked his boat, nose down, ass up, ass down, nose up, before rolling first one way, then the other. After a few moments, he was ready to go, but like me, he hung back. We both knew our place in the hierarchy: Lukas was near the top of his game, a rising star, and had been in several documentaries—that's how I met him—but Hobes was well past his prime, a half generation from obscurity, and he deferred to Lukas. Me? Even though I had paddled all over the Americas and Europe and co-owned a production company—albeit a small one, rarely in the black, that specialized in films about women in sports—I had never been a star, had never done any of the really big drops or fought a really big river or been an Olympian like Hobie, and therefore had less currency than either of the dudes.

The brahs.

Lukas nodded. "All right." With that, he leaned out and reached forward almost to the end of his boat and dropped his left paddle blade into the fast water. In one stroke he was in the middle of the narrow river and tearing away from us.

We had begun.

Hobie looked at me to see if I wanted to go next, and I waved him forward. He darted out, and I took a deep breath, counted to three, and gave a quick chop on either side to propel myself forward. As always, when I paddled or skied, I began to sing to myself, slowing whatever song was in my mind down to a chant, in rhythm with the water and each stroke of the paddle, and I shifted side-to-side, hips settling the boat into the roiling stream.

In a moment, from idling along the bank, I was racing forward, leaning into each pull, rotating my upper body, letting my core and shoulders do the work, the boat slapping and bouncing over and around rocks, an easy Class II leading into el Mezclador. Ahead, I could see Hobie, his paddle flicking now and then, only when necessary, as he relied on his hips and legs and the chines to chart his course. He was relaxed, agile, not bobbing along, but gliding, fluent, quiet, easing by rather than around obstacles. Further out in front was Lukas, an entirely different sort of paddler, all muscle and power and stubborn technique. He seemed to leap from wave to wave where Hobie flowed into and out of each trough. Hobie was about getting along with the water; Lukas was about dominance, about finding his own line and bending the elements to his will.

For my own part, I was more like Hobie than Lukas. A friend had once told me that when I was on a river I was more liquid than solid, fluid, flowing into spaces and around obstacles rather than trying to bend the world to suit my form or purpose.

I liked that: sinuous, lazy, lithe, yet ready to go.

As with riding a bike or driving a car, when you're kayaking, you're not paying much attention to where you are, but where you'll be. A few hundred meters downriver I could see the approach to the first left-right of the mixmaster. As we neared, Lukas now ten meters ahead of Hobie and twenty in front of me, the river narrowed to a torrent less than five meters wide. On the right hand side, the bank rose steeply, all wet-black, exposed rock with moss and the occasional fern or wild currant growing from a handful of loam wedged in a crack. Higher, where the sun could reach, were some pines, laurels, and entangled brush that appeared to glow, a blinding white-green. The trees and bare rock seemed to lean in over the river, a natural amphitheater. On the left side, the bank was lower, piles of broken rock and snags and foaming whitewater topped with a violent green, the scrub trembling with the spray and breeze in the narrow canyon. Overhead, at a glance, the sky was at peace, still, clouds immobile, delicate, absolutely unconcerned with the tumult below.

As the stream narrowed, it picked up speed and volume and for a moment I seemed to be riding uphill rather than down, the deck awash, bow disappearing beneath the waves only to dart forward into bright air. I took one more look at Lukas and Hobie as Lukas set his shoulders, hips, and paddle to make the sudden left turn into the first zig of El Mezclador.

I couldn't help myself: "Cinch 'em up, boys!" But of course they couldn't hear me above the roar of the water or through their walls of concentration.

In a moment, I, too, shifted my hips and leaned into the turn, my paddle nearly perpendicular as I pivoted around it. The banks, already close, narrowed all at once as I entered the left zig, my boat dropping into a trough, the rapids rising above my head on either side. In a few meters more, the trough closed out and the boat shot forward and I drove my right hand into the torrent, paddle again perpendicular and deep, turning as fast as I could, trying to arrest, for the barest instant, the headlong rush into a whirlwind of white and blue and black. Atop a wave, the boat spun perfectly, bow now cutting to the right, into the zag, and I was squared away and running right down the middle. I could feel the burn in my arms and shoulders and chest as I set up for the boof—a combination of power-stroke and deflection off the water rising from the rock—and the front of the boat was airborne, the back nestled in the cascade, and a three-meter freefall and a spine-snapping landing on water turned by the force of impact into wet concrete.

One case of ovarian torsion down, two to go.

With the river straight for a stone's throw, I glanced downstream. I could not see Lukas, but Hobie was setting up for the next sudden left, his orange and green boat seeming to slice effortlessly into a solid rock face. In a moment, I was there, and luckily, it wasn't a stone wall, just a tight, frothing gap, and I shot through, pivoted hard right, launching once more into the ether. A little sideways, I landed hard, hull, arm, shoulder, and right side of my head hitting the landing simultaneously, elbow jabbing into kidney, lungs seeming to pop like balloons, and I extended my paddle and snapped my hips, righting myself and drawing a deep breath.

Performing a quick diagnostic—no apparent damage, just the embarrassment of missing the boof and risking a yard sale—I set up for the left zig, the walls closing in, a dull black, the canyon narrowing to just a few meters across, the sunlight unable, this early in the morning, to penetrate this section of the gorge, the way ahead suddenly lost in deep shadow, the river barreling into yet another immense wall, and I sank my paddle and right arm up to the shoulder into the river, riding as high, and leaning over as far as I could while pulling the nose around, a perfect cut, the hull grazing the wall like a luge around the top of a steep bank, then two hard paddle strokes forward to be going faster than the river, a perfect boof around the last boulder and churning whitewater on the left, and I sailed out into space, suddenly back in the sunlight, blinded, weightless, an astronaut, the boat a meter or more clear of the waterfall and going further still, airborne, and a pillowy, perfect landing in the spume, and I gave a cheer and pumped my right arm: Take that, boys!

Seeing Lukas and Hobie idling in an eddy on the right side of the river, I spun in beside them and grabbed the gunwale of Hobie's venerable Dagger.

Hobie was smiling and bobbing his head. "That was great, and you really nailed that one!"

I couldn't help but agree. "That was awesome. Completely, utterly awesome."

Lukas shook his head. "Hobie said you missed the second set of falls, and tanked."

Hobie looked upset. "I said I thought Ollie might have landed on her side in that second one, but I just had a glimpse."

"And, so what? Who doesn't miss a boof, now and then?" I patted Hobie on the hand. "No worries, Hobes." He didn't roll that way. He was clearly old school, polite and good natured, more about supporting his paddling buddies, old or new, than making everything into a pissing contest. Besides, he had seen enough to know that I could paddle.

"Those were the easy ones."

Hobie looked Lukas in the eyes. "Not cool, man, not cool."

"Whatever." He nodded his head downriver. "We should get going."

Even in the few moments we had sat in the eddy, I could feel my body temperature dropping, and despite the exertions of the mixmaster, my teeth were beginning to chatter. I wanted to pull into the current first, but I waited for my turn.

Taking the lead once more, Lukas spun out into the current, followed, a few moments later, by Hobie. I let them get out well in front, and then slipped into mid-stream. The way ahead was narrow, but flat, a few large boulders here and there, and a few dead trees and bamboo angling from the banks and stabbing into the Class II rapids. Compared to the frenzy of El Mezclador, the ride, at the moment, was mellow, the sun beginning to clear the mountain tops in earnest and I was glad for the brim on my helmet. The water dazzled, but as we neared Gabriela Mistral, the walls of the canyon became steeper and higher on both sides, topped by colossal trees, and I was once more in the shade. Just in front of me, about ten meters before the edge of the waterfall, the river seemed to lean steeply to the left, the rock formation on the right pushing the water abruptly to port. Not strong enough to paddle uphill I was pushed up against the rock and the canyon narrowed once again into a true gorge, the walls only slightly wider apart that the length of my paddle. Lifted by the surging water, knees elevating the bow, I was launched into space, a beautiful, perfect huck.

Airborne, a G. Love song about becoming an astronaut spinning in my head, kayak bursting into sunlight after the deep gloom of the slot, waterfall blasting cold at my back and sun warm in my face, I felt about as good as a person could feel.

Elated. Weightless, wholly in the moment, with just enough reflection to know that it cannot get any better than this.

A fall of about half the height of a diving platform and then—

hull slamming into the water, entire boat submerging, spine compressing, head plunging as if it wants to ricochet off the front deck, arms and paddle driven upwards, and suddenly it's snap back to reality, ope there goes gravity, and the sudden exhalation of every molecule of air in your lungs—huhhh.

Waiting in an eddy at the edge of the landing zone, Hobie paddled over and gave me a high-five. "Nice. You really flew out there!"

While Hobie was offering his congratulations, Lukas had already turned and was heading downstream. This, I decided, was both the first and last time I would kayak with him.

II.

ABOUT FIFTEEN MINUTES LATER, when I missed, if only by a few degrees, my boof on Éxtasis and had landed hard on my side after a more than six-meter drop—thank goodness I had made the left side and avoided a plunge onto the broken rocks and debris on the right side landing—Lukas had reached into the water and, in one swift motion, had righted both me and my boat. Dazed, I found myself sitting placidly in deep, still water.

"What are you doing? What was that?"

Blood was pouring from my nose and I could feel it running over my lips and falling from my chin. My left ear was ringing as if someone had punched it and my jaw was aching. My left arm and shoulder, too, were throbbing and I was grateful that my lifejacket had absorbed some of the blow to my ribs. Even so, winded, I struggled to breathe.

No doubt tears were streaming down my face, but I was more focused on the blood than the humiliation and shock.

"I'm not the first person to miss a set-up."

Hobie was holding my boat steady and if he had had a handkerchief, he would have offered it. "Everybody gets banged around now and then, or you're not trying."

"Look, if this is too much for you—"

"What?"

"I said, if this is too much—"

I wanted to yell, but instead I looked at Hobie and pushed away, getting some distance so I could stop the bleeding and wash my face. Once apart from the others, I pinched my nose and tilted my head back for several minutes, and then scooped handful after handful of water to wash away the blood on my face, drytop, and lifejacket. The left side of my face was tender and there seemed to be swelling under my left eye.

Great. A shiner. A lasting reminder and, evidently, a source of scorn. As if a black, purple, and green L would soon be tattooed on my cheek.

I took a deep breath and swore to myself.

At last, after getting myself together, I nodded that I was ready to continue. Hobie asked if I wanted to take a break—we all had a dry bag with peanuts, granola, cheese, and weed stuffed behind the seat—but I declined. I was ready to go. More importantly, I wanted to get back on the river, and this time, I didn't wait for Lukas or Hobie to paddle out ahead of me.

Behind me, I could hear Lukas say he was glad I wanted to keep going.

Yeah, right.

Taking four quick strokes—my paddle, luckily, had not broken in the fall—I darted into midstream and aimed my boat forward in the easy water, bumping along, letting the current carry me as I tried to get back the good feeling I had had after nailing the earlier waterfall. I swung my hips from side to side, getting a sense of the strength and bounce of the riffles and, building up some speed, aimed directly for a large, mushroom-shaped boulder taking up most of the middle of the river. At the last moment, I eased the bow to the right and glided gently past the toadstool, once more assuming a course directly down the middle. A stone's throw ahead, the river narrowed, the rocks on either side becoming sheer. A moment more, and I entered the toboggan run, the way so constricted that I had to hold one hand just behind my back, the other reaching well forward, paddle tight against my hip. The slide was barely wider than my kayak, and it dropped like the beginning pitch of a rollercoaster. As I neared the end of the chute, I pulled my knees to my chest with all my might and was once more launched into the air. Rather than falling nose first into the washing machine and torpedoing to the bottom, I sailed over the bowl and landed in racing water, heading straight for an immense black wall of towering basalt, a monstrous blank face, devoid of even little plants clinging to pockets of dirt in cracks or along ledges. Waiting until the last moment before careening headlong into the slab, I pivoted right and blasted into a wide, lazy river.

I had run, with only a few mishaps—well, one goof and one serious miss—the upper Záncara. The left side of my face was still throbbing from the rough landing below Éxtasis, but I was also grinning from ear to ear, and so what if my nose had begun to gush again and maybe I had a chipped tooth where the paddle had collided with my face?

Turning into an eddy, I looked back as Hobie tore toward the wall and then made an easy turn to the right and bubbled out into the calm water beside me. After a quick handshake and hug, we looked back at the toboggan run.

Lukas appeared at the top, his boat slightly askew, and as the bow caught on the rock on one side, the stern banged into the other side and he scraped along. At last able to get the nose away from the wall, he overcompensated and knocked it into the other wall just as the slide ended and he tumbled headlong into La Lavadora, the hydraulics immediately sucking both paddler and boat below the surface. We could see the bright red kayak through the foam and spray, and it pinwheeled in the heavy, cycling current. Unable to right himself, Lukas bailed and, holding onto his boat with one hand, paddle in the other, kicked himself free of the maelstrom. Laughing, he waved at us as the powerful current swept him toward the cliff.

One moment, he was giving us a thumbs up and laughing and swimming with the current. In the next, both he and the boat disappeared as if into solid rock.

Hobie and I were about twenty meters away, and we looked at the wall and then at one another.

"Where'd he go?"

Reaching almost to the nose of his kayak, his paddle slicing deep, Hobie propelled forward and I followed.

As we ferried across the river and neared the wall, the force of the current kept pushing against the upstream chines and we had to paddle just to stay in place. Ahead of us, in the scoop worn in the wall, we could see Lukas, turned to face us, his arms reaching out and bracing against the wet rock on either side, the powerful current draining from La Lavadora running directly into his torso and legs, working to push him against the back of the scoop. With his shoulders and head above the water, he seemed stable and his boat, mostly submerged with just the stern sticking up out of the water, bobbed beside him.

As we stared, he yelled, and we heard him as if we were speaking to one another across a dinner table. "I can't swim out. The current's too strong."

Hobie looked at me. "Do you have a throw rope?"

"I don't."

"I gave mine to some young guys a few days ago on the Jarama, and I never got it back."

If Lukas had a throw, it was somewhere behind the cockpit of his all-but sunken boat. To find it, he would have to let go of the walls and we had no idea what sort of hydraulics were at play. Just by looking, we had no way of knowing how deep the scoop went or what its true shape or dimensions might be. We might be seeing all or most of it, or it might be five or ten meters deep or it might be the beginning of an underground passage that reconnected with the river a few meters downstream, or a few hundred, or maybe never. Whatever the case, the river ran in a straight, unforgiving line from La Lavadora to the small cave and as we watched, the current began to push Lukas backward, deeper into the shadows. He fought against it, but the walls were smooth and slick with icy water and as he labored to stay forward, the ceiling curved downward, forcing him lower and lower into the surge.

Clawing his way back toward the front of the cave, he once more locked his arms into place.

Hobie and I looked at one another, and then back at Lukas.

"Lukas, is the current pulling you down, or is it just that the walls are slippery?"

"There's some sort of undertow. I'm having a hard time staying above the water."

"If you let yourself be pushed to the back of the cave, do your feet reach the floor?"

"It's not like that. It doesn't end where the ceiling goes underwater, and when I was back there, I wasn't touching the bottom and there doesn't seem to be a back wall."

Already Lukas' teeth were beginning to chatter, and we could see his arms trembling from exertion.

"No worries. We're working on a plan. We'll get you out, buddy." Hobie turned to me. "You got any ideas, Ollie?"

Ideas? I knew the basics of self-rescue, and like everybody, I'd dropped into a hole and been held under for longer than I liked, and I'd seen paddlers held under by strainers and undercuts and I once saw a deeply stoned brah perform unintentional cartwheels after going over a shallow weir—he somehow managed to pop out and float to safety, beat-up, bloody, and minus both his boat and trunks—but I had never seen someone trapped in a cave with a river's worth of icy current bearing down on them.

"What if we floated one of the boats in? Maybe he could climb on top until we can get some help."

"I thought of that, but his head's almost touching the ceiling as it is, and I don't think there's room, even if he could somehow manage to get on top. And, without a rope to slow it down, it would be like firing a rocket, don't you think?"

I nodded. I slipped my fingers alongside of my neck, trying to unstick the gasket of my drytop. I was having trouble breathing.

Lukas called out. "Is there something we could use as a rope?"

I looked around. By now the sun had cleared the mountains and the air was beginning to warm and the sky was clear and the brush and trees glowed green and swayed in a languorous breeze. About a hundred meters downstream, a clump of bamboo arced into the river from the far bank.

"What if we cut one of those long bamboos? We could float it into him while one of us holds the other end?"

"Ok, worth a try." As Hobie turned his boat toward the main channel, I explained our plan to Lukas: we'll send in one end of the bamboo, while holding the other, and we'll pull you out.

In a moment, Hobie was back in the main current, paddling furiously toward the stand. Reaching up, he grasped the longest stem and worked his way, hand over hand, to the bank. Drawing the knife that was strapped to the front of his lifejacket, he sliced the plant near its base and, clenching the branch between his teeth, ferried diagonally to the far side of the river and began to paddle uphill toward the cave. The closer he got, the stronger the action of the water became, and he battled to move forward. At last, nearing the mouth from the downriver side, he took the bamboo in one hand but was immediately swept away, spinning, nearly toppling. Righting himself, and once more taking the paddle in both hands, he worked his way back, holding as tight to the sheer wall as he could. Once again near the entrance, he whipped the thick end of the bamboo around the corner and let go. The current immediately grabbed the bamboo, but rather than pushing it into the cave, it circled sluggishly and then picked up speed heading downstream.

Hobie, cursing and fighting the river, sunk the stern of his boat into the course, pivoted, and slammed the hull back into the rapid. He raced to retrieve the bamboo, already several meters away and he nearly toppled again, reaching into the water several times to get ahold of the slippery, now almost leafless branch.

When he finally pulled it from the water, it was bent in several places, and he threw it away in disgust. Paddling furiously, once more, for the bamboo, he cut another stem, this one somewhat shorter, and, once more, paddled laboriously against the current. Exhausted, he reached the cave for a third time, and in a single motion took the bamboo from between his teeth and threw it like a javelin into the opening.

Seeing it, Lukas unbraced his arms and immediately sank from view. He came up sputtering and wheezing and took hold of the branch even as the river propelled him deeper into the scoop. His head hit the ceiling, gashing his forehead, and he once more went under.

Spent, Hobie had allowed himself to be carried downriver, well past the stand of bamboo, nearly out of sight around a bend.

Not sure what to do, I paddled forward, as near to the entrance as I could without getting swept in, and Lukas' head bobbed up, his lips pressed almost to the ceiling, gasping for air. Blood was streaming from the laceration on his forehead, and he was fighting both to breathe and to stay above the water. As I watched, he edged his way forward against the current and once more braced his arms against either wall. But this time, rather than being shoulders and head above water, only his head was visible.

Behind me, Hobie yelled that he was going to find help.

From here, the scramble to the truck could take over an hour, and from there, he would have to hike along the road, hoping to run into someone with a rope. Lukas had the only key in the front pocket of his lifejacket, and Hobie might have to hike all the way back to the nearest village, a journey of several kilometers in slow, up-and-down terrain.

Maybe there was somebody on the river above us. Maybe they had a throw rope.

But maybe there was nobody on the river, and nobody on the road.

I called out to Hobie. "Should I pull out and see if there's a trail leading downriver? Maybe there's somebody below us?"

"I don't know, Ollie. Maybe you should just stay and keep him company?"

I signaled that I would, and Hobie took off running.

When I turned back, Lukas had once more let go of the walls and was violently trying to unbuckle and unzip his lifejacket.

I called out. "Lukas, I don't think that's a good idea."

"It's not keeping me afloat, anyway," he gasped, "and maybe without it I'll be able to swim out."

Rotating onto his back, he managed to raise his legs and feet to the surface and, digging into the rock with his toes, attempted to push off from the ceiling and backstroke his way clear of the cave. Repelled by the current, he was swept beneath the rock.

How long he was gone from view, I could not say. A minute? Two? But he reappeared, battling furiously, his hands and feet repeatedly striking the walls and ceiling. All at once, he stopped flailing. He looked at me and then the water took him and he disappeared.

Los Borrachos de Donostia-San Sebastián

I.

HE HAD NEVER SEEN such a beautiful place. From the esplanade overlooking the curving expanse of the horseshoe-shaped beach, he stared at the gentle waves rippling against the strand and then shifted his gaze in turn to the verdant hills on either side of the opening to the Bay of Biscay. To the west, upon the promontory, rose the steeple of a church partially hidden by the deep green of trees and at the base of the hill were several houses or low-rise apartments, a crane towering above them. To the east, upon the other promontory, stood a tower or lighthouse jutting above the treetops, and still more houses and low buildings flowed down the steep incline toward a small marina with a few dozen sailboats and fishing vessels. In the gap beyond the shelter of the harbor were a number of small ships and, in the remote distance, a freighter creeping east along the horizon. Two stories or more below, on the broad, smooth beach that ran for a hundred meters from the base of the esplanade to the water, were couples strolling at their ease, people playing with their dogs, and children splashing in the wavelets as a parent or perhaps a grandparent or nanny looked on. The mid-morning light made everything and everyone clear and bright and crisp. He spoke:

"Have you ever seen such a beautiful place?"

When neither his wife nor his daughter responded, he turned

and spotted them several meters away, giggling at a man posed and dressed as if he were the statue of a man leaning into a strong breeze. He tilted as if into the wind, his hair and tie swept up and back, his suit-jacket open and as if blown back, his face contorted, squinting as if the torrents carried bits of sand. Working up her courage, Ellie crept toward the man and dropped a coin into the upside-down tambourine the man had placed nearby and in which rested several coins by way of example and encouragement. When the coin hit the skin, the others and the jingles bounced and clinked and chimed and Ellie laughed and ran back to her mother. Once there, she turned and imitated the man; he grinned, bowed at the waist, thanking her silently for the appreciation, and then resumed his arduous, frozen course into the tempest.

Alec gazed at Ellie and Claire and recalled how, on a trip to Amsterdam not long after they had moved to London, they had tried to go to the Rijksmuseum and just outside the front doors was a man all in silver, standing in a box with only his upper body showing as if he were a bust set upon an elaborate pedestal. He was remarkably still, and they stopped and watched, and then he, too, and all at once, gently leaned forward in bow, and Ellie, between them, each holding one of her tiny hands, had screamed, turned, and run off for all she was worth, they in hot pursuit, calling her to come back. When they caught her, she could not be consoled and would not go near the museum:

"That silvery unreal man moved!"

When they tried to explain he wasn't really a statue, just a man pretending to be a statue, she demanded:

"Who chopped him in two?"

In the end, Alec had gone inside to see *The Night Watch*—and had been shocked at how immense, even monumental it was—while Claire had watched Ellie run around the grass alongside the museum. When he passed the silver man, Alec apologized and dropped a few Euro into the collection box. As before the man gently bowed without speaking and then resumed his perfect, motionless pose. He was really good.

Looking away from the handsome young statue and his girls, Alec leaned back against the balustrade running on the edge of the wide, curving walkway and admired the city, turning his head first to the east, toward the old city and its medieval-looking buildings and streets, and then slowly the full, long curve to the west, enjoying the apartment buildings, banks, shops, and large houses on the other side of the avenue paralleling the kilometers of esplanade. He then turned his attention to the people around him—most seemed to be locals—and then out at the people sauntering on the hard-packed sand or playing in the water. He wanted to reach out to an older couple as they passed by, to grab one of their arms and give it a gentle shake:

"Do you know how lucky you are to live here?"

The little city was magnificent, even perfect: modern and medieval, sheltered without being claustrophobic or too-crowded feeling. When Ellie and Claire joined him, he said:

"We should move here. It's incredible."

Claire smiled. He often wanted to move someplace new, never turned down a transfer, and when they traveled he was always speculating on what it would be like to live wherever they found themselves at the moment:

"I doubt Phantom Works will open an office here."

He frowned, but did not speak.

Ellie wanted to know:

"What's that writing? All the signs have Xs and Zs and Hs."

When Alec did not respond, Claire said:

"I think it's Basque. People only speak it around here and no place else in the world. Isn't that amazing?"

Ellie thought for a bit:

"Maybe."

In the meantime, Alec had turned and was looking back at the beach. Below him and to the west was a small group of men and perhaps a couple of women standing in the shade cast by the walkway above. The esplanade was supported by arches that sheltered alcoves, and the seven or eight people were gathered partially in the recess. Compared to the people walking on the beach, or above on the walk and in the town, they were shabbily dressed, and they passed a bottle or two from one to another, the bottles slowly making their way among the group. One of the men, thin and tall and dressed in baggy, dark clothes, spoke and the others laughed and a wild-haired and crazy-whiskered old man holding one of the bottles lifted it as if in toast to a bon mot and then raised it the rest of the way to his lips and took a long, slow draught. He roughly wiped the finish with the palm of his hand, and passed the bottle to the man who had spoken.

Claire, conscious that she had stung Alec a little, had eased to his side:

"What are you looking at? Oh."

He turned back and faced the city once more:

"Nothing. Just the beach. You have to admit, this place is amazing."

"Sure. Amazing."

Ellie said:

"I'm hungry. Does this place have food?"

II.

WHEN CLAIRE AND ELLIE headed for the old city in the early afternoon for some ice cream and shopping, Alec set out to wander around, as he often did, and to see what he could see. He climbed the steep hill to the lighthouse, and then zigzagged his way down to the quay and looked over the battered fishing boats and various sail boats, some new and sleek, others well-worn and in need of refitting and paint. He followed the curve of the esplanade all the way to the crest on the west and then went a few blocks into the city and let his feet take him where they would, stopping along the way for a coffee and some sort of fish sandwich. By evening, well after he should have gone back to the hotel and checked in with the girls, he found himself once more on the east side of the perfect harbor and, foot-weary, he rested for a time on a stool at a tapas bar, sipping beer and sampling the seafood and ubiquitous jamón serrano and ibérico. The beer and food made him drowsy, and he sat slump-shouldered and happy and gazed around him at the people in the crowded bar and those going by on the narrow, cobbled street. At last, stirring, he reluctantly pushed himself away and eased among the patrons to the street and then turned toward the harbor and the hotel. Moving at half-speed, somnolent and creaking like an old man, he shuffled among the tourists and locals and passed a wine and liquor store. Without thinking, he stopped and backtracked a few paces and stepped inside the tiny, bottle-crowded shop. Looking absently at the labels, he grabbed a likely-looking Rioja and a flacon of Oruju claiming to be, if his Spanish served him, over one hundred proof.

He hobbled from the old section and into a warm evening breeze coming off the water. Rather than turning toward the city and the hotel, he continued along the walkway, nodding now and then to other saunterers, and came at last to a set of stairs leading down to the strand. Without changing his pace, he swerved to the stairs and, his knees aching, stepped down and onto the hard-packed, level sand. Almost immediately, he came upon the drinkers. He stopped abruptly a few meters away.

No one of the group paid him any attention. Most were standing, looking across the sand at the waves, the tide coming in, passing a bottle of wine one to another. A man and a woman were sitting against one of the piers supporting the arch above them, attempting, it seemed, to fix some sort of pipe, all the while half-heartedly trying to give instruction or take it from the other. In the dark beneath the esplanade he could see other shapes and thought he could hear a man moaning.

"What the fuck do you want?"

Alec staggered back as if he had been struck.

Standing an arm's length away, suddenly there and towering over him, was the tall and thin man he had seen in the morning. His nose was smeared across his face as if he had been a boxer, and his shaved skull was long and narrow, his visage gaunt and leaden and covered with black and gray stubble. He waved a burning cigarette at Alec's face:

"I said, What the fuck do you want?"

"Nothing. I—you're English."

The tall man rounded his eyes in mock surprise:

"And yer a Yank. Ain't we a pair? Meanwhile, piss off."

As they had been talking, some of the others had wandered over, including the electric-haired old man. He said something in Spanish to the tall man, and the tall man smiled, his cheeks protruding as his lips curled up into a sneer:

"He wants to know if you're looking for company?"

Alec took another step back:

"What? No. I—"

The others were laughing. A young man with sores on his lips and neck flicked a cigarette past Alec's head and said something in German. A lank-haired, dirty-faced girl at his side burst into hysterical laughter and just as abruptly stopped and stared hungrily at Alec.

The tall man nodded at the pair and then turned to Alec:

"Do you want me to tell you what Fritzie said, mate?"

He shook his head and reached into the sack he was carrying and brought out the bottle of Oruju. He passed it to the thin man who, taking it in one hand, broke the seal and pulled the stopper with the other and took a long, slow draught. In the meantime, Alec had reached for the wine bottle and passed it to the young Germans who then turned away from the others, hunched over the bottle as if it were an ember they were trying to keep lit as they retreated toward the darkness beneath the arch.

When he turned back to the others, the gaunt Englishman

was standing even closer, holding the bottle in Alec's face:

"Drink."

"Oh, no. I'm ok. I've just been drinking beer over—"

The man took another drink and then shoved the bottle almost against Alec's lips:

"Drink."

He pulled the bottle back and took another long draught, and then grimaced and again shoved the bottle at Alec, this time tweaking his nose with the spout:

"I said, Drink."

Alec took the Oruju and drank deeply, taking an even longer pull than the thin man. He passed the bottle back, his guts clutching as the strong drink reached them.

"Now, there's a good little Yank."

With his free hand, he reached out and shoved Alec hard on the shoulder:

"Off you go. Wouldn't want to overstay yer welcome."

III.

AS PLANNED, they rented a car and spent a day in Bilbao and two more days following the coast back to Donostia-San Sebastián. When she was tired, Ellie would complain about the smell of the sea and how hot it was and if they had to climb one more hill or stop at one more place with a weird name—who would come up with a name like Txakolina?—her brain would explode, but for the most part the weather was mild and the breezes temperate and the steep hills and bay beautiful, and Ellie became a dedicated connoisseur of pintxos and was happy to decide which ones to order. Too quickly, they were back in their hotel overlooking the perfect harbor, and they were all weary and ready for a day of rest. In the late afternoon, Alec said he might go for a walk along the beach, did anyone want to come? When both declined, he decided he might go, anyway, though Claire thought it might be just as well if they all watched some of the World Cup as their favorite, Uruguay, was playing Ghana.

Without quite meaning to, he walked briskly and directly to the spirits vendor he had stumbled across a few days before. He bought two large, inexpensive bottles of the burning, clear Oruju and a smaller flask of pale green Izarra, and after paying tucked the flask in the cargo pocket of his walking shorts. From the old quarter, he walked to the harbor, to the stair leading down to the strand. A few of the drinkers from before were there—including the emaciated, tall Englishman and the wild-haired Spaniard sitting on the sand, sharing a cigarette—and some others that he did not recognize. He drew one of the large bottles from the sack, and held in out in front of him as he approached. The Englishman, showing yellow, irregular teeth, spoke:

"Well, if it isn't Monsieur Monde."

For a moment, Alec paused:

"Pardon? Oh. Well, I have been working out lately."

In turn, the Englishman seemed confused, and then burst out laughing and he reached out and curled long, knobby, dirty fingers around the bottle and pulled the stopper:

"Good lord, does it hurt to be such a fuckin git?"

Alec sat on the hard, warm sand and snagged the Oruju in mid-pass:

"I don't know what you mean."

"Of course not."

"What? Mr. Earth? Mr. World? Mr. A-Man-of-the-World? Mr. Worldly? Is that it? You got the world figured out, and I don't, because I don't smell like piss and own a toothbrush?"

The Englishman jerked the bottle from Alec's grip and put his long arm around Alec's shoulders, pulling him close. He leaned his face down until his lips were almost against his cheek:

"Where do you think you are, mate?"

Although the man was thin, he was evidently quite strong, and Alec could feel his fingers digging into his shoulder and could smell the alcohol and cigarette and something deeper and sour on the man's breath. He flexed his shoulders against the pressure and sharp nails:

"Do you want to drink or not?"

The Englishman tightened his grip until Alec's shoulders began to ache, and he felt small and had trouble catching a full breath.

"Your pretty little wife and little girl aren't here, are they?"

"What?"

"All by yer lonesome."

"Hardly. And what do you mean by—"

He pulled Alec even closer:

"Among strangers."

Alec tried to stand:

"Keep the bottle."

The tall man released his grip:

"You're fuckin right I'll keep the bottle, and the other one, and the one in your pocket."

The grizzle-haired Spaniard, who smelled like he had not bathed in years and who had dozens of little scabs and sores on his face above his beard and across his wind and sunburned and grimy forehead, had eased to Alec's other side and had put his arm around Alec's neck:

"We drink, ok?"

Alec nodded:

"Ok."

"Good."

The old man pointed at the Englishman, and grinned:

"'Ee's ass'ole."

The old man drank from the bottle and shoved it into Alec's hands and when Alec went to drink, he nodded gleefully and pushed up on the bottom of the bottle. Alec gagged, and the alcohol ran down his cheeks and chin and onto his shirt and shorts.

For hours, they sat and drank from the large bottles, others by times coming to join them, each, in turn, stepping into dark corners to piss. Alec, who rarely smoked, steadily puffed on bummed cigarettes, his throat and lungs burning, his head throbbing, and when he tried to walk into the darkness to relieve himself, he often staggered into a pier or one or more of the others sharing bottles. As the sun set, he lurched across the beach, almost falling several times, and walked into the shallow, cool water, his trekking shoes soaked through, until the water was above his ankles. He stood, swaying, staring at the darkening ocean in the distance, trying to smoke a cigarette that he had dropped in the water and then picked up and put back between his lips, now and then looking up at the stars as they appeared as a crazily swinging script of blue.

When he awoke, his head pounded so badly that he turned a little to his side and vomited, the side of his face falling into the voluminous, stinking puddle he had just made. He lay for a longtime, his head throbbing, course after course of vomit erupting and spilling out the side of his mouth and onto the sand and debris around him, onto his neck and shoulder and chest. With each heave, his ribs hurt incredibly, and he began to sob with each successive convulsion. At last, after the vomiting had subsided for a time, he forced himself onto one elbow and looked down as best he could at his torso.

He had been stripped of everything save his boxers. His shirt and shorts and shoes were gone, and even in the half-light beneath the esplanade he could see and feel that his stomach, ribs, and upper arms were covered in abrasions and bruises as if he had been beaten and kicked. He gingerly put one hand to his face—other than the hangover, his face and head seemed to be intact and mostly unscathed. In a panic, he reached behind him, but was unhurt. Gasping in pain at the torsion the reach had caused, he lay back in the sand and gravel and closed his eyes against the hammering in his skull.

IV.

SEVERAL WEEKS AFTER Claire had left with Ellie—back to their apartment in Toulouse, threatening to fly home to Seattle if he did not show within a few days, as soon as he was well enough to travel—his skull pounding, his tongue as if stuck to the roof of his mouth, his guts a churning nest of bilious snakes, one of the women from the front desk had knocked on the door, apologizing for the disturbance but explaining softly that his card, for some reason, regrettably, was not working and would he be so kind as to settle the bill, as soon as possible, in some other manner? Gathering himself as well as he could, he dressed and stumbled from the hotel to the bank around the corner. When he found that neither his credit nor his ATM cards worked, he waited for a teller and managed, for a modest surcharge, to get an advance from his DBS account, enough to cover the previous week at the hotel and to float him for a few weeks, or more, if he found a cheap place to stay. He returned to the hotel facing the harbor, packed, paid his bill, and wandered deeper into the city, following the directions provided by the thoughtful concierge to a modest, family-run pension near the old quarter.

That evening, at last feeling well enough to eat a little, he left his tiny room in the pension, and zig-zagged through the narrow, illogical streets until he found the tapas bar he had been in almost two months previous. The taberna was almost empty, and he took a table at the back, as far away from the street and the few patrons as he could. He ordered a large beer and asked for three or four plates of the waiter's choosing. His stomach still tender and prone to sudden, painful lurches, he sipped the beer when it arrived, pushing the small dishes to the far edge of the table. The beer, at least, helped, and he hoped that his guts would settle enough for him to manage a few swallows of food.

Since his night on the beach, he had avoided going anywhere near the harbor, and he likewise tried to avoid getting into conversations with anyone, either locals or tourists, who might want to catch a stranger's eye for a bit of news of the outside world or the pleasantries of where-are-you-from and what's-around-that-you-would-recommend?

That day, stinking and filthy and in considerable pain, when he had finally felt able to stand, he had forced himself, step by painful, gasping, fiery step, to totter from the alcove beneath the walk and out into the brutal, sun-searing day. There were the usual numbers strolling on the strand or playing in the water or leaning over the balustrade above, but he had had no choice and lurched to the bottom of the stairs, the sun seeming to rip his eyeballs from his head. Slowly, and in fear of falling backwards and tumbling down the concrete steps, he climbed his way to esplanade, the hot, smooth surface burning the bottoms of his feet. He had looked both ways and then shuffled forward, across the walk and onto a slight rise covered in grass and a small flower garden. Reaching the far side of the rise, his feet muddy from the flowerbed, he stood on the sidewalk running along the four-lane drive paralleling the long, gentle curve of the harbor, the traffic heavy and zooming in either direction, horns blaring in mocking salute. When a small gap opened in the nearest lane, he stepped out, forcing the drivers in the other lanes to slow and stop and let him pass. Once across, it was only a few meters to the front of the hotel, and the doorman helped him inside and called for security to take him to his room.

Claire, sleepless and sick with worry, soon turned grim and silent, but had helped him in the shower and then had called the front desk to call a cab to take them to the nearest hospital. Ellie had cried and cried and wanted to know what had happened to her daddy and had the police arrested the awful men who had hurt him? After the hospital, Claire had moved herself and Ellie to another room down the hall, and a week later had flown back to the Midi-Pyrenees. For all he knew, they were probably back in the States by now.

Still sipping at his beer and nibbling at the least exotic-looking of the tapas, a slice of cold, spiced beef on bread, he became conscious of a tall man weaving through the patrons at the front of the bar. Suddenly alarmed, he snapped his head in the direction of the moving figure: the man was tall, but modestly dressed in khaki slacks, a light blue oxford collar shirt and dark blue sport coat. His hair was slicked back, and he was clean-shaven and looked like a businessman on holiday in Spain. Even his teeth, as he smiled, seemed straighter and whiter, though his nose still twisted one way and then the other between his lean, well-tanned cheeks.

Alec exclaimed:

"It's you!"

"Well, if it isn't Monsieur Monde. You just never know who you'll run into."

His accent was plummier, less harsh and coarse. He pulled up a chair at the small table, signaled the waiter for two large beers, and turned to Alec:

"On the mend, are we?"

When the waiter arrived, the tall man reached into the inside pocket of his jacket and brought out a well-ladened billfold and set out enough to cover the beers and Oruju he then ordered.

"What the hell? Who are you?"

"Geoffrey. Geoff to my friends."

He offered his long, thin hand across the table.

"No? Won't shake hands with an old friend?"

"Where did you get that money? Those clothes?"

The waiter arrived with bucket glasses of the strong liquor, and Geoff raised one of them in toast:

"To my old friend, Alec."

He downed it in one gulp, and signaled for two more.

"Drink up. I have a plane to catch."

"A plane?"

"It's time for me to be getting back to work—and please don't say, Work? And, my wife expects me back—and please don't say,

Wife?"

Alec sipped at his beer and then set it down and picked up one of the Oruju:

"No kids?"

"No."

"You work in—"

"London, of course."

"And, you're on—"

"Holiday. Every year. I find the air and the light quite pleasing."

The tall man finished his second drink, stood, and pushed in his chair:

"If I ever see you again, I'll make it count. You understand."

The Sumerian in the Driveway

SOME WINTER NIGHTS, after hockey, with the Milky Way embedded in the tin vault of the great An who created and sustains the universe, the sky wagon, battle wagon, Ma-Gid-Da, as if falling from the heavens, its great, invisible horses in flight, armored, I used to grab a chair from the front deck and visit with the Sumerian who lived in the driveway.

"Tell me, Flynn," he would say, the massive darkness of the foothill looming above us, the Rattlesnake valley below, "are you not worried, this very night, about the fate of the people on the faraway island shaped like a leaping cat? Shall we not do our part to fight the tyranny that oppresses them? Shall we not do our part to lift their spirits and cry out in the name of freedom?"

The Sumerian, whose name was Akram, had an elaborate sense of humor.

"If you want a drink, just say so."

He was from the city of Ur, and although he wasn't a priest, he had a full, wavy, square-cut beard and a white tunic fringed with gold stitching and bracelets over his compact biceps. He wore thick-soled leather sandals and, as a caravaneer, had the muscly calves and thighs of someone who walked great distances in pursuit of trade. He never complained about the cold, but after I gave him an old North Face down jacket and a well-worn pair of ski pants that my daughter had left behind when she went away to college, he seemed grateful, yet he could never make up his mind whether the toque I offered did a better job inside or outside his bronze helmet. He wasn't tall—a little over five feet—but he had assured me more than once that, for a Sumerian, he was actually pretty tall.

When at ease, and when, perhaps, he thought no one was watching, he had the habit of standing sideways, legs wide apart, both arms raised.

One night, as I was rooting around in the side-pockets of my hockey bag for a couple of roadkill beers, he said that he thought that the all-but-frozen PBRs were evidence of Nanna-Su'en's goodwill toward the people of Ur:

"Can you imagine how good this would taste on a hot, dusty day in Susa, trying to get the Elamites to part with the sacks of tin they had persuaded the sand-blasted, idiot Mundigakians to trade for grain? I shouldn't complain about the Mundigakians, but, like camels, they go days without water and never take baths. They smell like rocks and feet."

"The Sumerians had beer." I know because he had told me, and because, after I noticed a Sumerian living in the driveway, I did some research.

"Sure, lukewarm, and we sipped it with straws from communal bowls. That's a lot of backwash, as you can imagine. Even so, Alulu, one of the brewers in Ur, made wonderful beer, even if it was thicker than porridge. I owe him for five Silas of his best that I took with me on our last trip. How much, after 4300 years, do you think that will be, with interest?"

After a couple of Kokanees, or a Cuba Libre with plenty of lime, he always wanted to play driveway hockey. "I'll be Number 4, Bobby Orr. And you take goal and be Ken Dryden of the Habs."

I had made the mistake of telling him about how, when I was a kid, we used to play hockey after school on the frozen, ice-rutted streets of north Edmonton. I told him about the hockey stars of those days, the ones we idolized and wanted to be, and I showed him video of a few games on my laptop. At first, he was alarmed—how do they move so fast? why are they so tiny? do they also use their sticks as spears?—but as he got used to the technology, he was hooked. When I got a new Dell from work, I gave him my old Toshiba. Whenever I was going through things and packing up boxes to take to Secret Seconds or Good Will, I'd ask him if he wanted or needed a trivet from Sweden or a pashmina from a street vendor in New York or a plastic pill crusher from CVS.

He'd shake his head. "I don't think so. What are they for?"

When he was online, he wanted to order things from Amazon, but since I didn't hassle him about the porn—did I know any of these women? did they live around here, by any chance? could gaba truly become so large, yet be so round and remain so near the collar bones?—he didn't press me too hard for my password or credit card number.

"Again? Grown men don't play hockey in the driveway, especially not at 1:00 a.m."

"I need the exercise. Besides, who'll see us?"

He was right. The driveway was sudden and steep and curved toward the garage before flattening out, and we were sheltered from the street by the retaining wall and arborvitae. Even if a car drove by, very likely they would only see shadows swaying like pine boughs in a strong breeze. Sometimes, the carrot-colored street hockey ball would ricochet off the goalpost or garage door and thwack the house nestled into the hillside a few steps below. As usual, he won. He had a hard, accurate shot, and he whipped the hard ball past my shoulder or just over my boot and stick and although he preferred to play out, he was very scrupulous about equal time—"You be Phil Esposito, and I'll be Gump Worsley"—and would dive about and crash onto the concrete without fear. He was a decent goalie, but I kept my distance since he would now and then swing the heavy goalie stick like an axe:

"You have to keep the crease clear so you can see the puck."

"Fine, but we're playing a friendly game."

"As in love and war, there are no friends in hockey."

"You hit me in the shins again with that goalie stick, and there aren't going to be any Sumerians in hockey."

After the game, I would shake the snow off the small Weber I kept beside the garage and pour a bit of white gas onto some scraps of wood. We would pull up our chairs and Akram would admit that it was a miracle, wasn't it, that even a measure of amber warmth from the country of my ancestors across the sea could be brought on ships and then on great, roaring machines across these United States of America, a wonder, indeed, that something as fragile as glass could survive such distances and that two friends, huddled near a fire, could revive themselves with that amber warmth, could settle around a fire and speak of things that need to be spoken of or of things that were nonsense but worthy of consideration nonetheless? Did I think that David Thompson, when he stood on this very mountain and sketched the valley, when he looked down at the place where the Blackfeet would lie in ambush for the Salish as they made their way east to hunt bison, had a drop or two to warm him on cold nights?

Akram liked Wikipedia.

"On the rocks?"

"Neat."

One night, as we stared into the sometimes crimson, sometimes violet coals, he asked if he had ever told me about the journey after which nothing was ever the same?

I shook my head.

He nodded, and said that maybe it was time. This is what he told me:

We were going to be gone for many months, maybe a year or more, a journey that, after years of toiling in caravans, would have allowed us to save enough that I could become a merchant and would not have to be away from my family for months at a time.

You understand? A journey to change our circumstances, after years of work and scrimping? To become a merchant, to be home every night, instead of trekking across countless da-na, across deserts and great plains of rock, all the time hoping, with each trade, to increase our wealth that one grain of gold more? The simplest thing in the world: one last trip to change our family's fortunes.

And, by then, my father a caravaneer, my grandfathers caravaneers, I had been on dozens of trips, knew all the routes, knew every river, stream, oasis, pirate town, and mountain pass. From Ur, packing grain and farm tools, we would follow the Id-Ugina north and west into the lands of the Akkadians, trading along the way, and finally, after a year and a half, back into Sumer and home—home!—to Ur.

Simple: trudge, trade, increase our wealth by one grain of gold each time, and, finally, reach home and begin our lives as merchants and not caravaneers. Let someone else do the walking, the bartering, the praying for water.

Except that on the tenth day after our departure my son, Naram, got a toothache.

Also a simple thing: a beginning soreness at the back of the jaw. At first, he had some pain, a little discomfort. Then, a few days on, the pain got worse, and there was some puffiness and his skin was, at first, warm to the touch, and then hot.

We were, as the saying goes, in the middle of nowhere. Before the fever began to spread, we reached a small village, but they had no wise men or women and when I looked in my son's mouth, all I could see was inflamed, mottled flesh: a new zu, no doubt, where there was no room for a new zu. What, then, was the best course of action? We set up camp and rested for a couple of days—and my son became neither better nor worse. We were wasting time, and I decided to send him home to his mother. We knew a man, in Ur, who could give my son something to numb the pain before cutting into the gum and yanking out the unwanted zu.

I gave Naram one of his cousins, a good man, as a guide and equipped them with plenty of food and water and a horse and while we headed for the north and the west, they turned to the south and the east. When I glanced back, not long after we had parted, they had vanished from sight.

The next several months went about as well as I hoped: no brilliant victories, but no inglorious defeats, either.

We had left in the fall, and by winter we had turned south and traded spices in Jericho that we had secured from Meluhha sailors the summer before in exchange for the tin we had wrangled, at great cost, from the Elamites. We debated, because we were doing well, whether we should push across the desert to the lands of the Egyptians, but decided to keep to our original plan: we decided not to press our luck.

By spring, we were almost in the lands of the Hittites. Hearing about the possibility of trade in this village or that, we had worked our way towards the Amanus mountains and finally, in need of rest, had set up camp along an all-but dry river bed that ran down from snowy, jagged peaks and out onto a great dusty plain. We had been pushing hard, and I decided that a few days respite and mending were in order. For the first day, we did nothing but doze and sip water from the little stream and cover ourselves from the sun although the air was thin and cold. On the second day, we pretended to re-reed some baskets and panniers and to repair the leather harnesses, but mostly we did as we did on the first day: snoozed and wished for beer and dreamed of women.

On the third day, at about noon, there was a faint rumbling from the mountains above us, and then, in what seemed to be only moments, the rumbling turned into a roar and a wall of water, rock, trees, and mud came cascading down the dry river bed and hit our camp.

As I think about it now, I believe that somewhere high in the mountains a hard and sudden rain must have fallen, or perhaps an ice damn broke on the river, and, all at once, where there had been no river, only a trickling rivulet, there was now a rushing, deafening barrage and it swept over us and drew us inside and churned us up with boulders and broken pines and sludge and it swept us a da-na and then another out onto the plain in a great filthy, frothing roar, dropping the bodies of my men and animals here and there as it lost its fury and spread out on the dry land.

We did not all die, of course. But no one was left unscathed. Of my twenty men, ten were drowned or torn to pieces, and of the remaining ten, most had broken bones and severe lacerations. My right knee was bent backwards and my left elbow was gashed and so swollen that I could not move it at all.

"Lucky for you I sustained those injuries, or the hockey wouldn't even be close."

"Don't kid yourself: I take it easy on you because you limp like an old dog."

Somehow, a few of the camels survived, but none of the horses and almost all of the carts were destroyed.

Worst of all, the small wooden box that contained all of our earnings had been swept away.

I sent the least injured man for help, and while the three or four who could not move were secured in ragged shelters in a new camp, the remaining few, however badly wounded, scoured the plain for the wooden box. Everywhere they looked, there was mud and debris, and they hobbled about as well as they could, and dug and guessed and while they never found the box, after three weeks of looking they found a vein several šu-du-a long containing about half our wealth, a mix of silver and gold coins.

I sent a prayer to An when I heard the news. All, then, was not lost.

Yet we were farther from home than we had ever been, and while the nearby villagers were kind to us, we had lost almost all of our goods and we were beat up and sick. In the early days after the flood, they could have killed us in our sleep.

We spent almost six months huddled against the mountains, recovering our strength and making small journeys in search of trade. Slowly, we recuperated enough to begin again in earnest. In the early fall, we organized ourselves into a caravan of about half our original size and strength, and we set out to salvage what we could of our original plan: we would resume trading as well as we were able, and we would follow our intended route and try, as much as possible, to gain back what we had lost.

I was not without hope, you see.

Yet it seemed as if our luck, like our wealth, had been scoured away by the flood. We would trade for a horse, and one of our camels would go lame. We would follow a rumor about metals to trade only to find an abandoned village: everywhere there were signs of life, but nobody, not even a stray dog, in sight. And, where, until our luck turned, we had been able to gain a little on each trade, now we lost heavily. For the next few months, the harder we tried, the worse we did.

Nevertheless, slowly, slowly, we won back some of our confidence, and by the time we reached Ur, almost three years after we had left, we had recovered most of what we had lost in the flood. By the time I paid off the men who had survived, and set aside portions for the families of those who had died, I had less than half of what I needed to open my business.

But it didn't matter, because when I arrived at my house, it was empty. Thieves, it seemed, had taken everything. My wife was nowhere to be found, my five daughters had vanished, and my son—my son, whom I had last seen as a ripple in the heat across an expanse of super-heated sand!—where was he?

I staggered around what had been our home, the cardinal point of our lives, and it was a ruin, our bedroom burned, the roof caved-in. As I stumbled about, weeping, one of my neighbors arrived at the doorway and he explained, as well as he could, what had transpired.

My wife, who was still beautiful and who had always been the subject of interest among the worst sort of men, found herself, he told me, beset by suitors. My wife, ever faithful, would not allow them into our home, but they became bolder and bolder until one night there was a scream, confusion, a lamp knocked over and a fire, and my wife was murdered, stabbed a dozen times, and with my wife dead and no word of me or my men, matters became worse and worse. The daughters were taken, and of the five, three were almost certainly dead and the remaining two held captive in Uruk, maybe, or Lagash.

My wife murdered because—

My daughters taken—

And my son—

Gathering what friends and family I could, we traveled to Uruk and Lagash and found my two youngest daughters, alive, not well, but alive.

We killed the men who had taken each of my daughters, and we killed their wives and children, and we killed their old ones, we killed them all, and the few of us who survived brought my daughters back to my house and what few relations and friends I had left helped me to rebuild our home and our lives and many years later, when we had, at last, prospered, I left many guards at my house and yard and I went in search of my son and nephew. I took my horse and my two most ferocious men, and I retraced the route we had followed on those first days of the caravan. When we located the impoverished village where they had no wise men or women, we turned around in an effort to follow what might have been Naram and his cousin's course toward home. Everyone we met, we interrogated: had they seen a boy, perhaps quite ill, traveling these years ago with another man who looked not unlike the boy?

Most said they had never seen such a pair; a few said, maybe, but it was so long ago and who could remember?

As you will have surmised, I never found him. I looked back over my shoulder, one day, as he was riding toward home and I was riding, I hoped, toward our fortune, and he as if evaporated into the air. I loved him dearly. He was a sweet boy, with no meanness, and he seemed happiest when he was living as his grandfathers had lived. And I don't even know what I did, what any of us might have done, to be played so by the gods or fates or whatever it is that pushes our lives this way and that.

I LEANED OVER and poured some whiskey into his tumbler.

"Over the years," he said, drinking, "I made many journeys, trying other possible routes, trying to find just a little bit of him and his cousin that I could bring home. And, one time, while I traveled alone, a sandstorm enveloped me and then, for reasons I cannot explain, I was here, in your driveway."

We sat in silence for a long time. Every now and then, I would add a few more scraps of wood to the fire, and the snow fell gently on our toques and shoulders and laps. At last, Akram spoke. "Do you know why I told you this story?"

I nodded. "You want to go home."

"And for other reasons."

I bobbed my head.

As we stared into the fire, we talked it over, whether he would ever be able to find himself at home again, whether he would ever be anywhere again. We talked it over—I told him he was welcome to live in my driveway until the day I moved away or died, and longer, perhaps, than that—but he knew, and I knew, that the time had come.

The next morning, I hitched up the old sailboat that my wife's brother had given us but that I hadn't used in years, and pulled it out of the driveway. I took it to Good Will and dropped it in the parking lot with a note, a bit of a dirty trick, but I had made a promise. Then, when I got back home, I took apart the cairn I had stacked on top of the retaining wall on the high side of the driveway one day not long after we had first moved in. For good measure, I cut down one of the arborvitae that stood between the street lamp and the driveway and that the deer had nibbled into the shape of a pinecone on a stick. Well into the evening, about the time I would be leaving for the beer leagues if it were Thursday or Sunday, I glanced out the front window at the driveway, bathed, as it always was in winter, in pale blue from the street light, the goalie stick leaning against the retaining wall.

Wreck on the Highway

I.

I recall the mix of terror and exhilaration that propelled me up the sleet-slick steps. I shoved open the porch door, bounded ahead, turned to the trailer door and banged into it, missing my grab at the handle. A second grab and in, but which way? Two steps to the right, down the short hall, and there would be grandma sitting at the kitchen table, sipping her cuppa, maybe on the phone to one of her sisters down home, maybe looking over the Hope weekly or a paper she had picked up in Chilliwack, maybe gazing up at the old clock that had belonged to her mother, thinking about whatever she thought about when she became quiet, her tea going cold in the green-with-black-circles mug she preferred. Or two steps to the left, the other way down the hall to the living room, where grandpa would be sitting in his recliner, the TV on but barely watched unless it was hockey, a *Maclean's* on his lap or a book by Mowat or Burton or Costain, Bay of Fundy, my cat, curled up behind him on the back of the chair, rocking as grandpa rocked, nails darting out, seasoned sea legs, to hold on should grandpa push down the handle and set the chair into crazy motion. I could hear grandma talking on the phone, so I zagged right. Grandpa was used to me flying around, and nodded as I skidded to a halt beside him.

"You're not going to believe it."

He looked up at me over his glasses, smiling his mild, ironic smile, and waited.

"No. No. I mean it. You're not going to believe it. You gotta get up and come."

I could see he was working out some quip about how, very likely, he wouldn't believe it, but his grin faded as I pulled on his hand:

"Believe what?"

"There's been a wreck."

"Where?"

Grandma stood behind me, phone in one hand, the other coming to rest on my shoulder:

"I thought I heard something. Was it down the road, towards the range?"

"Yes, yes, that's it. A wreck, a big truck all loaded down. It roared off the highway, Tommy said, and crashed into the ditch and up and over and spilled everything and rolled on its side. The tires were still spinning when I ran down there. Tommy sent me back to get you."

Tommy was one of our neighbors and he walked all the time as if he had someplace to go and he had been wandering in the woods at the foot of the mountains when the truck had lost control and plowed into the darkness.

"He says the driver's smashed up pretty bad and bleeding from this big gash on his head, and he says be careful when you're going down there because the truck spilled lumber everywhere and to bring some flashlights and don't break a leg or trip on the broken down trees or shattered boards. He said, Bring a blanket and some stuff for the guy's head."

Grandpa was already on his feet, stepping past me to get his jacket from the hall closet as I repeated what Tommy had told me to tell them.

"All right, Janey, you've done well. You've done very well. Go out on the porch and grab up the flashlights, my green raincoat, and that old sleeping bag, and you'll have to show me where all this is. Sile, get on the phone to Cerdic and tell him to get the ambulance out here right away, and tell him to bring the boys in case we need help, and to make it quick."

He slipped his slicker over his jacket and pulled his wool toque down securely:

"Tommy holding up down there? He keeping it together?"

I shrugged. Who could ever tell with Tommy? He was fidgety, like he always about to run for cover:

"I don't know. He seemed ok, and he was talking to that guy, telling him he was all right and that help was on its way and not to worry."

Grandpa nodded and nudged me toward the porch:

"Sile, you call Cerdic right away, and tell him to bring the boys, till we see what's going on."

Soon enough, we were outside and heading along the narrow dirt road that circled Traveler's Peace and its few mobile homes. When the road turned uphill towards the woods, we kept on straight, the Trans-Canada to our left, separated from the road by the ditch and a row of mangy cedar, ferns, and brambles. The trees and water-logged, always-unfurling ferns did little to block the highway din, and on wet nights like tonight, on their way to Vancouver or going the other way toward the interior and then Alberta and then across all of Canada if they needed to, the semis would howl by like enraged demons, their tires shrieking on the sleet-soaked pavement, engines throbbing, and you couldn't talk or hear above the roar until they were long past. Grandma claimed not to notice anymore, but I hated the screaming machines. On the other side of the four-lane was the railroad track, and beyond that, a kilometer or so, the mighty Fraser, as slate-dark and somber in the winter as the frozen rain highway. As always, it was raining hard, a cold November night, with wind gusting and heavy sleet alternating with the rain. Almost cold enough to snow.

We followed the path along the ditch, downhill toward the

wreck. We couldn't see any lights ahead or hear any voices above the wind and rain, and we kept on, and it seemed as if we walked forever and soon enough would be at the low, pink building that marked the entrance to the shooting range. Grandpa never said a word, and if he was beginning to wonder if I was lying, he never gave a hint, but kept going, head down, his heavy flashlight sending a steady, white beam ahead.

"Oh, my."

Grandpa stopped and put out his arm so I couldn't pass him. He played his light back and forth across the ditch. There were deep, churned-out grooves shooting from the highway toward the water flowing through the shallow gully. The tracks disappeared where the water ran, but on the other, steeper side, the ground was sheared away and sprayed outward, a trough cut through the bank. The truck had plowed off the road and continued on at high speed into the cedars and smashed and uprooted trees and bushes lay everywhere and we splashed through the ditch and up the other side, following the deep gouge and trail of debris. Twenty yards in, a hulking, twisted shadow in the darkness, the trailer lay on its side, its load of lumber burst open and flung everywhere, the crisscrossing, sometimes shattered boards glowing a slick, pale yellow. The cab was also on its side, well away from the trailer, the fiberglass shell torn from the undercarriage and wrapped in fragments around the base of a towering, ancient cedar. It looked like a giant's head cracked open, its severed and demolished body bent and broken, its thousand ribs cracked apart and strewn everywhere.

"Tommy said the driver lived?"

We navigated our way slowly through the mess and splintered, broken trees, our lights glinting off shards of glass and isolating for a moment on straps and chains and shrouds of white, flapping plastic wrap. In a few moments, we had picked our way around the trailer and stepped gingerly over the severed hoses and chunks of fiberglass and twisted steel covering the ground between the trailer and cab. At last, we came around to the underside of the engine, easing by the great tires jutting out above our heads, and there was Tommy, in a sweatshirt and jeans, shaking, whispering to a man slumped against the mangled base of the truck. Tommy had taken off his thin raincoat and laid it over the man. The driver moaned quietly and turned a bit to look at us with one eye and grandpa gently pushed my flashlight downwards to take the beam from the man's face. I couldn't tell how old he was, somewhere between Tommy and grandpa, and he had long dark hair and a pointy beard and he was big in the chest and gut and arms. He was soaked through, and shivering like Tommy, and seemed not quite able to focus on us. He nodded, and I could see a laceration running from the top of his head, over his forehead and eyebrow and continuing down his cheek. Blood ran from the gash and down his face and over Tommy's jacket, and his eye socket was mangled and swollen shut.

Grandpa knelt down and took the man's hand:

"You're all right young man. The ambulance is on its way. You hang in there."

He unrolled the old sleeping bag and covered the man and then reached into his pocket for an umbrella which he opened and snagged into the undercarriage above the man's head. The rain had once more turned to sleet, and thick droplets plop-plopped on the glistening nylon. When he was sure the umbrella would stay in place, grandpa turned to me and gestured for his raincoat and I passed it over and he passed it to Tommy.

"Tommy? You all right there, brother?"

Grandpa used one hand to help Tommy with the jacket even as he steadied the sleeping bag over the man. Tommy nodded gratefully, his teeth chattering:

"I'm fine, Mr. McLauren. Just a little cold and shook-up is all. I heard this helluva noise and found this fellow flung out and crawling in the mud. He's lost a lotta blood and maybe he's busted inside, too."

"You've probably saved his life, Tommy."

Tommy, skinny, hollow-cheeked, a skeleton-man, was shaking so hard he was almost clacking.

"I sure hope he makes it. This has scared the hell outta me, I can tell ya. You think he'll make it?"

The three of them huddled together as best they could, grandpa and Tommy speaking to the man, trying to keep him conscious, trying to reassure him, but the man looked frightened and he moaned and raised a muddy hand as if to wipe away the blood running over the mangled side of his face. Grandpa handed me his big flashlight, and told me to get over to the path along the highway and to wave the light so the ambulance and Cerdic would know where to stop. I walked gingerly over the broken tangle, slipping once on a sleet-covered crisscross of boards, and in a few moments I reached the path and ditch and looked up-and-down the highway. I waited and waited until, at last–I was sure the man was probably dead–I recognized Cerdic's pickup traveling slowly in the far lane and I turned on the flashlight and waved the beam back and forth. He swung a U-turn and he and two of his sons jumped out of the cab.

"Well, now, Janey, what have you done?"

Cerdic was grandma's brother and, like grandpa, enjoyed teasing me. He was tall and thick and had hands the size of hockey gloves, and the two boys, my mother's cousins, were built the same. One, Bill, was reaching into the bed and pulled out triangular reflectors and two sticks that looked like cartoon dynamite. He walked uphill along the highway, and set the reflectors down as he went. A little further on, he took one of the dynamite sticks and seemed to snap it in two, and it flashed out a bright and fiery red, and he laid it on the shoulder. Ron, the other brother, had gone into the trees, following the tire tracks. Cerdic watched him go, and then turned to me:

"Who's up there, Janey? That fella hurt bad?"

“Grandpa, Tommy, and the driver. He has a big cut on his head and he never said a word while I was up there.”

Bill walked past us, heading downhill along the highway, and popped the other flare. By the time he had made his way back to us, Ron emerged from the woods:

“We can get up there.”

Cerdic nodded:

“Right. Lock the hubs.”

Telling me to stand well clear and to watch for the ambulance, they climbed into the truck, backed it out onto the highway and then rocketed it into the ditch, following the semi’s trail. The truck careened through the gully, flinging clumps of mud and grass and torn-up fern, and then shot up the far side, the engine growling, the taillights swinging crazily side to side and up and down as the truck fishtailed along the muddy, sleety ground. In another moment, flashing lights appeared at the crest of the hill and swooped down, slowing at the last moment before making a U-turn across the highway. When the paramedics jumped out, I told them what I knew: who was up there, and about the man and the brutal slash and how he seemed awake but not talking, and about how Cerdic and Bill and Ron had managed to get their truck up there and could possibly carry the man and a stretcher in the back if that would help. The paramedics listened, asked a few questions about how wet it was back there, and decided to leave the ambulance where it was. They grabbed their kits, flashlights, and a board with handles and waded across the ditch and set off along the churned-up, newly-made road. The pair had been gone only a few moments when Tommy appeared:

“Janey, your grandfather said I should walk you back to the trailer.”

He looked sad–he always looked sad and cadaverous and afraid to make eye contact–and his teeth still chattered and as small as grandpa was, Tommy looked like a drowned kid in a man’s coat.

We decided to walk back to Traveler's Peace along the highway. Tommy seemed to be all jacket and skinny legs as we walked, his shoulders hunched, hood up, chin down on his chest, not saying much. I glanced over at him and thought, not for the first time, how much he reminded me of my mother's friends. Or maybe friends wasn't the right word. Grandma had called them her crowd, or those people. They were all skinny and sly, and the men all had lurid tattoos on their arms, and some of them on the backs of their hands or across their knuckles. Usually, they were home-made, and you couldn't always read what they said. The women were skinny too, usually, and they all looked like they needed a shower and some decent food, and they all talked in a muffled, yet hard way and laughed in short, staccato bursts, seemingly at random. No one seemed to make eye contact and they seemed mostly to be talking to themselves, all at once, rather than to one another in turns, but all that was a long time ago. As Tommy and I neared the entrance to Traveler's Peace, an RCMP cruiser, coming from the east, swept past us, its break lights glowing, the flares and reflectors clearly visible down the long, shallow grade. On the other side of the highway, in the distance, more flashing lights, Mounties from Hope, and they swung across the road and pulled in behind the ambulance.

"That man'll make it, Tommy. Grandpa said you probably saved his life."

Tommy half nodded and half shook his head:

"I hope so, Janey. I sure hope so. Hate to think of anyone dying that way, maybe far from home. And if he lives, that's nothing to do with me."

We reached Traveler's Peace and followed the road going to the left. To the right it led to the residential campground and its permanent camping trailers and old RVs with shelters built over them or little porches added on and some even had crooked little fences around their tiny lots. People rented the sites year-round but only stayed in them during the summers, on weekends or holidays. We kept going until we reached the first trailer, grandma and grandpa's, on the right. Tommy waited in the road, watching to make sure that I got inside and that grandma was there. He waved and grandma called out did he want a coffee or tea or something to warm up? but he seemed not to hear and slouched his way across the road and up a few trailers to his place. He kept it neat, but it was so old and rundown and needed paint or new siding that it seemed as if it would soon sink into the soft, moss- and puddle-covered ground.

Grandma hustled me inside and helped me to take off my soaking jacket and told me she would run a hot bath, and I followed her into the little bathroom with its little tub, telling her about the man and the slice across his head and face and grandma said that she was glad I was home, safe and sound, and out of that weather and that I wasn't to think about the wreck. She sprinkled some beads into the steaming water and eased past me. I locked the door behind her and struggled out of my wet-through jeans and I was surprised to find that I was shaking, like Tommy. I could see the driver's face so clearly and how he had tried to look at us when we first arrived and how his one good eye tried to swivel around and find us. I slipped into the scalding water and sank under the surface trying to think of other things. I don't know how long I lay there, but when I got out and dried off I was still shaking, or shaking again, and I pulled on my pajamas, drained the tub, and called out to grandma that I was going to bed. She came down the hall from the kitchen and helped me pull back the covers and smoothed them out over me.

I recall, now, how in those nights I used to think of those beautiful young men from the movies, private schools and blue blazers with crests—did such places really exist, and where were they?—unimaginable money and families, hopping onto desks to declaim poetry, jawlines as straight and dangerous as skate blades, cheekbones and chins sharper and more dangerous still, the boys I knew nowhere near as graceful or sculpted, all somehow less finished, less in focus, not heartbreaking, just vague, droopy and damp, the girls the same, peevish, lumpy. Yet on that night I could not bring those crisp, beautiful young men into focus, did not even try.

II.

I SLEPT LATE THE NEXT DAY, Saturday, almost to noon, and I awoke to the sound of saws and hammers and men talking. I got dressed and found grandma in the kitchen, on the phone, and she pointed to the fixings for sandwiches on the table. I helped myself, and grabbed a pop, and went to the porch and down the steps into an unexpected blue light. The air seemed to glow silver-blue and the backs of my hands were the color of summer sky. I looked up. A tarp was suspended overhead, attached to the side of the trailer and the roof of the porch and tied to tent poles driven into the ground a few yards away. Another tarp was lashed to it and extended out over the front of the trailer, held in place by more poles and rope. There were several saw horses here and there and Cerdic's truck backed up in the driveway, its bed so full of lumber its blunt nose stuck up in the air like a bear trying to catch a scent. Grandpa's little pickup was parked beside it, hunkered down with more boards heaped under the topper, the lawnmowers and tools for his yard business pushed as far under the truck as possible to keep them out of the rain. Between the trucks were bags of sand and gravel. Cerdic's sons were busy filling and tamping shallow squares cut in the grass with the gravel and sand, and into each square they set a pyramidal concrete block. Grandpa, intent on his work, cut a two-by-four with his circular saw while Cerdic held the board. Tommy, looking bewildered and soggy, held a hammer in one hand and a bag of nails in the other. When grandpa saw me, he smiled:

"We were beginning to think you'd never wake up."

Cerdic called me Sleeping Beauty and nodded to Tommy:

"If you like, you can go around behind the porch and dig those last few holes where we marked them out this morning. Not too deep, and pack 'em tight."

Tommy nodded, glanced about and, searching for a place to set the hammer and nails, handed them to me. He picked up a shovel wandered off around the side of the porch.

I stared at grandpa and then looked at the two rows of blocks into which Cedric's sons were setting four-by-fours. The blocks and posts went in regular lines around the front of the trailer, the first row less than a foot from the walls, the other three or so meters out. I walked to the corner and followed them around front and part way down the other side. I emerged from beneath yet another tarp and looked up. The sky was gray, with tattered, low clouds caught in the trees and steep, jagged peaks on either side of the valley. A light mist swirled in the air, cool droplets stinging my face and hands. Behind me, I could hear the pit-pit of drops on the tarp. I kept going along the side of the trailer that faced the road and the row of cedars and the highway, past the rock and flower gardens grandpa had heaped up in the yard, and around the back end, passing between grandma's clothesline and the shed grandpa had built to hide from grandma and to try out his hand at painting and making mosaics out of stones he polished in a little tumbler. I turned the corner and saw Tommy near the back of the porch, gripping the handle in both hands, driving the narrow-nosed shovel deep into the soft, soggy topsoil. I watched him dig for a moment, twisting the blade this way and that to pry loose a rock. I told him about the sandwiches and offered him my unopened soda, but he refused:

"Gotta get these holes dug."

I watched him struggle for another moment, and then headed for the front of the trailer, passing between the porch and the Schull's trailer only a few feet away and running at the same mildly oblique angle to the gravel road out front.

When I got back to where grandpa and Cerdic were working,

grandpa nodded and grinned. I grinned back:

"New deck, right?"

Grandpa nodded:

"New deck. A place to sit out when it's nice."

Retired for a few years from the car dealer where he had worked as a mechanic, he had often talked about how he would like a deck and how he wanted to reinforce the porch and get the lean out of it and maybe replace the stairs.

"Grandpa!"

He shrugged, and looked sheepish. Cerdic snorted. They were enjoying themselves immensely.

They set me to work measuring boards according to the plan they had sketched, while grandpa and Cerdic continued to cut and carefully stack two-by-fours. After a time, Mr. Schull from next door showed up with another circular saw. Normally, he and grandpa avoided one another, as most of the folks at Traveler's Peace avoided one another despite–or perhaps because of–the proximity, but grandpa set him to work right away, running an orange extension cord out the kitchen window since all the porch outlets were already in use. When I next looked up, Mrs. Schull was sitting on the porch steps with grandma, both wrapped in sweaters and jackets. They were friendly, though grandma often referred to her as poor soul when it was just me and grandpa around. Mrs. Schull had few teeth, and she seemed to be embarrassed about it and rarely went into Hope and never to Chilliwack, that I knew of, to shop or go for dinner. Mr. Schull was always talking about how much money he had and all the people he knew in Vancouver, and grandma said that if he had so much money and knew so many important people, why didn't he know a dentist who could give his wife a full set of teeth?

Not long after that, Mr. Pulliquin, who lived on the far side of Tommy, appeared and spoke with grandpa and Cerdic. Soon, they were laughing out loud, enjoying themselves more and more. Mr. Pulliquin was telling them some sort of story, gesturing widely, his face and arms and hands scarred, his sinewy, curled flesh the color of beef jerky, his right hand boasting only the pinkie and thumb and three yellowish stumps. Pretty soon, he was holding boards for grandpa while Cerdic and his sons joined the posts with heavy one-by sixes. I kept at my job, and when I looked up again, a bottle of CC and a case of beer had appeared, and the ancient, ghostly man with the strange name from across the road–for reasons I never understood, he always waved at me and called me little Hugh–was sitting in a chair beside grandma and Mrs. Schull, and someone had hung a couple of trouble lights from rivet holes in the tarps. The day had grown more overcast and dull and the sun had disappeared behind the mountains. Still later, a string of white Christmas lights circled the far edge of the tarps and grandpa had clipped a beat-up aluminum lamp to one of the saw horses so he and Mr. Pulliquin could see to work. Another bottle appeared, another case or two of beer, and people I barely recognized began to appear from the gloom, wraith-like, furtive, a little like dogs afraid of being kicked, and soon they were milling around and helping out, and grandpa had pulled the barbeque from the shed and was grilling hamburgers. When the hamburgers were ready, the work ceased in shifts and more chairs and cases of Molson and Keith's showed up and Cerdic's boys had kicked some of the gravel mound into a circle and piled the cut ends of boards in a heap, poured gasoline on it, and started a fire.

When at last I had measured all the boards Cerdic had set out for me and drawn lines across them in pencil and stacked them under yet another tarp–they seemed to be reproducing on their own–I put together a heaping plate of food and pulled a chair up to the improvised fire pit. Despite the mist and droplets of rain, flames shot high into the darkness and the smell of woodsmoke was deep and warm. All around me, our neighbors were talking and laughing. Mostly, they were older, past retirement, and there were no kids in the trailer park save me, and I never knew of a party or a picnic–usually they sat on their porches, playing cards, not calling across the way, not joining one another for a coffee or a cigarette. Mostly, everybody seemed to be waiting for cable to reach this far up the valley: how many times could a person watch *Love Laughs at Andy Hardy*, about the only movie broadcast on the one grainy channel that the owners of Traveler's Peace provided via an immense and ancient satellite dish near the front entrance. But tonight, a cold, drizzly November night, it was a party of sorts, a building-party, a party of two Crown Royal and five cases of beer. In one day, we had gained most of a new, wrap-around, enclosed deck and the beginnings of an addition to the porch. Grandpa, somewhere in the course of the afternoon, had promised me my own bathroom. Cerdic had added:

"A girl needs her privacy."

"Quite a scene, huh?"

Tommy pulled his chair up next to mine, balancing a paper plate with a hamburger and chips and salad in one hand and a cream soda in the other. When he sat down and got his dinner settled on his lap, I asked him:

"Tommy, why'd you move to Traveler's Peace? It's all old folks here, and it's in the middle of nowhere."

He looked startled, but he often looked startled:

"Gotta live somewheres."

"You know what I mean. Why here?"

He stared at the fire and shook his gaunt skull side to side, as if in argument with himself.

"Like everybody says, 'We all live just beyond Hope.'"

"That doesn't make any sense—"

Before I could ask him again, flashing blue and red lights flickered through the trees from the far side of the highway, lighting up the tall cedars and reflecting off the rain-slick walls of the trailers and vehicles and faces, and everybody turned to watch the lights as they slowed and two Mountie cruisers turned cautiously into Traveler's Peace. I looked around to say something to Tommy, but he had eased his chair away from the fire and into the shadows.

Working My Way through High School and College

Against reason, I ran myself into the knocking box with two hogs, and when I shot the first, the other, because hogs are smart, started squealing and thrashing, and because I'm at least as smart as a hog, I started squealing and thrashing, too, trying to get free, but then I stunned the other one and shot myself in the forehead, opened the knocking box door and tumbled onto the kill floor where I slit my throat, tied a chain around one ankle, winched myself into the air, let the blood drain, and then dropped my corpse into the scalding tank, the water brown with blood, feces, clumps of hair, and the odd toenail. From there, I flipped myself into the dehairer, threw the switch, and I began to clang in place for a moment in the rack until the short arms with rubber paddles and metal teeth began to catch, tearing off hair and the outer layers of skin, and spinning the bright pink me round and round. For an instant, as I saw the floor between the metal bars of the rack, one arm slipped through, bone snapping, compound, forearm and wrist held by shredded tissue. All the while, as I spun, I held a blowtorch to my face and head and to my ass and crotch to burn away hair. Pressing the off switch, I waited a moment for the paddles to stop, and then scraped jowls and ass-crack with a knife to get rid of the stubborn stubble. I then cut slits between the bone and the Achilles and hung me on a spreader, gutted myself, pushed me down the line, split myself almost in two, and then washed the sides with a pressure washer and pushed what was left into the chill cooler, head dangling by the meat and skin of the back of the neck, ears jutting out, mouth hanging open. Later, I made some of me into hams and bacon.

The Pintlers

The first time I became aware of Jeanette was at the Black Sands Art Show, part of Anaconda's annual Summerfest. Local painters, photographers, ceramicists, craftspeople, and merchants had set up awnings, tables, and booths throughout Washoe Park, with walkways looping and meandering among the stalls and temporary galleries. In one corner, local restaurants, pitmasters, and service groups like the Sons of Norway and Daughters of the Mines had stands and mini-restaurants with church or picnic tables and the odd umbrella to cast a bit of shadow, and in another, the I-have-a-cool-old-car-and-you-don't club had classics in a row, hoods up, their owners, primarily middle-aged men with guts and grins, glad to talk with whomever came along. Water hoses and extension cords criss-crossed the paths, and most were covered and secured by rubber cord guards, and folks milled about, on the whole happily and lazily, checking out the wares and trying to decide between noodle bowls, empanadas, barbeque ribs, elephant ears from the Episcopals, or pork chop sandwiches from the Baptists. The Anaconda Volunteer Fire Department had a display on summer fire hazards in the urban-rural interface, and leaflets on defensible space and the home ignition zone.

One company, a hot tub and ceiling fan seller from Missoula or Bozeman, was nestled among the arts and crafts booths and had an industrial hose and extension cord running diagonally across a walkway to supply water and power to their demo models, and although they were covered, the guards didn't sit particularly flat on the trampled grass. I was standing a few yards behind one of my officers, who was chatting with a trooper from the MHP, and was about to tell him to go over to the booth and ask them to nail or stake down the rubber cover strip when a woman, perhaps in her thirties, turned and stepped away from the man she was with. The man had evidently wanted to take her picture, backdropped by black and white photographs large enough for a livingroom wall of Yellowstone bison in winter, their hides crusted with snow and steam from a hotspring rising in the background. Just as the woman stepped back, she caught her heel on the guard and, naturally, tumbled at once onto her bottom and then onto her back. She made an audible thud and gasp as she landed hard on the dry, compact ground, and as her momentum carried her onto her back, her legs went up into the air and her dress, a loose summer cotton, billowed out, a perfect mushroom cap, and then crumpled around her waist.

By then, I was only a step from my officer and the trooper.

"Whoa!"

"'Whoa' is right," said the other. "Did you see that?"

"I did," the trooper jibed, "and, I tell you, from now on, I'm flying with her."

"What?"

"If the plane gets into trouble, you could use those underwear as a parachute."

I put a hand on each of their shoulders and gave them a shove:

"Rather than gawking, how about helping?"

"Yes, ma'am."

They both looked sheepish, but before they could cross the few yards to assist, the man, who could not have been more than 5'3" or 5'4" and who was as spare as a fencepost, had stooped over and gently taken her arm and placed it around his neck. In a single motion and seemingly without effort, he lifted her from the ground and set her on her feet. She cried out as her ankles took the weight and all but crumpled again.

Even from a distance I could see that her left ankle had begun to swell, and I pushed past the two lunkheads and asked the couple if I could help. The woman, in tears, gratefully acknowledged my offer and I slipped her other arm around my shoulders and she hopped as we supported her to a nearby picnic table. After a bit of maneuvering, her ponytail at one point slapping me across the face, she dropped onto the bench and leaned back against the top. The bench sagged with her considerable weight, and creaked as she shifted this way and that trying to get comfortable. She held onto my hand the entire time, thanking me over and over again between gasps for air. Her dress had fallen, as the man had lifted her, back into position, but as she sat, she kept tugging on the hemline to pull it down.

The man, his wispy, thinning black hair slicked back from his widow's peak and temples in the style more of the 1950s than the 2000s, his skin dark and tanned and deeply lined, his face handsome in an awkward, uneven way, was perhaps likewise trying to thank me, and he had his right hand out as if to shake mine, but I couldn't understand a word he was saying. He spoke just above a whisper, and if he was speaking English, French, or Spanish, or all three at once, I couldn't pick out any words. I reached out, his rough hand, stones wrapped in leather, dwarfed in mine, and he pumped my arm like he was trying to get water from deep in the ground.

I told him that I was glad to help, that my name was Helen Ross, and that I was chief of the city-county police. Whether he understood me, I cannot say, but he kept nodding and pumping. I disentangled my hand and turned to the woman to introduce myself to her.

At last letting go of the hem, she began patting at the material covering her thighs and waist. “Oh, that was embarrassing.”

She was crying softly now, and I activated my shoulder mic and called for a couple of paramedics to join us—discreetly, no stretcher, no scuttling through the crowds—and to bring some ice packs, wraps, tape, painkillers, a few bottles of water, and a pair of crutches. As we waited for the paramedics, I learned that her name was Jeanette and that her husband’s name was Jean-Baptiste.

A couple of weeks later I stopped at the Phillips to gas up my cruiser and stepped into the shop to see Gus about finding a time to get an oil change and alignment for my Tundra. Jacob and Gus had been great friends and hunting partners, and when Jacob died and Ellen went away to college and never looked back, it somehow came about that I became Gus’ hunting buddy. Mary, Gus’ wife, didn’t mind—Gus was like a brother to me—and we got out a few times a year. While we were talking about elk hunting in the fall, Jean-Baptiste, wearing overalls and covered in grease, came up to me and took my hand and began pumping it and bobbing his head and saying something. When I asked how Jeanette was doing, was her ankle doing any better, his eyes glistened and he shrugged his shoulders and held his hands palm up, his elbows tucked against his ribs, and I smiled and was none the wiser: maybe she was in a cast, or maybe she was jogging every day. He jounced my hand once more, and just as quickly as he had appeared, he disappeared beneath an Outback on a lift.

When I turned back to Gus, he was laughing:

“Ain’t he the damnedest guy you ever met?”

“I can’t understand a word he says. Can you?”

“He’s not so hard to follow, once you get to know him, and he can fix anything: car, motorcycle, lawnmower. I just wish I could get him to work full-time for me.”

I told Gus about the accident at Summerfest. He had never met Jeanette but had perhaps heard about her tumble? “He was telling me something about someone who fell, but he talks so damn fast in that whisper of his, I mostly just nod. I think he told me, one time, that someone shot him in the throat."

At that bit of news, I pointed towards Gus' small office in one corner of the garage and told him he was buying me a coffee:

"I'd like to know that story. Call it professional curiosity."

Jeanette and Jean-Baptiste, it seemed, were real life Cajuns—that much I had deduced—straight from small town Louisiana, yet what they were doing in Montana, or how long they had been here, or how long they planned to stay, Gus didn't know.

"He wandered in a month or two ago, and at first I thought his old Ranger needed repairs, but somehow he made me to understand that he was looking for work. I didn't really need someone, but I offered him a couple of days a week and he talked me down to one. Or, at least he's been showing up on Mondays. I keep trying to give him more days, but he prefers to work for himself, as a landscaper and handyman."

The couple, according to Gus, had lived in St. Benedict, a dot on the map north of a stream bearing the wonderful name of Venchy Branch and across Lake Pontchartrain from New Orleans. Jean-Baptiste had been a part-time groundsman and maintenance worker for an abbey on the south side of the creek, and otherwise did whatever odd jobs he wanted, including helping his old ones with their nearby farm. In the wake of Katrina, skilled and unskilled labor had been in high demand and Jean-Baptiste and some his brothers and buddies, after doing their part to get St. Benedict back on its feet, had gone into the city to do what they could and to earn some extra money. They worked demolition in ruined neighborhoods, and helped to clear downed trees and upended or flooded-out cars and houses in the worst-hit neighborhoods. They also served on repair crews tending to salvageable homes and commercial buildings, often working one job during the day and another at night.

One night, while tearing out moldy, rotten drywall in the offices of an electrical supply company on the New Orleans side of the 17th Street Canal, several police, or at least individuals in police uniforms, had broken into the attached warehouse in order to steal all the copper, widgets, tools, and machines they could get their hands on. Jean-Baptiste and his brothers and buddies wisely ignored the cops and kept about their jobs, but the NOPD officers decided to ensure their silence with a modest display of firepower.

"Stop right there: a crew, maybe cops, is robbing a warehouse, and you decide to keep tearing out ruined drywall and stinky carpet in the front end? No way."

Gus shrugged:

"Different time, different place. The world had gone sideways. Or maybe the cops told them they were moving the supplies to a safer place."

"You're just making this up."

Gus grinned:

"You want me to tell you what I know, or not?"

As the cops were leaving with their loot, having filled a 26-foot Ryder with everything from fittings to fans to a Daewoo standup forklift, they went into the office space, drew their weapons, and shot at the unarmed workers, men who were very deliberately looking the other way.

The might-be cops had opened fire with pistols and shotguns, not to kill, perhaps, but to impress upon the men the necessity of minding their own business. They may not have intended to kill, but they murdered two men, anyway, including one of Jean-Baptiste's brothers, and Jean-Baptiste had been hit in the windpipe with the shot that had blown through and past his brother's face and skull.

It was when they called for an ambulance that things really got interesting.

Jeanette, it turns out, was there that night—after the hurricane, she refused to stay alone while Jean-Baptiste went away to work—and after her husband had crumpled to the floor, she tried to stop the gush of blood, pressing her hand over the holes blasted into his neck. In between tearing her jean jacket into make-shift bandages and plucking a shard of his brother's cranium from Jean-Baptiste's chin, she used some of the broken plaster to elevate his feet in order to fend off shock for as long as she could. In the meantime, the brothers and buddies had rushed outside in order to grab whatever weapons, mostly hunting rifles and skinning knives, they had in their rigs. When the ambulance finally arrived the paramedics refused to enter the building until the cops or National Guard showed up and secured the scene, which, given the widespread strife, dislocation, and violence of the time, could have been whenever, and the men ordered them in at gunpoint. As the first cops, responding to 911 reports of shots fired and paramedics held against their will, pulled into the parking lot and began to climb from their squad cars, Leroy, the next oldest brother after Jean-Baptiste, pumped a shell into the chamber of a 12 gauge:

"No damn way. No damn cops."

To make his point, he fired into the grill of the nearest prowler.

At that moment, as even more police screeched into the parking lot, including some who may have been involved in the robbery, events seemed ready to spin out of hand, with the cops yelling for the workers to drop their weapons and Jean-Baptiste's crew replying with obscenities and threatening, with their deer knives, to skin them right down to their souls.

While all of this was going on, Jeanette picked her little husband off the floor, as if he were a bride about to be carried across the threshold, and directed the two paramedics toward a side door, forcing them to lead the way. When they refused to open the door, in fear of getting shot, she turned a little sideways and forced her left arm away from her torso, using the inert Jean-Baptiste's feet to kick at them as forcibly as possible, which couldn't have been much.

I see the moment clearly: his head lolling over the crook of her cradled left arm, neck exposed, the crude bandages soaked and heavy and slipping away, exposing a dozen, two dozen killing gashes and punctures, his small, slight frame a sagging V between her trembling, struggling arms, his legs from the knees dangling from her elbow. For all she knew, he was dying, perhaps already dead, and she had to use him as a sort of feeble battering ram against the paramedics.

"You're crazy. We open that door and we're dead."

Somehow, she made them comply, made them open the door and lead the way around the corner of building and into the middle of the fray. Somehow, they scuttled into the parking lot, open and exposed between two groups of angry, weary-yet-adrenalized, well-armed and impatient antagonists, without getting shot. Once they reached the ambulance, one of the paramedics jumped inside and with the last of her strength, and help from the other, Jeanette half lifted, half pushed Jean-Baptiste onto the gurney. Spent, both physically and emotionally, she staggered against the fender and collapsed.

"At the hospital, the cops arrested Jeanette and handcuffed Jean-Baptiste to his bed and charged him with robbery and felony murder for the deaths of his brother and friend."

"Ok, that's the first thing you've said that I can believe. The rest of your story is horse shit."

After poking holes in Gus' story for a while, and making a mental note to put a call into the NOPD, I set my empty coffee cup on his desk and headed through the garage and back toward my cruiser. As I passed Jean-Baptiste with the Subaru still on the lift, he was looking up at the underside of the engine, holding a trouble light in his right hand and moving it and his head this way and that to get a better view of whatever he was working on. Sure enough, with his chin elevated and a bright light only inches from his face casting precise, almost surgical shadows, I could see a dozen or more scars and dents sprent across the front and side of his neck, as if a herculean, monstrous child had jabbed him with tiny, malicious, sharp fingers.

He also had a pinkish scar on one side of his chin.

Some days later, while I was supervising a speed trap just east of town on Highway 1—and was therefore bored out of my mind and not thinking about anything in particular except for needing to pee—it occurred to me that I had perhaps seen Jeanette and Jean-Baptiste before the fall at the fair. Since, evidently, we want to wait until the sun can push tourists into the parched earth like a giant, asphyxiating hand, and since, apparently, we like to give the fire season a chance to really get going and perhaps turn the sky as brown and raspy as the inside of a smoker's lungs, Anaconda Summerfest takes place on the first weekend in August. In early April, I had been in Missoula for a meeting of Western Montana Chiefs of Police, and during a lunch break had wandered along the Clark Fork, across a footbridge, and onto campus. I drifted by a dog park and football practice field and eventually became tangled up with a small crowd heading into a fieldhouse. In the time-honored way of cops, I gained admittance by flashing my badge. By chance, I had stumbled into a powwow, and the floor of the arena, no doubt usually a basketball court, was full of fancy and grass dancers in full regalia, the air vibrating with drums and the eerie, otherworldly chants of the drummers. The lower stands around the court were full, and I climbed into the second tier to watch the bright, energetic movements of a hundred or more performers.

I was enjoying the dancers so much that, save for the entrenched habit of scanning the faces and body language of those around me, I might not have noticed a couple who emerged from the concourse through one of the many tunnels leading to the stands. The man, who may have been Jean-Baptiste, looked more or less as he did on that day in Anaconda when I first became aware of them, but the woman, who might have been

Jeanette, looked nothing like the disheveled, teary woman with the painfully swollen ankle whom I had helped to a picnic table.

A head taller than the man, she appeared ebullient, energetic, and her hair, a bright, brittle blonde, was cut short. Even from a distance, her eyes seemed to shine with bonhomie and something more than casual interest, and once they emerged from the concourse tunnel and she could see the dancers and hear the drumming and chanting, she was riveted. She all but ran to the railing on the landing above the first tier of seats and leaned over to get as clear a view as possible. She scanned this way and that, appearing to try and take in the entire spectacle at once.

She was entranced, almost giddy, but what struck me most as I thought about it, roasting in my 100-degree car and wondering why, at my age and rank, I still took turns in the field, was that she was painfully thin. So thin, in fact, that while she was clearly buoyant, she also had the look, perhaps, of someone recovering from a long illness. There were the remnants of dark half-moons beneath her eyes and her skin seemed, at least in the greenish, industrial lighting of the arena, inelastic, waterless, stretched a little too tautly over the bones of her arms, shoulders, and neck.

As I observed her and her seemingly undernourished partner, like any cop working in rural America, I thought, and perhaps even spoke, what immediately came to mind:

"Tweakers."

They were both so thin, and if the man appeared calm, the woman seemed fidgety and amped, as if she were willing herself not to scramble onto the floor and join the dancers. But if they were tweakers, unless one or both pulled a knife or gun or jumped from the landing onto the folks below, they weren't my problem and no doubt the university cops had already spotted them. I watched the dancers for a while longer, and when the time came to head back for the afternoon meetings, I worked my way along the edge of the floor and towards a large tunnel that I guessed led to the foyer. As I turned the corner onto the downward sloping ramp, I almost ran into the man and woman.

Although the air was filled with rapid and dramatic singing and drumming, they were dancing, waltzing, slowly and closely, to a music of their own, and the man moved effortlessly and seemed almost to carry the woman in his arms. He was smiling and murmuring something to her, and she was giggling and moving almost as gracefully, she towering over him, a kind of joy brushed over her sallow, desiccated skin and dark, almost bruised eyes, he looking up at her with such artless happiness and affection, and no doubt I paused for a moment to watch their dance just as I had watched the fancy dancers.

They were no concern of mine, so I stepped past them and weaved my way through the others in the passageway and returned to the dry, yet necessary mill of how best to police small towns and rural communities. By the time I reached the hotel, I suppose, I had all-but forgotten them until, unbidden, the image of the dancers came to mind while I broiled in my cruiser.

Could that really have been Janette and Jean-Baptiste?

A few weeks later, in coordination with the AVFD and a dozen state and federal agencies, and along with Park Rangers, the MHP, and every other sheriff, tribal police, and game warden in Montana, we were making efforts to update folks in our counties on the fire situation, the worst in a string of bad years. The fire west of Absarokee had reached nearly 300 square miles, and a string of several smaller yet uncontained fires hopscotched west from there, with the nearest to us just south and east of Bozeman. With out-of-control wildfires in Oregon and Idaho pouring even more smoke into Montana and an inversion choking the valley, the sky was brown and low and you couldn't see the Pintlers from town. With dry lightning storms forecast for Deer Lodge and surrounding counties, we hoped that people had their photos, valuables, and animals ready to go should an evacuation order be issued, and we were trying to warn people, using every media possible, that their world could become catastrophic, even deadly, in a matter of moments.

As part of our overall strategy, and especially in an effort to alert the outliers who lived beyond the reach of newspapers, television, and the internet, we were posting notices on county roads and accesses to public lands about the increased risk of fires in the area. More, after hearing reports about a French couple buying a cabin on a few acres in one of the drainages west and south of town, and after putting in a call to the NOPD—the detective I spoke to, a guy named Robicheaux, said they were still investigating but the case had stalled: despite two dead bodies and an empty warehouse, all charges against Jean-Baptiste and his kith and kin had been dropped due to a lack of evidence; when I asked about the cops-as-robbers angle, Robicheaux, who sounded a bit hungover and gloomy, hesitated for a moment and then admitted that, very likely, it had been cops and that he knew who they were—I was curious to see if it was Jeanette and Jean-Baptiste who had bought the cabin, and I was curious to see how they were doing. I was also, frankly, a bit concerned that they might not wholly grasp what it meant to live on a remote property at high altitude in fire season. After work, I signed out one of the department's 4X4s, grabbed a sheaf of the fire warnings and a staple gun, and headed west.

Once on the highway, I drove a few miles and, just past the junction with Lime Spur Road, turned south into the Barker Creek drainage. I followed the logging road as it meandered uphill and down in the general direction of the creek, and then kept on, heading more or less south on the east side of the stream until the road branched and I swung back to the east and north, climbing steadily up a steep foothill. Just short of the summit, I turned onto an even more poorly maintained logging road and followed it, first to the northeast and then to the southwest, through thick forest. The road was a rough mix of washouts, ruts, collapsed cuttings, and abrupt fallaways, and, one hand on the wheel and the other braced against the ceiling,

I bounced along, following it as it circled a sheer and sweeping clearcut. Everywhere was long, dry grass and slash, prime biomass for a fast-spreading fire.

Down to a few miles an hour due to the road, and wondering if the straining, superheated V8 might spark the sward, I made slow progress until the road began to improve as it rose toward a tree-filled ravine. Not only was the road getting better, but the grass and saplings on either side had been cut back several yards. Rather than following the V of the ravine, the road meandered like an old stream among the ponderosa and doug fir, blocking any sight of what lay ahead. At last, I emerged into a small, mostly level clearing shaped like an elongated diamond. In the center stood a smallish, smart-looking one-and-a-half story log cabin with gables and a blue steel roof. The road, well-graveled and without potholes or ruts, circled in front of the cabin and matching detached garage, and parked in front of the garage was a small Ford Ranger with Louisiana plates. Beside the Ranger was an old VW bug convertible with its top down.

How had they gotten that thing over that road?

To the right of the house, in raised beds enclosed by chainlink, was a thriving vegetable garden, and behind the garden was a wall-less shed full to the ceiling of herringbone-stacked split logs, enough for both a fireplace and a woodstove for two long winters. Beyond the shed at the top of the clearing was a tidy stand of quaking aspen.

I tapped the horn and when no one appeared, I climbed out of the rig, a bit seasick from the hour and a half on washed-out washboard, and staggered over to the Ranger and looked through the back window of the canopy. Inside, in an orderly fashion, were two lawnmowers and landscaping gear as well as three plastic tubs of what looked to be everyday handyman tools. I continued on to the front door, and knocked.

A few more steps, and I peered in through the large front window. The floorplan was open, with an amiable livingroom giving onto a dining area and kitchen with an island. On the dining room table, in a clear glass vase, was a single, apparently fresh cut rose. I walked around the house, but nobody appeared to be home. I returned to the 4X4 and, grabbing a fire warning flier and one of my cards, I wrote that if they had any concerns or wanted to discuss their options should they have to leave in a hurry, they could call me or speak with anyone at the police department or volunteer fire station.

Taking one last look around—save for a couple of shade trees, they, or the previous owners, had cut a more than substantial enough fire break around the house, and they had likewise thinned the trees nearest the structures—I climbed back into the truck and gritted my teeth: past seven, the sky old copper and lowering and the light in the clearing a peculiar, eyeball-wrenching aquamarine, I wouldn't get back to town until nearly 10:00 or even 11:00 p.m., by which time I would be exhausted, battered from the drive, and cranky.

Still, Jeanette and Jean-Baptiste had a wonderful place, the very picture of the Montana dream.

As I drove, I remember, I thought about fires, and about how damn far from anywhere or anyone Jeanette and Jean-Baptiste had landed. I had read somewhere that Katrina had generated winds up to 175 mph, a force I cannot even imagine, and it had evidently hit the couple so hard that they had been borne aloft, twisting and tumbling amid the wreckage and ruined lives, only to land, to wash ashore, more than 6000 feet up the side of a mountain in western Montana. Now that's a hell of a storm, one that can uproot you from family, from all you know, from your history, and drop you as close to the middle of nowhere as you could imagine.

I have never been trapped by a fire, but I have worked in the heart of them, directing evacuations and driving pell-mell down roads choked with black smoke yet raging with cinders and falling, blazing branches, fiery debris pelting windscreen and windows, homes on either side roaring, bursting with fire, propane tanks fire-balling, the air shuddering and quivering, the vehicle thrown this way and that from the concussions or fire-generated winds, the whole time trying to see the road, to stay on the road. Fires, as I suppose most folks in the West know, make their own weather, and I once saw a tornado of flame rise above a forest, vaporing trees in what seemed like moments. That sense of panic: this is more than I can handle.

By the time I reached town, dropped off the 4X4, and dropped onto my own couch, whiskey in a tumbler with two cubes, I was, as predicted, cranky.

The fire season, as all fire seasons do, passed when the first real snows came in November and doused the flames. And from early November, it snowed steadily and heavily at elevation, and anybody living above 5000 or 6000 feet either had to snowbird it someplace more livable or hunker down for the winter, pretty well-stocked for food and supplies. Expert snowmobilers can get around in the mountains all winter, but they have to deal with snow so deep it can bury a machine that slows down too much, or they can disappear in avalanches, their bodies unrecoverable until, in some cases, early summer.

Although I never saw Jeanette again, and perhaps had only seen her that one time when she fell so painfully, so mortifyingly at the fair, and although I never saw Jean-Baptiste again after that time at Gus' garage, I was able to piece together, from different folks and reports, that their Montana adventure did not end that summer, or even that long, cold, snowy winter. Rather, in the late spring, they moved back to Louisiana to be with their families and friends.

Yet that winter, long after anybody could travel easily, or even at all, in the mountains, Jean-Baptiste caught a cold that turned into pneumonia. He probably caught the cold at the hospital in January, and had been battling it for a few weeks only to become sicker and sicker. Since they were so far away from town, and since, perhaps, Jean-Baptiste was like most guys and preferred to suffer rather than to get some help, his lungs began to fill with fluids, and he developed a roaring temperature and endless cough, and after a while of that, burning up, he slipped into semi-consciousness.

I like to think that he was very apologetic about it all. Hoarse from coughing, and struggling to breathe, he no doubt asked Jeanette not to worry about him, explained that it would pass, that he would get better soon, that he was sorry that he was not able to help more around the house and yard, not able to clear a path to the woodshed or to the garage, not able to go into town should they need anything.

Of course, had I been there, I would not have understood a word he was saying. Already a whisperer in other languages, I wonder what he sounded like while he was slowly drowning and crackling for air?

One day, she must have told him:

"That's it, I'm going for help, to find someone to help me get you into town. You need to see a doctor."

Whether, by that point, he could argue or even respond at all, I cannot say, but Jeanette made about the only decision she could. She bundled up, went out to the garage, hit the automatic door-opener, and pulled the starting cord on the ancient snowmobile. It started immediately, since Jean-Baptiste took such care of his machines and tools, and grabbing a shovel, she let the sled idle while she dug and compacted a long ramp to the top of the deep, heavy snow. Once satisfied that the ramp was gradual enough to get up to speed before hitting the powder and becoming bogged down, she bungeed the shovel to the back of the sled and went back into the house in order to swaddle the baby, Lisa-Marie, in a number of layers. She then stuffed the bundle of baby between her breasts inside her coveralls.

A wool cap beneath her hood and goggles to protect her eyes, she climbed onto the snowmobile, a twenty-five year old Arctic

Cat that now sits behind Gus's shop, for sale, a much better machine than people realize, revved the engine, popped the clutch, and shot up the ramp.

I like to think she caught a bit of air.

She proceeded carefully and steadily, erring on the side of giving it too much gas rather than not enough. Nevertheless, she was an inexperienced snowmobiler and, after several miles, yet well short of the highway, she submarined into a snowbank and interred the Cat. She buried the sled, but not, after a long and exhausting struggle, its riders. Using the shovel, she cleared away enough snow to be able to stand on the snowmobile's seat and survey the terrain.

Talking happily the entire time to Lisa-Marie, Jeanette took her bearings, jumped from the seat into the snow and immediately sank past her hips. Soaked from her labors, she unzipped the coveralls to her waist, moved the bundle to one side to keep the baby safe and, rotating at the hips and swinging her arms, began to plow through the snow and along, she hoped, the road. Hours later, and quite a bit off course, she stumbled on a house at the north end of Nelson Gulch. They knew someone with a snowcat and would take them directly to his place.

The baby, I discovered, had been born, following the plan and the natural course of things, at the Community Hospital in Anaconda, and so was, by birth and by dint of experience, a true Montanan. Jean-Baptiste recovered, evidently none the worse for the wear, and once spring rolled around they sold the cabin and acreage and moved back into their old house, which had not sold in that time, in St. Benedict. That next winter, a bit out of the blue, they sent me a Christmas card and pictures of Lisa-Marie, and I have not heard from or about them since.

The Dying Albertan

Part I.

1.

Back in the day, O'Keevan had been touted as the Glenn Gould of Stone, but that had been twenty-five years ago, and although he had had successes—considerable successes, in fact—as a sculptor and painter in the years since his first dazzling works, his older self had never quite equaled the daring, brightness, and volatility of his younger self. He was known in contemporary circles as a sometimes irascible and remote, if technically gifted artist. He was perhaps equally well-known as a keen, if often mordant critic of Canadian culture and the arts, and in addition to a number of essays, radio pieces, and television appearances on everything from the Group of Seven to the Tragically Hip—his most louche publication, no doubt, was a short essay ("Peggy Bakes Cookies") comparing Margaret Atwood's public persona to one of those monkeys at the zoo who craps in its hand and throws it at the visitors; he closed the article with a line about how she was even less genial to her friends—he was also the subject of a number of essays, studies, and problematic interviews.

Problematic because he was a notorious fabulist. Worse, he had no tells. Perfectly straightforward seeming if he wanted to be, he never let on when he was spinning tales, and if an interviewer hadn't done their homework, his dissimulations had a way of finding their way into print or onto the TV screen. A few years ago, in the course of being interviewed about a showing of his latest work at the Power Plant, he spoke enthusiastically about a lesser Tom Thomson painting, *The Bridge*, describing it in detail and affirming how Thomson's technique had been profoundly inspiring and influential on the series now on display, particularly in O'Keevan's homage, *The Causeway*. The interviewer and fact-checkers at *Maclean's* didn't catch the fact that Thomson had never painted a work entitled *The Bridge*—he had done a watercolor when he was seventeen that was referred to in some catalogs as *The Bridges*, but it bore no resemblance to the work O'Keevan had so lovingly described—and they quoted at length from the ekphrasis. As it turned out, *The Bridge* was actually one of O'Keevan's most recent canvases, one that the curator at the Power Plant, for reasons of her own, had decided not to include in the showing. The artist did not approve. The magazine, caught out the instant the article appeared, published a correction in the next edition, but by all accounts O'Keevan was jubilant over both his little con and jab at the curator yet played the innocent in a follow-up with the *Toronto Sun*: evidently, there had been a misunderstanding.

He also hated to talk about his past or personal life, and he rarely told the same story twice. Sometimes he was born in Halifax, sometimes in Antigonish, but his birth certificate—a matter of public record and not difficult to verify—said Moncton, New Brunswick. His mother died in childbirth. His mother lived in Sarnia. She lived in Istanbul. His father died in a boating accident before he was born. His father lived in Cape Breton. His father was rumored to be Jean Beliveau. O'Keevan remarked that he was an only child. He wasn't an only child. His brother had played for the Brandon Wheat Kings. His brother had drowned in Canoe Lake at the age of two years and seven months. His twin sister was a gynecologist in Toronto. He had no sister. O'Keevan said he had been married three times. He had never been married. He had been married, for a month and a day, to

Margo Timmins. He had no children. He had a grown daughter. He studied in New York. He hadn't studied in New York, a matter of considerable regret. He had studied in Munich. He had never been to Munich. He had lived in Paris. He was friends with Mavis Gallant. He had never met Mavis Gallant, a rather difficult thing to do since as far as he knew, she had died before he was born. He had a cabin in the Cariboo that he loved above all places. He hated the bush—too many mosquitoes and black flies—and would only live in cities. He detested cities and would only live in small towns—small towns like Vancouver, where, a little research would reveal, he had lived for the past twenty-some years.

Worst of all, if I were to take the job, was that he was a story-changer when it came to talking about his influences and the inspirations for and meanings of individual pieces. The Group of Seven had had the most profound and lasting impact on his art, no question. He wasn't really a fan of the Group of Seven, too much snow. Too cartoonish. The Group of Seven never saw a twig they didn't want to paint, and then paint again. Emily Carr was a tourist. Emily Carr was a genius—seeing her work, the actual canvases, had changed his life, made him want to be an artist. Emily Carr never had an idea of her own. Elizabeth Wyn Wood was the first Canadian to know the beauty of the sculpted line; works like *Gesture*, *Dead Tree*, and especially *Passing Rain*, taught him everything he knew about being a sculptor, about passion and seeing and fluidity and grace. Elizabeth Wyn Wood was overly influenced by the Group of Seven. Elizabeth Wyn Wood never saw a twig she didn't want to sketch, paint, or sculpt.

Probably O'Keevan's most famous painting, *Cumberland Heights*, was a landscape in blues and greens and mustards of a gentle, rock-strewn and lichen-covered rise (in the foreground and taking up most of the canvas) overlooking a black and menacing Queen Maud Gulf (in the background) while (at the top of the canvas) a snow squall was churning and building on the horizon. He said it was a painting about the resiliency of the small, of life. He said he wanted to create a painting about the way lichen felt when one brushed it with one's fingertips. He said it was about the feeling of great satisfaction he achieved when, on a trip to the Arctic, he and his companions had finally reached the bay and sat upon the easy, wind-burnt rise and watched a storm lash across the gulf while they sat in warm sunlight, a soft refreshing breeze at their backs. He said he had never been to the Arctic, and had painted it after a postcard of someplace in Norway that someone had sent to him from Granada, Spain. (This latter story earned him considerable enmity, for a time, among Canadians who want Canadian things to be Canadian; he later denied that he had said that, and all was forgiven, if not already forgotten.) He said it was about his second wife's mental illness. He said he wanted to capture the sound of the wind from the water reaching the land. He said it was about color. About proportion. About the way the irregular compels the mind. He said it was just a landscape, and didn't mean anything. He said he had no more idea than anyone else did what it was about, if it was about anything, but that he had other paintings for sale: buy a painting and you can say anything you like about it.

When the Arts editor at *The Orb and Post* left a voicemail asking if I would be interested in interviewing Niall O'Keevan (b. Neil Kirvin, 29 March 1961) on the occasion of the 25th anniversary of the first showing of *The Dying Albertan*, one of his most anomalous, yet most talked about works and no doubt one of the most infamous sculptures ever produced by a Canadian—*The Province* declared at the time that the *enfant terrible* of Glace Bay had made something "too ugly and too beautiful to be art"—I didn't call him back right away. Although *would you be interested in* is most often pro forma when directed to a freelancer—of course I would be: I prefer to sleep indoors, to have enough to eat, Toronto's an expensive city, I love my little apartment and never, ever want to live with my parents, again, etc.—I held off returning Bailey's call for a number of reasons. For one, I was no doubt pretty far down on his list; the others, including at least a few who lived in B.C., had turned him down. Two, I had no particular desire to battle O'Keevan for some kind of truth; he didn't like to talk about himself or his work and I could respect that. (Actually I couldn't—if you want to be in the public eye, you have to expect a few personal questions; you want to sell your whatever, you're going to have to talk about it—but I had no desire to go toe-to-toe with a cranky giant.) Three, what was the thing called, anyway: generally, it was known as *The Dying Albertan*, but it seems to have been listed, for some exhibitions, as *The Dying Athabaskan*—he meant, he once remarked in an interview, someone from the region of the Athabasca tar sands—and whenever anybody asked about why he had never quite settled on a title, he would call it something else altogether, *The Dying Québécois*, *The Dying Haligonian*, *The Injured Maritimer*, and others. Four, both O'Keevan and the statue were in Vancouver; if I waited to reply, say a day or two, then Bailey might cough up more money and a better per diem; that way I could get a couple of extra days out of the trip and visit my brother and his wife in Delta, see the new niece.

Did I really want to get lied to, pushed around, and probably belittled, to boot? I did not.

I texted Bailey that I would let him know tomorrow, and poured a glass of wine for Janelle, my best friend, and Sasi, my sort-of-cousin—he was, he would explain if I asked, my mother's brother's wife's sister's son; I could never figure out if that meant we were related or not—and plopped down on the couch beside him:

"Well, what should I do? Should I take the job?"

Sasi was of the opinion, from what I had told them and from what he had read and seen on TV, that O'Keevan was an asshole and not worth the trouble. Janelle thought he was quite handsome and, after all, he was on TV and had met the Queen and any number of prime ministers and movie stars and artists, and he couldn't really be as bad as everyone said.

"You're not helping. Besides, do I really want to spend a day or two with him and with that damn sculpture? It's not ugly, it's just so sad and forsaken, or something."

Sasi looked at me:

"I think it's about hate. I mean, look at what he does to the body. Whoever he had in mind, he must have hated him."

"You think it tells a story?"

Sasi considered:

"It seems so personal, as if he were trying to say something about someone rather than about something. As if he were not trying to capture an idea, but an emotion. Then, again, I'm a mathematician and don't really understand these things. For all I know, it's about his mother, or his balls, or about nothing at all, just something that popped into his head for reasons that nobody will ever know. Probably even he doesn't know where the idea came from."

Janelle said she thought it was about love:

"You wouldn't show such agony, such vulnerability and sorrow if you didn't love the person, and you wouldn't allow yourself to come so close to such devastation unless that person mattered so much to you that you had to bring yourself to try and understand what they were feeling and knowing as they were dying."

Sasi and I both giggled. Janelle had been an English major before going to law school.

"What now?"

"You feel things deeply. Very deeply."

Janelle flipped the bird, and the way she looked at Sasi suggested to me, once more, and despite her denials, that she had a thing for him:

"You guys suck, and I hate you both."

A bottle and a half of Malbec later, Sasi thought we should get to the heart of the issue:

"How's your bank account?"

I called Bailey in the morning and told him I would take the gig. We haggled over money, the number of days, how much extra for the photographs, and he told me that it was all setup and that I was to meet O'Keevan next Friday morning, 10:30, his studio:

"On Thursday evening, you'll be admitted afterhours to the Vancouver Art Gallery so you can photograph the monster. I'll fax you the addresses, contacts, and contract, and you're good to go. Oh, and there's a bonus if you can get him to tell who he's sleeping with. Have fun."

Have fun? I had only a few days to finish a 1000-word article on natural gas-fired power plants and new CO2-capture technologies for an industry trade journal—freelancers may be the last of the generalists—remind myself of O'Keevan's corpus and recent showings, research what I could about his life (knowing he would tell tales), write my questions—some standard, most tailored to the subject—make sure I had plenty of paper, new batteries and backups for the recorder, pack my cameras, lights and stands, reflectors and diffusers, and brace myself for an unpleasant experience—followed, if all worked out, by some family-time and Kavita's wonderfully old world food extravaganzas.

Have fun?

A gig's a gig.

2.

O'Keevan, as I knew from my research and from seeing him on TV, looked a little like Harrison Ford, only shorter, rounder, less rugged. He was also not wearing a fedora or toting a whip when I arrived at his studio, a two-storey, suitably industrial-looking brick building on Beach Avenue. A sidewalk led from the street to the south side of the building and after I pressed the buzzer, he met me at a the door which opened directly into the studio. He was wearing a blue blazer, white oxford collar shirt, jeans, and Italian shoes—he was, after all, worth a fortune, but apparently more from wise investments than commissions and sales—and he was very polite in greeting me, very old-school Canadian: courteous, demure, smiling, offering no clue as to what he thought of me or the occasion. Besides, he had been interviewed dozens of times, and at worst I was just another reporter he had to engage for an hour or two. At best, I might know something and not prove too dim about art, or about his work in particular.

The space was very much a working studio, one large room with a well-worn hardwood floor and industrial lighting suspended from the high ceiling. The back wall was taken up by a loading dock and although the back quarter of the chamber was given over to benches and tables stacked with the tools and equipment of sculpture, there were no works-in-progress; in the old days, O'Keevan, like Michelangelo, had done his own carving, but these days, like many wealthy artists, he contracted out the stone-work to professionals in Pietrasanta. The rest of the studio was set up for painting, with a number of easels of various sizes and scores of canvases stacked here and there against the walls. Some of the canvases were immense, large enough to hang in the lobby of a corporate office or in a prominent place in a gallery or museum, while others were small enough for private collectors. A work-bench ran along the south wall and above it were several paintings that I had not seen in any of his catalogs or exhibitions: some were very likely new and there for his contemplation or for the contemplation of his visitors. One or two paintings on easels were covered in cloth: unfinished, perhaps, or at least not for my eyes.

At the front of the studio, beneath the wall of windows overlooking English Bay, was a generous conversation area, complete with couches and comfortable chairs set around a coffee table. Not too far away on the north wall was a kitchenette. He gestured for me to sit on the couch facing the windows and the water, and asked if I would like a coffee. Wearing one of my two professional suits—the black with the conservative-length skirt and well-tailored jacket—I eased into a comfortable position and looked up at him:

"Just a regular coffee?"

"Oh, well, I could step out for a moment, to the corner, there's a Waves. . . . I see you're joking."

"Any coffee would be fine."

He returned from the kitchenette with two mugs and set one on a coaster on the table:

"A dear friend gave me one of those fancy machines where you drop the little plastic thing in, close the lid, push a button, and wait, but I couldn't pronounce the name or find the little plastic things, so I gave it away—don't report that, in case she reads it."

He eased into a chair, and we talked for a bit about the view and had I spent much time in Vancouver? I had, family in Delta, loved the lower mainland and Vancouver Island, and while we chatted, I dug out my notepad and recorder and set it on the table. After a time, he leaned forward:

"You went over to the gallery?"

I nodded and activated the recorder.

"What did you think?"

What did I think?

I had spent several hours the previous evening—under the watchful eye of a rotund and unfriendly demi-curator—setting up and photographing *The Dying Albertan* from any number of perspectives, low and high, near and far, in-between, fixing details in close-ups, retreating to put the details in context, moving the lights and reflectors, creating different intensities and contrasts, trying out the best angles and distances to capture the overwhelming, difficult-to-look-at anguish in the twisted, destroyed body, front and back, and, in particular, its puzzling, dramatic, yet almost serene, beatific face.

As the title suggests, O'Keevan modeled the perhaps one-and-a-half times life-sized nude on *The Dying Gaul*, the famous second-century AD Roman copy in marble of a lost third-century BC Hellenistic original thought to have been cast in bronze—O'Keevan seems to have been attracted to the provenance of the form and the ironies attendant to a copy of a lost original that had itself, over time, become the subject of many more copies and variations—and like the Gaul, the Albertan sits on the ground in collapse, his weight forward on his right buttock and bent right leg, torso twisted, right arm reaching down to the ground, sharing the weight and agony. Also like the Gaul, O'Keevan's dying man—with its somewhat Native, perhaps Asian, facial features?—has spiky hair but in the place of the torq he wears a thin chain with a cross. The similarities do not end there, but the differences matter more.

Where the original has his left hand on his right knee to help support him, the left arm of the Albertan has been completely severed just below the shoulder and lies across his lap. Strangely, while the right arm, like the Gaul's, appears lean and well-muscled, the severed limb—I know, I measured—is too big, too long, as if it doesn't quite belong to the body. More, although the humerus, radius, and ulna have clearly been broken and smashed in several places, the intense, thick muscles seem to ripple as if still firing. Stranger still, the left hand outsizes its counterpart, the fingers meaty and twisting, the palm thick and padded, the implement of a small giant. Similarly, while the Gaul's left leg retains its shape, strength, and poise, the Albertan's left femur, though still attached, has been snapped a small distance below the hip and the many-times shattered, zig-zagging leg has collapsed on top of the right. Where the Gaul has been stabbed with a sword or spear through the right side of his chest, just below the clearly defined pectoral, the Albertan's entire left side has been smashed in, as if struck by something massive, furious, malignant. Ribs like knives jut through the shredded skin, the ribcage otherwise collapsed; the muscles, soft tissue, and guts are also stove-in, and the right side bulges as if the insides have been violently and permanently driven sideways. The genitals, like the severed arm, are also oversized, as if not belonging to the body; the baseball-sized head of the penis and long shaft rest on the right thigh.

Yet stranger and stranger: the closer one looks, the more irregularities one sees throughout the body. At first glance, only the arm and genitals seem not to belong, seem out-of-place, but upon closer inspection some of the toes appear undersized, the right side of the jaw a little distended, the smashed kneecap too large and knobby, the un-smashed hip too protrusive, the buttock raised partly off the ground too thin, too boney, smaller than the other. Plainly, these distortions preceded whatever catastrophe befell the Albertan and drove him brutally to ground. Alive and well, standing, the Albertan would have been an oddity, a bizarre, already misshapened figure.

Then, there's the face.

The Gaul, in mortal pain, knows he's dying. His body retains its defiant strength in the moment frozen forever in bronze, and then stone, but he knows the spear has pierced his lungs and heart and he's doomed. His eyes are wide, he grimaces, his brow heavy, miserable, wishing he could undo his defeat, his death.

The Albertan, despite the fact that every detail of his face seems slightly off (the eyes are not level; one appears to be en route through the base of its brow—the nose, almost Roman in its line and narrowness lies slightly crooked, as if aligned toward the left corner of his chin rather than the dimple; it also seems to have slipped, just barely, down onto the lip—a crazy tooth, just one, almost protrudes from the open mouth—the pupil of one eye is a pinprick; the other appears to have no pupil at all—the left ear appears to be creeping its way, just, toward the back of the skull; the right appears to have slipped, just, toward the jawline—the nostrils are not the same size—the cheeks do not quite match—where everything else about the body suggests a shattered vibrancy, the lips seem plastic, not quite right, as if taken from a giant Mr. Potato Head and reworked and adjusted to fit, almost), seems almost serene, almost at peace, despite death closing in, despite the force of whatever has destroyed his entire left side. At a glance, one perhaps feels slightly unsettled about the face—you have to look, to consider, to notice the sum incongruity of the details—but the longer one looks the more one sees until unease becomes alarm, or even fear. No doubt about it: O'Keevan was good, really, really good. Yet why the sense of serenity? Endorphins? Some secret knowledge? A visitation that we cannot see? A sought-for peace unexpectedly arrived? A sought-for peace pursued? found? called into being by the Albertan himself? What? What!

Of course, people began to notice these things very quickly once the statue had been unveiled, and all of it had been the source of considerable curiosity, speculation, scorn, debate, analysis, and more.

"What do I think?"

He nodded.

To say, it's overwhelming—which is how I felt while I was studying it, photographing it, trying to see it and bring it into focus in my lens and mind—would be to say nothing. O'Keevan knew it was overwhelming; it must have been overwhelming to him (unless it was some sort of joke that only he knew the punch-line to). To say, it's brutal. Sad. Strange. Bizarre. Upsetting. Bewildering. Cruel. Vicious, even. Frustrating. Maddening. Elusive. Powerful. Moving. It made me shudder. Made me cry. Made me long to be cast back a moment, before whatever happens happened, to intervene, intercede, to change the course of what was about to ruin this young man. It made me want to turn away, close my eyes. All of that—known, expected perhaps, old, tired, obvious—would be to say nothing.

I sat, still trying to process, as I had been processing all night, barely able to sleep—both upset and needing something smart to say:

"I think you must have loved him, whoever he was. And hated him. Very certainly, very clearly, very viscerally, hated him. And something else: his face: it has the ghost of you, even though it's clearly not you. And the nose: it's too small for the face; it belongs to a woman. Maybe also the cheekbones."

I looked at him as he sat back in his chair, his eyes fixed on mine:

"I think it tells a story, but no one can read it—except for you and—"

3.

He kicked me out. In the politest, nicest possible way, he kicked me out despite my protests: I came all this way for an interview; Bailey will be incensed; you made a deal with *The Orb and Post*; this is very unprofessional; I hit a nerve, that's a great start; who is it?; your missing father?; dead mother?; somebody else?; who's the woman?; give me an hour; a half-hour, and we'll call it square; would you stop pushing!

At about 52 kgs and 1.7 m, I wasn't much of a countervailing force as he steered me toward the door. Once at the door, he opened it and gestured for me to step through and into a beautiful early spring day. The tulips on either side of the walk leading to the street, some solids, some variegated, all perfect and resplendent, swayed in the warm breeze coming off the bay. Tankers and sailboats rode the horizon.

"What? That's it? Seriously?"

As the door closed, he murmured:

"I hope you have a nice visit with your family."

You hope I have a nice visit with my family? What about my job? What about getting paid? What about holding up your end of the bargain? As I stumbled toward the street, I considered what else I should have said by way of threat:

"I'll write whatever I want and attribute it to you.

"I'll redub you the "Glenn Gould of Stone"—I know you loved that!

"I'll—"

Nothing, that's what. I got to the curb and called Bailey:

"He kicked me out."

"Ok."

"I didn't get the interview, or photos of him."

"Ok."

"That's it, 'Ok'?"

"I can't remember the last time he gave a proper interview about himself or his work. He's always walking out in a huff or saying he has another appointment or talking nonsense, and I was surprised when he agreed in the first place. I thought it was about 50-50 whether he'd answer the door. Still, it was worth a shot, and we'll give you a kill-fee of one thousand, and cover your expenses."

"What? Wait—you knew—"

"Keep the car while you're there, visit your brother, come home as planned, and the check's in the mail. Think of it as a paid holiday."

"No, you don't understand. I'm onto something. About the statue—there's a story there, about someone he knew, and maybe a woman."

"Did you get some decent pix of the monstrosity? Tell you what: you write something to go with the photographs, and I'll pay you for that, plus the kill-fee. And, listen: don't be upset by this—the art world's full of strange people—you know that. All sorts of misanthropes, ego-maniacs, frottagers, Howard Hugheses, and everything else. Forget about it. And, when you're back, I'll find you something straightforward with someone early enough in their career not to be a creep or nutjob. Call me next week."

What is it about people?

I stood on the sidewalk, trying to decide what to do: to the north, a few blocks away, was Stanley Park: I could drive to the Teahouse and sit on the deck and have a Cosmo—at, let me see, 10:32 a.m.; behind me was downtown: I could go shopping; to the south and east was Granville Island: I could kick around the market and galleries for a few hours and decide from there what to do; further south and east was Delta: I could go to Jaspal and Kavita's and see the baby and enjoy being auntie for an extra day; to the west was the university: I hadn't been to the MOA in years; to the north, Whistler: too far to get in a half-day.

I thought of Sasi. A professor at York, he had been born and raised in Mumbai and spoke perfect Indian English and had perfect manners, both of which he exploited every now and then by saying something filthy. I could hear him as if he were standing at my side:

"In these situations, Ritu, you sometimes have to look these people right in the eye and say, 'Go fuck yourself! I'm going'— well, many women might say, 'shopping,' but in your case, probably 'to the library to look something up about tractors or fracking because I have 3000 words due to *Tractor Digest* or *Go Green, Or Die!* by Monday.'"

If I were going on a research trip or to take pictures at a wedding, concert, rodeo, or trade fair, Sasi would sometimes go along, so long as he was able to bring a book just in case the people or products were boring or the bride and bridesmaids homely. In a way, he was better company than Janelle: she was expensive to be around. In the evenings, she wanted to go out for a drink or dinner, or dancing on the weekends, and she always wanted to go shopping and try everything on. Why not? She had a beautiful figure, and looked good in anything, and even as a young lawyer seemed to be making fistfuls of money.

"A beautiful day."

Puzzling over my options, I had not heard O'Keevan approach. He seemed bemused, as if he were trying to remember where he knew me from.

"In these situations, Mr. O'Keevan, one must say, aloud and confidently—"

He looked at me politely:

"One must say. . . ?"

"Go fuck yourself! You're an asshole."

As O'Keevan gaped for a moment, and then burst out laughing, I gazed upon my stylish, more-than-respectably-priced shoes (I had sworn never to be caught out as Clarice Starling had been). It was one thing to say such a thing among friends, but my mother would have gasped in horror, and then giggled. Although she detested cursing, she loved Sasi's potty-mouth because he didn't mean what he said; usually, he was just making fun of how my father talked when he became angry about politics or about Nazem Kadri's propensity for bad penalties. More, she would love telling her friends how I dared speak like Sasi to such a great man.

"C'mon, I'll buy you lunch."

After flagging a taxi, O'Keevan directed the driver to take us to a place called the Twisted Fork. The host greeted O'Keevan warmly and sat us a small table just inside and behind a half-wall and across from the bar. After ordering a double of Mount Gay Extra Old, on the rocks, in an ice-cold glass—the server nodded: the usual—O'Keevan drank it down while I sipped a Diet Coke. After his second arrived, he looked across the table at me:

"So, you want to know the story of *The Dying Acadian*?"

The Dying Acadian?

That was a new one.

"Is it fiction?"

He feigned a hurt look and shrugged:

"What isn't?"

4.

Have you ever been to HUB Mall at the University of Alberta?

As an undergraduate, I loved that place, and spent a lot of time there. In those days, winter was still pretty long and miserable, and most of the campus buildings were connected to their neighbors via tunnels or skywalks, and since most of my classes were in either Fine Arts or Humanities, the best way between them in the winter—or if you wanted a coffee or to watch people—was via HUB. I also had a part-time job at the Rutherford Library, and another walkway led from the middle or so of HUB to there. Some days, I seemed never to go outside. I think there was an underground tunnel from Rutherford to SUB, the Student Union Building, and somewhere down there, behind a nondescript door with a little radioactive warning sign, was a nuclear reactor called the Slowpoke? At any rate, a person could move around campus without ever seeing the sun, and I would be there all day until it was time to go back to my little apartment a dozen or so blocks off campus, not far from Whyte Avenue and another of my favorite haunts, the Princess Theatre.

If you've never seen HUB, it's a rather amazing and unlikely place for so ugly and haphazard a campus. It must be three or four blocks long and it's barely wider than the road it straddles and that runs the entire length beneath the structure. You could enter the building from any number of doors on the ground level, and stairwells led up to the mall level; from the ground up, on either side, were so-so apartments, but the coolest ones were the ones higher up in the building, the ones overlooking the mall. The upper apartments had these great sort of Laugh-In cupboard door-things—you don't know Laugh-In, do you?—that you could swing open and look down on the mall or up at this wonderful glass ceiling. The mall had shops and restaurants and coffee shops on either side, and the walkway ran right down the middle—it was really narrow—and every few meters was a support post or giant ventilation shaft. At its narrowest points, probably four or five people could walk side-by-side, two going one way, two going the other, and then you had to contend with people popping into and out of stairwells or shops, stopping to talk, folks without a class next period and in no hurry at all, and, in the winter, everybody bundled up to twice their normal diameters.

I loved it. Best of all, there were a couple of great book stores. I wish I could have lived in the used book store—the dry-dusty-warm smell of that place!—and it was packed with books, floor to ceiling, random, crazily-tilting stacks on the floor, the isles narrow and zig-zagging this way and that. I used to go in there, and the clerks who knew me would let me stay and read if I bought them a coffee or muffin once in a while, or a beer if it was evening. In those days, I read everything—Janson, Gardner, Gombrich, science fiction, mystery, Jane Austen, Morley Callaghan, Ovid, Farley Mowat, Margaret Atwood—I read the entire *John Carter of Mars* series, with these incredible, sinewy-sinister, dry-haze, earth-tone, slightly out-of-focus cover paintings by Gino D'Achille, leaning against the edge of a plywood shelf. By chance, one time, I found this little book, *The Double Hook*, sitting on top of some others, and I stood there for hours one day and hours the next and it blew the top of my head off so far I haven't seen it to this day. Do places like that bookstore exist, anymore, or do you have to buy an eight dollar coffee and sit in somebody's mocked-up idea of a Parisian café?

Forgive me.

It is something to have been young, and to have felt completely at peace in a place that suited you so perfectly, and to have friends and lovers—who wouldn't do it all again if they could?

The only other place in HUB that I have to mention was a bar called Ralph's. Can you imagine? A bar named Ralph's in the middle of a college mall! Brilliant. I spent a lot of time in there with my stumblebum crew, mis borrachos! What must a glass of beer cost in those days? Seventy-five cents, a buck? So, for a pitcher, four or five—or about what your Pepsi costs here? Heaven, and a steady stream of women walking to and fro on the mall.

I suppose it wasn't all a parade and fuzzy beer eyes and friends—it was also a lot of work, and even in those days the university was huge and impersonal, and I took lots and lots of classes where I didn't know anybody, and some of it was as tedious as hell. There was this history prof, and each day he brought numbered shoeboxes to class, and in these shoeboxes were numbered envelopes and in the envelopes were numbered note cards—which he sat hunched-over and read aloud as if to himself, class after class, and it was a two-semester course! I thought I would kill myself, or paper-cut him to death with those damn note cards. A couple of us had his class until 2:00, and then we would fly directly to Ralph's where we would discuss ever more elaborate ways to drive him mad—steal his cards; replace them with recipes; erase the numbers, spill the works on the floor, and shuffle all ten thousand together; assemble a team to translate them into a hundred languages and burn the originals; most insidious of all, master his handwriting and introduce subtle, slightly confusing errors and paste photographs of nudes on the backs so we could see them but he couldn't.

Do you want a drink? What will you have? Fred: a Cosmo, and another of the same for me.

At the far end of HUB the shops ended and the space opened up at the intersection of the breezeways to Humanities and to Tory and Earth Sciences. There were places to sit along the walls, and a few high, round tables with decent chairs if you were lucky, and I would sit and read, waiting for the next class, or just watch the people and sketch—covertly: people don't want you to draw them anymore than they want you to take their photograph without permission.

One day I was sitting at one of these high tables, doing my thing, looking up every now and then to take in the flow of humanity—I suppose it was early in the fall semester—and I noticed this guy making his way very, very slowly down the mall toward the breezeways. I remember thinking that I had maybe seen him before, somewhere on campus, who knows, and I tried to watch him approaching without being too obvious.

He had clearly been in some sort of catastrophic accident, probably a wreck. Whatever had happened, he had been hit as hard as a person could be without it killing them. And, clearly, it had happened some time ago—because here he was, a student, strong enough to take classes and get around on his own—but it had all but destroyed him. He was crippled, smashed to the point where, if it had been just a little worse, a little more awful, they wouldn't have been able to put what was left of him back together, back into any sort of shape or form recalling his earlier self.

His left arm was missing, the sleeve of his coat folded and held to his chest with a safety pin. More, from the way he walked, I had the idea that he must have also lost his left leg and had some sort of prosthesis. He seemed to have to hike it around and forward, his foot dragging as if it could bear little or no weight. In his right hand, he held a cane and he teetered side-to-side in short steps, keeping the cane in sync with his unbending right leg: evidently it had been smashed and had not healed well and he had no strength in it. He seemed to tremble as he staggered slowly forward, as if moving at all were so difficult that his muscles shook from the sheer, painful effort.

Most telling of all—and I see him clearly to this day, and it bothers me still though it was never my place to feel sorry for him—was the look on his face. His hair was wild and curly, blue-black shot through with gray streaks, bangs hanging almost into his eyes. His eyes were round, staring, almost unblinking, and below them were enormous black circles, and his face was gaunt, even skeletal. He was clearly underweight, as if his guts and insides had knit back together as poorly as his bones. There was pain about his eyes and the grim set of his mouth, and exhaustion, but also something more: he looked haunted, as if the specter of whatever had hit him hovered in the space before him as he walked, always there, always threatening, always about to crush him again. He looked like somebody who had seen death, had felt death take his hand, had very likely died at the scene, only to be brought back, and who was now in such physical and emotional pain that he wasn't sure he wanted to have survived, wasn't sure he wanted to be alive.

He was a ghost. An afterimage, but everybody saw him, and he seemingly saw no one as he made his way, staring straight ahead at the invisible-to-us menace a few paces out in front and towards which he must inexorably stagger, day after day after day.

As I say, I had no business staring, no business pitying him—who, in his position, would want that, even as anyone who ever saw him must have cringed at the sight, at the thought of what must have happened to this poor young man—no business thinking anything one way or the other about a fellow human being. I was nothing to him, just another gawker at the periphery, just another maudlin, furtive, fearful, floor-creeping, floor-slithering soul, thinking, Thank Christ that's not me.

I watched him lurch along, swinging his dead leg around the double support of his barely living leg and cane, putting what little weight he could on the prosthesis, just enough and just long enough, to be able to force-flop his right leg and the cane forward one more step. Little by little, he passed by, and eventually disappeared among the Tokyo-subway-throng heading to and from Tory.

In those days, I drank for fun; today, if I were seeing him pass by for the first time, I would have fished for my flask: terrible, terrible things happen, and there are some things you never come back from. Never. And, regret, not pity. Grieve, not grief. That person, first, yes, absolutely, but also that person and you, not just that person alone, separate, inviolable. That person and you and everybody else.

Well, except for the fuckers, which, after all, is almost everyone.

Wasn't that what you were saying earlier? No?

I suppose I saw him a few more times somewhere on HUB that semester, slowly, anguishingly limping his way between classes, people avoiding him, giving him space as if he were surrounded by a bubble, a force-field that pushed others to the side or that warned them to step aside and that they were only too happy to comply with—as if, perhaps, they didn't want to get too close to a wraith, as if it would be bad luck to do so. The next semester, as far as I can recall, I didn't see him at all, and it wasn't until the fall semester of my third year that I caught sight of him again. I was meandering my way, as usual, toward Fine Arts and I nearly ran into him. I had just stepped around some folks getting coffee at a stand and, thinking about what I wanted to work on in sculpting class, I wasn't paying much attention. I believe I was also thinking about a woman in my sculpting class, Briony, when I violated his buffer, his bubble, and it was only by chance that I looked up and came back to myself just in time to pull up short:

"Sorry, man. I was daydreaming. . . ."

He had also lurched to a halt. I had never been this close to him, and I couldn't seem to get my eyes to focus, as if I could only take him in from ten meters away, and I stepped back in alarm. He looked at me:

"Whatever."

Still unable to bring him into focus—it was as if I were able to see only one part or piece of his face at a time, and that part was instantly replaced by another in a bewildering, kaleidoscopic, incoherent torrent—I also wasn't able to decipher his tone: was he angry? angry at almost being run into? angry that people thought he was so fragile that a mere bump would kill him? angry at being forced into a permanent distance by the fear and anxieties of others? angry in the regular way one can be angry when someone almost collides with them? not angry at all? He lurched past me on my left, and I stood rooted, no doubt slack-jawed, like a fool.

You see, I knew who he was.

That is, I knew him, even if he didn't recognize me.

5.

NO'K His name was Brice.

RA I'm sorry to interrupt, but I just want to be sure: his name was Brice?

NO'K Yes. Brice St. Denis. I met him at a summer hockey camp when I was in high school. At that time, I was living with my no-chin uncle and his ugly-in-every-way wife and even uglier-in-every-way children in Peace River, and the Edmonton Oil Kings major junior team held a series of camps at the old Edmonton Gardens, including one for players from northern Alberta. That's where I met him, though I had seen him play the winter before that in a bantam double-A tournament in Grande Prairie.

RA His name was Brice, and the woman you were thinking about when you almost ran into him in the mall was named Briony? Like the girl in *Atonement*?

NO'K Wasn't that a wonderful, sad book? Was the girl named Briony? I had forgotten.

RA So, Brice and Briony?

NO'K Is that odd? I could change her name if you like, but it was Briony MacDonnell.

RA Then, you said that you were living in Peace River when you were in high school, but I'm sure I read you went to high school in Halifax?

NO'K I did. I began high school in Halifax—at Saint Paddy's—and I finished there, but I did a year and a half at Peace River High. You see, my mum got sick and couldn't take care of me, so she shipped me out West to live with her step-brother and his awful family—everybody smelled like cigarettes, even the baby, and nobody had a job.

RA Didn't your mother die in childbirth?

NO'K She did. I never knew her.

RA She died, but later on she became too ill to care for you?

NO'K I'm sorry—I thought you knew all this. When I say "mum," I don't mean my biological mother, but the woman who raised me—that's mum.

RA So, your mum—

NO'K Rose Marie Kirvin

RA —raised you. And, where was your father?

NO'K I have no idea.

RA Did I read somewhere that he disappeared before you were born?

NO'K That's right. People say his last name was Campbell, and that he lived for a time down the street from the O'Learys, but that's all I know about him.

RA The O'Learys?

NO'K My mother's family. Her name was Francis Lydwine O'Leary. Franny.

RA Just so I have my facts straight: Franny O'Leary was your mother, and maybe somebody named Campbell—

NO'K Oh, I like that: Maybe Campbell! I'm going to call him that from now on.

RA —was your father, and after your mother died, you were raised by Rose Kirvin, and she was. . . ?

NO'K My mum—didn't I just say? I could write this all down for you, if that would help?

RA No, I mean, who was she to your biological mother and the decamped Mr. Campbell?

NO'K Oh, I see what you're getting at, but I'm not sure there's a word or a phrase for the person who raises your child after you die trying to give birth to him. Materfamilias-once-removed? Maternal-superseder? And, as for Maybe Campbell, I imagine he never gave the matter any thought. And, like Franny, Rose—she was the seventh of thirteen, by the way; can you imagine: eight sisters, four brothers! or five if you count the one who died before he was born ("Little Tommy," they called him, after Tommy Douglas), so the eighth of fourteen, really—Rose never married.

RA What?

NO'K Tommy Douglas was an interesting man, flawed in many ways, but in others ahead of his time. Still, he was no Joey Smallwood.

RA I see. So—you met Brice at a hockey camp?

6.

I was shocked when I realized who he was, realized that we knew each other and that we had sort of been friends, and I panicked, couldn't see or think straight: he had been such a brilliant player, with such gifted hands and quick feet, and here he was only a few years later all smashed up, almost unrecognizable, almost literally a ghost of his former self. When I had known him, he had been a star, maybe not big enough or strong enough or fast enough for the NHL, but among the players at the camp, even the immune-to-pain, over-sized farmboys, he was one of the best and made many of us look like we were playing a different game. He was well on his way to being a great forward, at least in the WHL: he could take face-offs, play the wing, make the pass, make a move, dig it out of the corner, take a hit, see the ice. He seemed to have it all, and we became friends, if only a little, during that week.

At first, I thought I had no business being at the camp until it became obvious, at least to me, that several of us had been invited along to be the b-team. Once I figured that out—during drills the first morning—I was fine with being there and quite enjoyed it. You can see that I'm not very big or built, as one of my brothers used to say, like a brick shithouse, but I was a decent skater and good for getting smacked around and knocked flying. That way the players who really were there to get looked at had targets, or guys they could make look silly, or make look brilliant by setting them up. We were the Generals to their Globetrotters, and for a week away from the smoking baby and the lazies, I was glad to play my part in fostering the national pastime. Mostly. There were a handful of guys who had impulse-control issues and who were there to show they could break bones, throw a punch, or excise a kidney with a Sherwood and a few flicks of the wrist. Usually, they fought with one another, but during scrimmages, everybody was fair game for a blind-siding, spearing, or slew-footing (though we didn't call it slew-foot back then).

There was this one guy, Danny Rebarr, who would run at someone from across the ice, just to nail them, and he took particular aim at the goal-scorers—probably with the coaches' encouragement: to weed out the weaklings—and as fast as Brice was, and as nimble, everybody gets hit, and Rebarr lined up Brice every chance he got. He even crushed me a few times, too, though I couldn't have been very high on his list.

The camp began on a Monday, and on Wednesday Brice dropped into the seat beside me at dinner. Generally, I'd kept pretty much to myself—I was never very adept at being a guy or talking guy talk—but we'd both been clobbered in the late-afternoon scrimmage, and he gestured toward Rebarr at one of the other tables:

"Fucking Rebarr."

I could only agree:

"He needs his head driven through the boards."

For good measure, I added:

"The fucker."

He nodded sympathetically: we both gave away thirty pounds, and a lot of meanness:

"The thing is, I can't handle that guy alone. And you can't handle him alone."

I looked at Brice—he was perhaps Métis, Cree and French, judging from his last name. He had dark hair, pock-marked skin, Roman nose, jet eyes, crooked smile, a few chipped and crooked teeth—to see if he was serious. He nodded, grinned, and put out his hand.

During end-of-drills scrimmages the next day, whenever Rebarr set blade on the ice, one or both of us would run at him. No matter where we were, we made a beeline and hit him as hard as we could. If he came at us, we slashed him; if we cycled behind him, we cross-checked. If he hit us from behind, we got up—when we were able—and went after him. If he was on the ice, we didn't play hockey: we attacked Rebarr. If he dropped his gloves, we skated away, offering insights into his character, intelligence, parentage, hygiene, and more. On a couple of occasions, we even managed to hit him at the same time, and when we all went flying, we tried to pile on and punch his head into the ice, the whole time telling him we were going to kill him in his sleep. If I had to say, that was probably my happiest day of hockey.

To his credit, Rebarr seemed to be enjoying himself as much as we were, and for the last couple of days, the three of us were buddies. If another of the goons tried to smash Brice, Rebarr ran them over or punched out their lights. Later, I heard they both made the team, and that as a rookie, Brice was one of the point leaders. I didn't see him again until I saw him that day in HUB.

What's that? Rebarr?

He played a season or two for Philadelphia, but was considered too easy-going to be a Flyer.

Fred? Both, again, please.

The thing I liked about Brice—in addition to admiring his play—was that he was straightforward. He played seriously, and well, and when he approached me about double-slamming Rebarr, he got right to the point. With that in mind, I determined, later on the day that I almost ran into him, to speak to him the next time I saw him. No doubt he had undergone a terrible ordeal that had made him into someone different, at least outwardly, but I was more or less the same and he must have recognized me, any number of times, among the gawkers on campus.

Yet he had chosen not to speak, not to say hello.

I suppose the why is not too mysterious.

Of course, the next couple of times I saw him in HUB, I looked away, made some excuse to myself. Finally, on the third occasion, I found the courage—when my sister was little, she used to say that her courage was in her foot and when she needed it, it took a while for it to work its way from her foot to her heart—and stopped in front of him near the breezeway to Rutherford:

“Brice. Hi. Do you—“

He had been staring into the far distance, and he shifted his gaze:

“Neil. How are you?”

“Fine, great. How have, that is—and you?”

He smiled wanly, his eyes sliding from my face and refocusing on whatever it was he saw in front of him:

“As you see.”

His voice was thin and whispery and he seemed to struggle to draw enough air to speak.

“I’m sorry I haven’t said hello before this. I’ve seen you around, of course, but I didn’t recognize you.”

“Well, we all change.”

“Right. What?”

I studied his expression. The skin was blotchy and tight, as if stretched from behind over the brittle, crackling bones of his face, and his eyes were half-closed and ringed with black. Up close, I could see that his jaw must have been broken in the accident, and his mouth on the left side seemed slack and droopy. The more I stared, the less he seemed to see me.

“Listen. Some buddies and I are going to Ralph’s later today for a beer, and I was wondering if you’d like—“

“I can’t drink.”

“What about a coke?”

“No, thanks.”

“If you change your mind, we’ll be there about 3:00—we like to get an early start. You know, make sure we have time to talk things through, understand one another’s points of views on the important issues of the day.”

“That’s swell. See you around.”

I stepped aside and he continued on his way toward the

north end of the mall.

I watched him for a time, then looked down at my hands. I found that I was trembling and I felt as if a weight from above were trying to press me into the floor. If I remained rooted, perhaps I'd eventually fall through to the street below. I gave myself a shake, and tried to recall where I needed to be and what I should be doing. Not quite able to get my bearings, by default I turned and headed toward Fine Arts and then wandered into the used bookstore. Kylie, the dark-haired beauty who never said hello and always appeared slightly pissed-off, was at the cash, and I wove my way to the back of the shop and stood in front of the art books:

"Good lord."

I'm not sure why I found the encounter so stressful and upsetting. I am not a particularly brave person, nor am I particularly fearful, and even then I didn't care too much about what other people thought of me. Nevertheless, I was badly shaken, and I hid in the stacks for several minutes, collecting my wits as if they were coins that had fallen from my hands.

I don't remember much about the rest of that day, save I somehow managed to make it to my afternoon classes. At last, I found my way to Ralph's a little after 3:00 and sat down with Peter and Grimes, and signaled for another pitcher. To my surprise, Brice showed up at around 4:00 and made his way gingerly around the tables and fell back into a chair:

"I hear that beer makes you feel better."

Peter, our ringleader and never one to miss an opportunity, was also one never to miss a beat, and Grimesey and I followed his lead:

"Beer makes me feel better about not having better quality friends."

"Beer makes me feel better about Peter not being funny."

"Beer makes me feel better about poisoning my mind and body with beer."

Brice said:

"Beer makes me feel better about drinking beer with guys who will never get laid."

Peter raised his glass:

"Hey. The new guy is one of us!"

With that, Brice joined our informal fraternity of would-be artists, poets, and happy drunkards, though he rarely did more than sip at his beer, his doctors having forbidden him, due to damage sustained to his liver and kidneys in the accident, to consume alcohol. And, with that, Ms. Agarwal, I must bid you good afternoon. It was a pleasure meeting you. Can you find your way from here?

7.

I followed him out to the street:

"Not so fast, Mr. O'Keevan. That's not the whole story."

He waved for a taxi as traffic roared by on Granville:

"Don't kid yourself: there's no such thing as the whole story."

"Was there ever a person named Brice?"

He shrugged, concentrating on flagging down a cab.

"Listen: I know you never went to the University of Alberta. I'm not a complete fool, and I did my homework. You went to the Art Institute in Chicago, and you were Artist-in-Residence at Alberta for one semester, but that was ten years after you sculpted *The Dying Acadian* or *Albertan* or whatever it's called. So what the hell was all that, that whole story?"

He put down his arm and turned toward me:

"Just as you say, a story. What are you so upset about? You came here looking for a story, I gave you a story, and now you can go home and write some version of it, and you'll get paid and your editor will be happy."

"Was there ever a person named Brice?"

"No. Of course not."

"You made it all up?"

He shrugged:

"I made it all up."

"No friend smashed in some sort of horrible accident?"

"No Brice, no accident, no Ralph's, no good old college days in Edmonton."

"No way. Too many particulars, too much fine detail. Some of it has to be true. And there must be a woman in there, somewhere, a Briony, someone."

He stared like he felt sorry for me. I changed course:

"Why all the distortions in the Albertan? The mismatched

limbs, the migrating eyes and ears? Why does it have your face? Is there a woman's face there, too? Why? Who was she?"

He turned back toward Granville, once more intent on catching a taxi:

"You want it to be about someone, you want an explanation, you want the inside story, but there isn't one. It just doesn't work that way. Most things just are, and there's no why about them. They don't mean, or you say a thing means, but what you're really talking about is yourself and not the thing. So, if it makes you feel better, make up the rest of the story. Make it about those friends you were telling me about, the mathematician and the lawyer. A triangle—the classic conflict."

A cab had pulled up the curb, and he yanked open the back door.

I was fuming: no way! No way! I wished Sasi were here: I couldn't think of a good enough curse to unleash in O'Keevan's face. I stammered. I seethed. I wanted to punch him in the nose.

He was about to climb in when he pulled back and, in two steps, was standing in front of me. He reached into the hip-pocket of his blazer and pulled out a maroon-colored case. For one moment, for reasons I cannot explain, I thought he was going to propose. Using both hands, he opened the case. Inside was a large silver coin, a proof, intricately struck.

"Here, this is for you."

I gazed at the coin, but could make no sense of it.

"The RCM has a subscription series this year, National Treasures, a dozen coins, each featuring a 'Famous Work of Canadian Art.' They selected 'Cumberland Heights' as the coin for June, and this is the 0002 of 8000. You can have it. Call it a memento."

He snapped the case closed, and dropped it in my hand. It felt warm and soft and solid and heavy all at once.

8.

I remember, early on in my second-year lit class, the professor—a chubby guy with glasses who was half-funny and enthusiastic if mostly a time-waster—projected a slogan on the screen that we were to follow if we were to "read and interpret well": Always historicize! We were always to think historically about literature and art and culture if we wanted to make sense of them.

Fine.

So, 1982, the year *The Dying Albertan*—"The Dying Whatever," "The Dying Whoever"—made its debut.

According to Wikipedia—I can hear Sasi's snort of scorn, but a body has to start somewhere—Pierre Trudeau was Prime Minister of Canada. (I knew I recognized O'Keevan's lifted shoulders: he was impersonating Trudeau's classic Gallic shrug.) René Lévesque was Premier (Prime Minister) of Quebec. Elizabeth II was Queen. (When has she ever not been Queen?) The British Parliament passed the Canada Act, declaring that Canada was now out of short pants. Dominion Day was renamed Canada Day. Guy Vanderhaeghe won the Governor General's Award (English; Fiction) for *Man Descending*; Roger Fournier (French; romans et nouvelles) for *Le cercle des arènes*; John Gray (Drama) for *Billy Bishop Goes to War*. Joy Kogawa won the Books in Canada Best First Novel Award for *Obasan*. Anne Murray and Bruce Cockburn won Junos for, respectively, Female and Male Vocalist of the Year. Ouch: Loverboy won for Group of the Year. *Ticket to Heaven* won the Genie for Best Motion Picture. Rocky, now called Rambo, went to B.C. and shot the hell out of Hope. (Sasi as Groucho Marx: *Which, if you've ever been to Hope, you completely understand.*) Gilles Villeneuve was killed during qualifying for the Belgian Grand Prix. Percy Williams, winner of two gold medals at the 1928 Amsterdam Olympics, seems to have committed suicide. The semi-submersible oil rig *Ocean Ranger*, not long after signaling Mayday, sank off the coast of Newfoundland during a storm, with a loss of 84 souls, everyone aboard.

On October 4, at the age of 50, Glenn Gould died in Toronto, a week after suffering a massive stroke. That same day, Niall O'Keevan unveiled *The Dying Albertan* at the Canadian Post-Avant-Garde Salon in Saskatoon.

Kristen Kreuk, Seth Rogan, and Cobie Smulders were all born in Vancouver. Anna Paquin was born in Winnipeg. Scott Hartnell was born in Regina. Jeffery Buttle was born in Smooth Rock Falls, Ontario. A-Trak was born in Montreal. No mention, however, of the birth of one Ritu Agarwal in Toronto. An oversight, I imagine.

Farther afield, the planets aligned on the same side of the sun, *Thriller* was released, the UK went to war with Argentina, Indira Gandhi was Prime Minister of India (again), Gabriel García Márquez won the Nobel Prize in Literature, Grace Kelly and Ingrid Bergman died, and it was the Year of the Dog.

Sure, now I see.

Part II.

9.

At night, sometimes, in the small hours she would sing softly, songs without words, low moans made into melodies, and when she began to sing he would awaken instantly, hearing her both inside his head and in the air above the bed, feeling the vibration of her voice-not-voice in the bones of his skull and down his jaw and into his neck and chest, the vibrato soft, the breaths-not-breaths shallow, for how could she breathe, yet a mezzo so clear, so caliginous, so anguished, a vibration, a lamentation, felt as much as heard, and he would pretend to be asleep, would try to quiet his heart which thumped and jumped in his chest like an engine trying to break its mounts, his heart her heart, would try to keep his own breaths shallow and steady so she wouldn't know he was awake though of course she knew-not-knew that he was awake for she must know, mustn't she, for who could say otherwise, not he, even as he was unsure of how much he knew of her, if any of her thoughts-not-thoughts were his thoughts or his thoughts her thoughts-not-thoughts and he would try not to move, not to stir, hoping she would sleep-not-sleep once more, her songs ebbing and flowing and ebbing away at last, after hours of singing her songs-not-songs, into a noiseless, mournful gasp-not-gasp and then into silence-not-silence for even if her aerations ceased he could still hear and feel them in his chest and in the bones of his skull and in the night-air, and he was afraid that the faint melody would give way to the sudden, terrifying, gnashing of teeth, the rasping, grating, grinding, clenching-unclenching of teeth, for what else did she have save her voice-not-voice, her breaths-not-breaths, but her teeth, teeth and gums and not quite lips, little else save the gnashing, gritting, clamping of teeth for minutes at a time, seem-

ingly furious, frantic for reasons-not-reasons until she subsided, at last, into sleep-not-sleep, and he could breathe again, his heart chest shoulders mind beginning to unclench and if never quite unclenched, at least quieting yet always watchful, jumpy, jittery until he could exhale, the tension loosening as if unwinding knots from a wire coiled and tangled in his chest and back and spine, and, if he were lucky, a few hours of half-sleep.

Or else she might not sing, might not smash her jutting, crooked, intertwining teeth, the strangely perfect O of her mouth a circle of crooked, spiky teeth, but rather move her lips, the thin-line, scar-tissue of her lips, as if trying to shape words, as if trying to have her say, at last, then his scalp twitching and pulling this way, then that, and he trying to judge the shape of the words, trying from the twitching and pulling of his scalp to understand even as he did not want to know, to understand, what she wanted to say, perhaps most wanted to say—to whom? to him? for whom else could she know?—as she murmured voicelessly to the icy air, the walls of the old trailer thin and poorly insulated, the gaps around the windows that his uncle caulked and re-caulked to little effect as the trailer torqued as the seasons changed as the sun was near and fiery or far to the south and silvery admitting the damp and cold and, when the wind blew hard, or storms came from the north, a keening of snow and stinging needles of ice or, when the sun hung heavy and languid and unmoving in the stifling, still, superheated air of dead summer, dust from the road and poplar down turned brown and brittle from the sun and the languid pong-taste of marsh-peat and sulfur and tar from the heating and sun-heated oil sands tanks across the river.

When Brion heard his uncle tap softly on Andrew's door, telling him in a murmur that it was time for breakfast, they had better eat and get to work, he swung his legs over the edge of his bed and reached onto the floor for his jeans and lined lumberjack shirt and down vest that he had repaired many times with duct tape. He pulled his wool toque down until it covered his ears and seemed to rest on his eyebrows. Normally, he avoided his older cousin, but today he was distracted and stepped into the narrow hallway and almost collided with him:

—Watch it, freak. And, what are you doing up, anyway?

Brion stepped back into his room to allow Andrew to pass. He waited until he heard him pull out a chair at the tiny kitchen table and then hobbled silently in his wake. As he emerged from the hall, his uncle nodded and smiled:

—Practice this early?

—Naw. Got some errands.

—Sure.

He had a plate of eggs and toast in each hand and he set one before Andrew and passed the other to Brion who passed it back. He grinned at his uncle:

—I can get my own. And, I'll get Janey up and take her to Mrs. Kinnaird's.

Brion poured himself a cup of coffee and when Andrew reached over to take it from him, he grabbed his cousin around the wrist. Although Andrew was a head taller, and nearly twice as thick, Brion held him easily as he tried to yank his arm away:

—Would you like me to pour you a cup, cuz?

—No thanks, freak. I'll get my own damn cup—

He stood, towering over Brion, and tried again to wrench his arm free, but Brion did not even sway as he tried a third time, putting his entire strength and weight into the effort. He glared at his cousin, and then looked at his father. Brion let him go and turned back to his coffee.

The uncle, who had been watching the struggle keenly, exhaled and pushed his plate away:

—Andrew, we'd better get going.

He was a small, gentle man, and when Brion's mother, his baby sister, had died while giving birth, he had taken Brion home with him because who else was there and what happened to a Métis kid would he go to Grande Prairie or Edmonton and be placed with a white family or were there still orphanages who knew? but there was no question anyway and he brought the brand new baby home and Marie, as he knew she would, objected, but to her credit it wasn't until later just after Janey was born that Marie disappeared, saying, I'm going for a pack of cigarettes do you hear me I'm going for a pack of cigarettes, and stepping out the trailer door into a snowstorm and the last he heard maybe she was living in Grimshaw or Spirit River or up in High Prairie and he wished he missed her but he did not and though he loved his son the boy had enough of his mother in him that he was sure he did not miss her though a boy and a daughter especially a daughter need a mother, and Brion had nobody, his mother dead, his father, whoever that was, nobody knew nobody said, and so, how to count, it was him and the two now men and Janey and Andrew angry all the time sure to move out leave go away maybe to Edmonton or Calgary or who knew and the family would

Brion shook his head.

He sipped his coffee and the family would

or the family wouldn't that was the thing and all at once the clacking of teeth the interlocking of yellow canines jutting this way and that snapping clamping frantic frenzied the detonations quaking the bones of his skull and down his spine and into his chest

He twisted his head violently, as if trying to throw the clattering into the air.

Over the noise and tremors, he thought he could hear Janey calling to him, and he stood, trembling, both palms on the table to steady himself, and pushed away. He staggered down the narrow hallway to the cramped living room where Janey slept on the couch and dropped into the recliner, his uncle's chair, his chest heaving, his guts sour and churning, sweat trickling from under his toque and into his eyes and down his cheeks.

He couldn't see well, but he thought Janey was sitting up on the couch, staring at him. He blinked and tried to rub the stinging salt away with his fingers:

—Hey. You could sleep for another half hour, if you want. I'll get you up.

She wrapped herself up in the quilt her grandmother had made and moved to Brion's side and then climbed onto his lap. If Andrew was like his mother, Janey was all father, quiet and kind:

—Can I visit with Sister?

—Better not, Janey, she's upset this morning.

—I know. I can hear her.

With her tiny fingers, she pushed up the side of Brion's toque and then began gently to root through his long, shaggy hair, so black it was almost blue, softly parting strands and holding them apart, clearing a space.

—Be careful, Janey, she's furious. She'll bite.

Yet he knew that was not true: for whatever reason, she always quieted when Janey was near.

He could feel Janey's fingers grip one of the snapping teeth, and instantly the clacking and shocks ceased:

—Are your hands clean? You always have you fingers up your nose.

Brion could feel his scalp relax as the mouth stopped twitching, the jagged teeth still and calm, and he could feel Janey's breath and lips almost pressed against the side of his head. She murmured that it was ok, that Sister was all right, that she was safe and there was no need for anger. He could feel her running the tips of her fingers over the interlocked teeth and then he could feel the little tugs and foldings of his scalp as if his sister were responding, replying, and he could feel Janey shift her weight and turn her head, her ear brushing up against the teeth and thin, scarred lips.

—What's she saying, Janey?

—Shhhh. I can't hear her if you're talking.

The story, the story the doctors had told to his uncle when Brion was brand new, and that he, in turn, had told to Brion when he was just a boy, but wanted to know, was that due, very likely, to malnutrition and the hardships put upon his mother's body by cold—it had been a long, cruel winter, and summer had never really arrived—and by the stress of twins, or possibly triplets, his twin had encased within him, and x-rays had shown that the mouth, the only emergent part of Sister, had no supporting bone structure, merely a tangle of muscles, ligature, and tissue, and led to no windpipe or esophagus, but was connected to something like a clot of brain or withered brainstem by a tightly knotted strand of nerves and vessels. Further x-rays and, when he was in junior high, an MRI had revealed that most of the remaining parts—bones, a spider's web of muscles and tendons, a half-formed rib-cage and spine, primitive intestine, calcified heart and lungs, and something like a stretched-thin umbilical cord that snaked around his ribs and encoiled his abnormally large heart and lay snarled on his diaphragm—had entombed mostly on the left side of his body (which accounted for his peculiar limbs and perhaps for his extraordinary strength). The MRI also suggested that nerves radiated from the brain fragment throughout his body, intertwining with his nerves, possibly even connecting, and there was some evidence to suggest some strands penetrated his spinal column, but the docs could not be sure. The nerves trailed out into fibers too fine to see, if they were there at all.

The MRI also suggested that there may have been more than just the twins, and that a third had likewise been absorbed, but so early on that only traces and anomalies suggested its existence.

—Sister wants to know.

Brion could feel his guts go watery and clench:

—Know what?

—She's whispering to me. She doesn't want—

Brion put his hands on Janey's tiny ribcage and stood, holding her away while he folded in the footrest and then setting her down on the floor:

—That's enough, Janey. Not everything is her business.

—She's scared.

—She needs to mind her own business.

He swung her under his arm as if she were an all-arms-and-legs football, and carried her toward the kitchen:

—What would you like for breakfast? Pancakes? Toast? Eggs?

Janey was not so easily deterred:

—Brion, don't do that. Don't try not to listen and be pretend happy.

—I'm not pretending. I am happy, because I get to be with you. And I am listening, but I don't want to talk about Sister. And, besides, if Sister keeps getting angry, she's going to chew through my toque.

—Stop it! Stop it! Sister told me!

10.

"You want to know the truth about the so-called *Dying Acadian*? The truth is that Niall O'Keevan—I knew him as Neil Kirvin, of course—did not—how shall I say?—originate *The Dying Acadian*. I did."

We were sitting at a tiny, two-person table in the tiny kitchen of small, dark green house with shake shingles covered with a thick blanket of gone-red cedar and pine needles from the towering trees that surrounded the house and obscured it from view from the road. I had had a difficult time finding the place, and when, at last, I spotted the mailbox all but invisible among ferns and nettles and pulled into the curved, narrow, all-but-overgrown driveway, there had been a small, faded gold and white pickup truck parked near the house. An older couple, certainly past retirement age, were sitting in the small cab, with the engine running, and the woman was pouring coffee from an old, metal-tartan thermos into the plastic coffee cup lid and handing it to the man. The cab was so cold that the coffee steamed, and the steam drifted up, creating a cloud on the inside of the windscreen. Rain and droplets from the overhanging trees ran heavily on the front of the window, mostly obscuring their faces.

I had pulled over as much as I could in order to leave the narrow drive open. When I got out, I waved, but they did not wave back. The man seemed to be using a paper towel to rub some of the moisture off the inside of the front window.

The rain was steady and cold, and the kitchen, though scrupulously clean and tidy, was clammy and cold and there seemed to be a film of damp on the counters and tabletop and the windows were beaded with moisture. When my hostess gestured that I should sit at the tiny table, she had urged me to keep my jacket on and would I like a cup of tea for warmth?

Although I am no Sherlock Holmes—Sasi is a much better reader and judge of people than I am—even I could deduce that she did not seem to suit the house. Or, rather, the house did not seem to suit her: although casual, her blazer, blouse, slacks, and boots were tailored and expensive, her hair was cut to the latest style, and she was both immaculately groomed and elegant. Her clothes, diamond earrings, and—platinum?—wedding rings cost a great deal more than the truck parked out front with the old folks in it.

"You'll forgive me, but that's shocking: O'Keevan stole the idea for *The Dying Albertan* from you?"

And she was beautiful. She had high cheek bones, cat's eyes, full lips, and a wide smile of perfect teeth.

"Really? Is it that you can't imagine O'Keevan stealing? Or that you can't imagine a man stealing from a woman? A white person stealing from a black? A 'friend' stealing from another 'friend'?"

"No. I can imagine all of those things. What shocks me is that I haven't heard this before, not even a rumor. All these years, and not even a murmur that one of the most famous works of Canadian art was actually created by a woman born and raised in Trinidad? Either you never said a word about it, or you did and no one listened or wanted to listen. I don't know you, so I can't judge whether you would ever have told anyone or confronted O'Keevan, but I can believe that if you did, your accusations probably were not well-received by lots of folks in the art world."

"I never accosted O'Keevan. He knew very well where the idea for *The Dying Canadian*—it was originally to be *The Dying Indian*—came from, so what would have been the point? But I did tell some of the people in the program, including some of the professors."

"You studied at the Art Institute at the same time as O'Keevan?"

"Same years, in fact. But all that was so long ago, what does it matter now? And, anyway, I didn't have the technical ability to realize such a sculpture, so it would never have existed if he hadn't taken my idea and done all the work."

"He got all the credit."

"And all the fame and money."

"You haven't done too badly. As a painter, I mean. I've seen your work for sale in galleries in Toronto, and know that you've had showings and been collected in Europe and Asia."

She concurred:

"I've done all right. Nothing like his success. Yet I've done well."

"So: what's the story of *The Dying Indian*?"

"More tea?"

"No thanks. But is there a heater in this place!"

11.

Peter raised his glass:

"Hey. The new guy is one of us!"

"That's just mean."

"Anybody can tell he's a lot better than we are."

"Peter, we've talked about this before: stop insulting people by trying to be their friend."

Peter said:

"Brice, ignore them. And, I, for one, am glad you're here, not the least as a witness. Because I have an announcement: as soon as we finish this pitcher, we are leaving Ralph's. Perhaps forever."

Grimesey and Neil feigned outrage:

"What! Leave Ralph's? They love us here, and we love them and this place, full of character and characters. Why, just look around!"

They looked around. The walls were bare concrete, the blindless floor-to-ceiling windows smudged and streaked, and the floor was covered with a dingy, stains-on-stains ever-wear carpet. At several tables were groups of young men like themselves, empty pitchers accumulating on the tables as many of the drinkers stared forlornly or inconsolably into half-empty glasses, their winter boots resting in puddles of filthy water and slush. Most were still wearing down jackets and toques or Oiler caps. As they looked at the table beside them, one of the strangers reached up under his toque, scratched half-heartedly, mumbled to himself, and then reached for a nearly empty pitcher.

Brice said:

"There are no women here."

"What? What about that hot chick behind the bar, the one. . . ."

They looked. There were two men their age tending bar. One of them was quite bald, save for a sparse tonsure and desperate patch just above the center of his forehead.

"Wow. This place sucks. We suck."

Peter nodded:

"That's what I was trying to say. Anyway, I ran into a woman I know—"

"You know a woman?"

"Are you making this up?"

"Would she like us if she knew us?"

"I ran into a woman I know from high school, and she's tending bar at the Esquire, on 109th near the bridge, and she said we should stop by there and she'd buy us a beer. When I asked, she said actual women go to that place. Actual women."

Grimesey and Neil said they thought going to that place was a good idea.

Brice began to reach for his backpack:

"I don't have a car, and I can't walk that far. Thanks, anyway."

"Nonsense. You're with us, now, and that means we all go in Grimesey's Hyundai. And, no bullshit about taking a bus home, wherever that is—the Hyundai's about the only reason we allow Grimes to hang with us—sorry, Grimesey, but you might as well know the truth—and he'll give us all rides home or back to campus, or wherever you want to go."

While Peter and Grimesey went to get the car, Neil walked with Brice to the end of the mall and into the walkway between Fine Arts and Law to take an elevator to the ground floor.

Neil said:

"This is my home ground."

"You're in law school?"

"No. Not at all. I paint and sculpt, or at least I hope to be a painter and sculptor. I get to use a corner of one of the studios in the basement, and I take most of my classes in Fine Arts. I love the feel of the place, and its sounds and the smell of paint and stone. The industrial sculptors give me a headache—too much pounding and metal on metal—and all they can make are rusty carbuncles, but other than that, it feels like home. What are you studying?"

"I don't even know. I only take one or two classes a semester—it takes me all morning to get ready before my aunt drives me to school. I sometimes think I might major in geology, or maybe anthropology, but I don't expect—"

Brice trailed off.

"You don't expect. . . ?"

"What's that? Nothing. Just mumbling to myself."

"Sure. My little sister talks to herself all the time; she narrates her life even as she lives it."

Brice swayed in place:

"Peter and Grimes seem like decent guys."

"They mean the world to me—"

I can hear Sasi hoot:

"Young Canadian men, Ritu, do not talk like that. They say, Look at the boobs—and they don't say 'boobs'—on that! Or they talk about hockey and about 'how many beers' they're going to drink before, during, and after the game."

"They're ok, but I sure hope this woman Peter knows has big tits and a sweet—"

"Too far the other way: they're mostly crude, and sexist, but this group would be milder, a little more indirect, a little more circumspect."

"Do they say 'tits' or not?"

"We've been buds since first year when we all lived in the same dorm. I never know anyone in my classes."

Brice nodded, and Neil opened and held the door as the car pulled up to the curb. Despite the heavy snow, falling in large, lazy clumps, they reached 109th in a few minutes, and Grimesey dropped off Brice and Neil in front of the Esquire, and then he and Peter drove off to find a parking space. The traffic on 109th was heavy and slow, with headlights and taillights glowing in the swirling ice crystals and low-hanging exhaust. Cars were lined up for blocks to take the High Level to downtown or Walterdale Hill down to the Kinsmen and across the North Saskatchewan.

"We should go in—they could be twenty minutes."

The Esquire was long and narrow, with a gleaming, dark wood bar running almost the entire length on the left and low booths running along the wall and windows on the right. A brass rail added some glow atop three sides of each booth, and all of the booths were taken, crowded with four or five people, with still others standing in the narrow passage. Nearly all the places at the bar were taken, and more were standing one or two deep behind them. Peanut shells littered the floor.

Neil spotted a tall table, available in the back corner beneath a TV broadcasting hockey:

"Shall we brave the gauntlet?"

Brice looked pale, his eyes deep and wreathed in black.

"Christ."

Neil hesitated.

"Let's not. When they get here, we'll send them back for the car. Trust me, they won't mind—this place is hip enough to make them uncomfortable. Too many attractive women."

"No. I'll follow you."

Neil shrugged and began to weave his way amid the cram, nudging the tumult to the left or the right with his shoulder, trying to make space. Several gave him dirty looks until they saw Brice, and then they moved away as much as they could. Brice, for his part, was having difficulty swinging his left leg around his right, and his cane kept becoming entangled among legs and boots and it took them three or four minutes to navigate the thirty feet. Once there, Brice had a difficult time trying to land on the tall chairs, and Neil took him by the elbow and shoulder and lifted him into place.

Brice apologized:

"That was like playing against Rebarr all over again."

"Whatever happened to that guy, do you suppose?"

"He played for the Flyers for a few years, and I heard from somebody at home that he's coaching a junior team in Ontario. Supposed to be a pretty vicious team. Wonder where they got that from?"

Brice exhaled, and scooted back on his chair as well as he could. He struggled with his coat and hung it over the back of the chair. Neil could see the perspiration on his forehead and trickling down the side of his face and neck and he seemed to be having difficulty catching his breath.

"You have a hard time."

"Crowds. Crowded places freak me out: what if I fall, or someone knocks me down, and I can't get back to my feet?"

Neil was about to reply when Peter and Grimesey arrived, and with them was a woman.

As he climbed onto a chair, Peter said:

"Guys, this is Briony. Briony, the guys."

She was of average height and thin, with short brown, straight hair. Her nose was slightly crooked, and looked to have been broken across the bridge and healed badly, and her face was uneven. Her smile seemed higher on one side than the other. She was odd looking, yet clear-eyed and attractive. She reached out her hand to Grimes, who was sitting closest:

"You must be Grimesey—the curly hair. Peter says you're really smart."

"Me? Who says? That's nice to meet you."

She looked at Neil:

"And you I know: you're in Painting II, right, with Hornsby? Right after lunch?"

Neil nodded:

"Painting II with Hornsby, right after lunch."

While Briony introduced herself to Brice—she reached out and touched the sleeve of his coat—Peter leaned over to Neil:

"Is it being a penniless orphan with a Newfie accent that makes you so eloquent?"

"At least I did better than Grimesey: 'That's nice to meet you'?"

"It's a wonder he was able to speak at all."

As they turned back toward the table, Briony was explaining that she had promised Peter that the first pitcher was on her, but they were on their own after that. They watched her walk away. When she was out of eyeshot, their shoulders drooped and they turned to one another.

"We just spoke to a woman, and she's buying us beer. An actual woman."

"Did you see the dirigibles on that! The umlauts! The headlamps! The ta-tas! The—"

"Would you stop, already."

"I told you. An actual woman. And you guys couldn't even talk!"

12.

ACT IV

Scene III. The Daily Drip, HUB Mall.

(NEIL, amid others, ordering coffee. Enter to him BRIONY.)

BRIONY	What the hell?
NEIL	I'm sorry?
BRIONY	You heard me.
NEIL	I don't understand, but can I at least get my coffee, and then you can explain what's wrong?
BRIONY	Right here is just fine: what the hell were you thinking?
NEIL	At the moment, I'm thinking why in the hell are you asking me what in the hell I was thinking? Oh, and I'm happy to see you, too?
BRIONY	Cut the crap. I just ran into Brice, and he tells me he's going to model for Painting III.
NEIL	Ok?
BRIONY	What do you mean, "ok"?
NEIL	I don't understand. Why are you so upset that Brice is going to model for class? And, why are you yelling at me?
BRIONY	You're a creep, you know that? A real creep, with real problems. I feel sorry for you.
NEIL	I'm a creep because Brice is going to take his clothes off in front of our class, and get paid $50? Why am I a creep? If you have a problem with it, talk to Brice. It's got nothing to do with me.
BRIONY	You put him up to this.
NEIL	Not me.
BRIONY	He said you suggested it to him. That's sick.

You're sick.

NEIL I did no such thing. He was asking me about the class and about what I was working on—and about what you were working on—and I told him that for the past few weeks we've had a series of models, nudes, so that we could work on forms and the body. You know, like we do? Models come to class, and we sketch, and draw, and paint them? That's how we learn, by practicing? And, in exchange for sitting at the front of the class for an hour, the program pays them. You have been to class, right?

BRIONY You set him up. You're preying on him. You have some sort of weird fascination with him, and you're trying to expose and humiliate him. You want to see what he looks like, to see just how badly he was hurt, and to see just what's left of him. You're sick. Mental. A predator.

NEIL What are you even talking about? It was his idea. I didn't suggest it to him, and I don't understand why you're so upset. If he wants to be a model, that's his business, not yours, not mine, his. And to hell with you for saying those things to me. You're the one with the sick mind.

BRIONY Are you in love with him?

NEIL What?

BRIONY I said, Are you in love with him?

NEIL You're crazy. Get away from me.

BRIONY Is this the only way you can get close to what you want? To do with your eyes what you don't dare try with your hands?

NEIL Are we talking about me or you?

BRIONY You're trying to turn him into some sort of Elephant Man for others to stare at and feel pity so that they can feel better about themselves.

NEIL You've lost your mind if you think I had any thing to do with this, or that I'm somehow turned on by the dying, or that I want to fondle his junk or that I think he's the Elephant Man. What's your problem?

BRIONY He's not a person to you. I'm going to Hornsby.

NEIL Fine. Go to Hornsby. Tell him what you want, that somehow I manipulated a cripple into embarrassing himself in front of a room of strangers and creeps. That it's all some sort of sex-thing for me, a real hard-on to see a buddy without his clothes. Hornsby will know in a minute that you're loony.

BRIONY I hate you.

NEIL You hate me? To hell with you! To hell with you.

(Exit BRIONY. NEIL, aghast, looks at the other patrons who, horrified, stare back at him.)

13.

On most mornings when Brion walked her to Mrs. Kinnaird's, Janey chirped non-stop, remarking on what she saw along the way, or telling stories about the other kids at the daycare, or retelling as if they happened to her the adventures he read to her in the evenings, or simply narrating what they were doing:

—Now, we're getting ready to cross the street, but only at the corner where it's safe so cars and trucks can see you and not run you over and squash you which would really hurt, and we look both ways and when we're sure—Brion has a good grip on my hand and I have a good grip on his hand—we step off the curb and now—

—Ready, Janey?

But today she did not murmur a word. Sister, on the other hand, would not be quiet and he could feel his toque jouncing as she chewed furiously at the wool. He swatted at her and felt her sharp, crooked teeth through the knit and he could feel and hear-not-hear her moan rise by times to a shriek, as if a howling winter wind, rising and falling, ceaseless, manic, hateful, screaming at him.

if you don't shut up, I will take pliers and a needle and thread and you can suffocate for all I care

He felt Janey let go of his hand. He looked up and they were standing in front of Mrs. Kinnaird's bungalow.

—I can walk from here.

—You mind your Ps and Qs, and take your boots off on the mat.

—I can walk from here.

He whispered:

—Be good and have fun.

He watched her go up the sidewalk and concrete stairs and ring the doorbell and go inside when Mrs. Kinnaird opened the door.

Mrs. Kinnaird waved and he lost sight of Janey as the heavy door closed against the cold and swirling snow.

Sister seemed to be gasping for air as she gnawed and gnawed at the soggy wool, as if the damp material were choking off what little air she could find in the superheated space. He reached under the toque to scratch at his sweaty, irritated scalp, careful to avoid the slashing fangs even as beneath the panic and wild lacerations he could feel her dead-snakeskin lips forming-not-forming shapes as if sounds, as if, yet again, always, trying to have her say trying to tell him something to speak and even as he wished Janey were here to tell him what she was saying he formed his hand as if into a cup and pressed it around the hacking, slicing tines as if to muffle her voice-not-voice & clacking teeth as they rattled the puzzle-bones of his cranium & jaw and reverberated along his spine & hips & legs waves fostering waves amplifying harmonic resonate bones becoming waves jumpswaying coiling twisting wavebones waterbones elastic yet as if about to come undone & cascade to oceanearth below all I want as he pressed his palm downward is to be alone can you imagine that Sister is that what you want to be alone & who is that other so far down so remote in blindalleys of flesh meat cul-de-sacs of no-light yet there & what others were they you or me or us & are you howling as I am howling for just one moment of silence of stillness of peace & apartness that finality of the skin that space that gap that end of me that end of you unbridgeable to be like everyone else & how many others those calcified specks with invisible spiral arms intertangled in darkness encapsulated in heat filaments reaching worming ivying rampant with desire desires desiring trying to speak to say all intertwining knotted the furious unending clamor of us when it should be me or i or you-not-me they-not-us they-not-i the superheated sun of voices-not-voices the clamorthrob of unbeating-beating stonehearts unfiring-firing stoneminds debitage alight with blinding sunthoughts-not-thoughts who can say & the communication of atoms this atom striking that that the next speckspeak along qua-

vering wires indiscernible yet felt in molten darkness the quiver of us all at once & just wishing isn't it what you want what i want one moment of just-me me-not-you, not-us-we not-us-them isn't it not too much to ask to want & you eating my favorite toque, my Oilers toque which I don't wear because I want to keep it so to hell with you with them all however many i feel them vibrating longing whispering-not-whispering calcified entrails entangled & somewhere in the superheated blindness sounding would-be-words

—Would you please, for one damn moment, be quiet. And stop eating my hat!

Brion looked up.

His feet, of their own, had led him across the bridge and before him, massive, was the refinery where his uncle and Andrew worked, a crosshatch of pipes, tanks, and chimneys churning out sulfurous black smoke and soot, the particulates churning in the air, mixing with the snow and ice crystals, eventually falling to earth, coating everything and everyone. As far as he could see, there were no living trees or bushes, and the snowdrifts were layered with ash and grit, carved by the wind into ridges and razorbacks and long, smooth oblong bowls. Behind him, the river was clogged with immense blocks and shards of ice piling up one on the other and creaking and groaning in the dull, harsh light. Parallel to the bridge, less than a kilometer away, was the train bridge and several engines strung together labored to pull a seemingly endless string of oil cars south for further refining.

He struggled to come back to himself, trying to remember where he was going and why. He looked from the refinery to the oilfields and the tar sands beyond, the snow melted to filthy ice around the clanging pumpjacks and pools and small lakes where the tar bubbled to the surface.

Right: practice. Light morning practice before the game this evening. Talk of scouts, his reputation as the best player in northern Alberta, probably too small for the NHL, but fast and strong and without fear. A natural scorer and playmaker. His coaches told him he would be drafted, no question.

He still had a couple of kilometers across the bitumen fields to reach the arena.

A few moments passed before he realized that Sister had fallen silent. The others, if there were others, had also fallen silent even as the aftershocks of the tumult rippled along his arms and legs. His ears ringing, head pounding, he felt ill and weak, and the sky was low and heavy with smoke from the refinery and flare stacks. He ignored the NO TRESPASSING signs and began to trudge along the winding, mazelike trails cut by others who had likewise ignored the warnings and followed the long-used paths. To the east was the town, shrouded in snowfall and haze, and to the north and west the tar sands stretched to the horizon. Dotting the expanse were the tireless oil horses and several of the more complicated injection and fracking pumps where they had found pockets of natural gas amid the sand and shale, and he could hear but not see megalithic earthmovers, excavators, and trucks with tires bigger than houses scraping and hauling the clotted earth to the refinery. Even with a strong breeze, the air smelled of ozone, rotten eggs, and diesel exhaust, and his headache grew worse. The glare from the dirty-coin sun seemed to be pulling his eyes from their sockets. Several times he stopped to spill his coffee and breakfast on the dirty snow.

The trainer would give him something, but he did not feel like practicing.

i could lay down & hold my eyes in my hands and shut them from the light for a moment

Sister, for whatever reasons, seemed to love skating and hockey and would sing as he glided and twisted over the ice, would warble like a bird in spring as he feinted and dodged his way toward the goal. As he slogged through the slush and muck, he thought that she would not sing today, that he would not feel the pressure of her joy pounding like an extra heart in his chest.

14.

"Before I tell you the story of *The Dying Indian*, tell me: why did you come looking for me?"

"I took an assignment from *The Orb and Post* to interview O'Keevan about *The Dying Albertan*, and I made a foolish, beginner's mistake: when he asked what I thought about the statue, I said that I thought that it told a story about people he had known, and from that bare suggestion he began to spin out, on the spot, this long story about his college days to account for the origins—and meaning?—of the monster, of all that pain and sorrow. Halfway through, he stops, gets up to leave, and when I confronted him with the fact that I knew he was lying about at least some of it, he claimed that none of it was true but that I should be glad that he had offered me anything. Then, the best moment, he tells me that if it would make me feel better, I should make up the rest of the story and make it about my friends. What—as a friend of mine would say—a colossal asshole! At any rate, as part of the story, he mentioned a woman named Briony, and although he claimed that she wasn't real, the name stuck: I knew it from someplace. I did some detective work, and found out that I was sort of right: Niall O'Keevan's work had been exhibited on a number of occasions with the 'bright and daring island images' of one Brionne de la Bastide and a handful of other famous Canadian artists. I wondered if you were somehow connected to the piece, and here I am."

"He betrayed himself."

"Betrayed himself?"

"He made up a story to explain how he came up with the idea—or ideas—for the sculpture, and he named one of the 'characters' Briony? It's as if, after all these years, some part of him wants the truth to come out."

She spoke softly and slowly, with currents of French and Spanish and the soft *as*, hard *is*, and *ds* for *ths* of Caribbean English.

"He wanted me to find you? In effect, he told me to look for you?"

"I don't know, but it seems possible. The mind has a strange way, sometimes, of saying what it otherwise doesn't want to say."

"So we're supposed to play a part in some sort of weird confessional? He sets me on a course to find you, and you're supposed to tell me the truth about the statue, and then what? He gets to enact some sort of penance, and all is forgiven? He's a piece of work, and it's all rather incredible, even for him."

"I have no idea, but in a way, I'm probably more sympathetic towards him than you are."

"He's crazy, a pathological liar and manipulator. And he stole from you!"

"I know that better than anyone, but I'm not talking about theft right now. Think of it this way: what if you were an intensely private, even shy person—for whatever reasons—yet your career requires living a very public life, going to openings, giving interviews, being available to potential clients, getting your name out there and trying to make a living, pedaling your wares. I can see how that conflict could cause a few—distortions. Very few people can make a living as an artist without putting themselves out there, at least now and then. And, in O'Keevan's case, he doesn't want to talk about his personal life, yet people keep asking him or wanting to know what the relationships are, if any, between their art and their private lives and experiences. I can see getting fed up with it all."

"But he's rich. He didn't have to meet me, or give any more interviews, and he can leave the rest to his agent and publicity people and accountants."

"There's the still deeper struggle between the private self and the ego. Say you want to be a painter, an artist, you think you have something to say, something people will want to see, to own, so you have to believe in yourself, you have to want people to look and look again and believe as much as you do."

I thought about it:

"I'm not sure about any of this—I need to think about it—but I can say this: to hell with O'Keevan. You were going to tell me about *The Dying Indian*."

Brionne smiled:

"I can see why O'Keevan tried to get rid of you: you're quite persistent. Well, the dogged Miss Agarwal, if we're going to do this, I'm going to switch to wine, and you can join me if you like. And, let's move to the living room—it won't be any warmer, but at least we'll be a little more comfortable."

"Sure, I'll have a glass of wine, but I'd like to make an additional proposal: I mean it when I say to hell with O'Keevan. Even if he somehow schemed for me to find you, I don't want to play any part in his contrition. I want to know about your work, not his, about you, not him, and I can trust you, right, to tell the truth, and not to make up some phony story? Because if you're going to make something up, tell me now and I can get back in the rental—which has a heater—and get out of here."

"No need to worry: I'll tell you the truth. Besides, it's not much of a story—in fact, it's not a story at all, but an idea I had—and I have no reason to lie."

I imagine Sasi peering over my shoulder as I sit at the small table in my sister-in-law's kitchen, so stuffed from dinner and wine and conversation and babies and the late hour that I am becoming drowsy:

"I can't wait to see where you're going with this."

What to do with a snoop?

"Be patient."

Have you ever been to Trinidad? No? Then, even if you know someone from the islands, you can't really know what it's like.

It's incredible. It's as if the histories of half the world needed someplace to collide, a pinpoint of intersection where bodies from half the world, once set in motion, couldn't help but run into one another and smash together and intertwine so furiously that they never looked or acted or thought the same again. Like atoms smashing, they broke apart and reformed, taking an arm from one, a leg from another, an eye, a cheekbone, a word, a sign, a desire, a need, anything, until you had the most beautiful Frankenstein monsters, all living on a tiny island, nobody one thing or one person, but ten, one hundred, a thousand, palimpsests of palimpsests, palimpersons of palimpersons, languages and sounds so bizarre that a person could say your mother's name, and unless you were from there, you wouldn't hear a thing, just a sound without meaning, a vibration in the air.

And nobody, no matter what they tell you, is telling the truth because they don't know the truth, even about themselves. In Port-of-Spain, you have Jews convinced they're minor Catholic royalty from Vienna, Indians—I mean once upon a time from India—sure they're the great-great-great grandsons and -daughters of Castille, Englishmen who don't speak English but the French of Martinique, blacks—the children of the long-ago children of slaves—speaking Hindi as if Hindi was what they spoke in Jamaica, I an I ahn a weh ya baan, my coolie bredren?

Arawaks without Indian blood—I mean Indian from South America, long ago, not from South Asia after the emancipation of the Africans—Caribs who dream in Taíno, bemused Courlanders who speak Lithuanian at home, Polish on the town, and public school English at work and among strangers, Leeward Islanders who were born on the Windwards and Dutch Somalis from Haiti who feel in their souls that they're the direct descendants of Bolívar. Everybody is dougla, garifuna, or wicked jahabibi who confuse even themselves—Afro-Carib Muslims, can you imagine!—and everyone boasts a skin of motley, has one blue eye and one the color of sand or the sun, the rainforest or hurricanes.

Well, Miss Persistence, that's half the story, half the idea I had for *The Dying Indian*. You understand me so far, yes? Then, do you want to know the rest or shall we go into Victoria for lunch? No?

Another glass of wine? A blanket?

Everyone is someone else, some uncountable numbers of someone elses, but it's not as if all those collisions were without their traumas. There was a lot of violence, even viciousness, involved in smashing all these peoples together, in remaking them into these shimmering, kaleidoscopic, beautiful monsters. The Caribs and Arawaks were displaced by Europeans, then the Europeans brought Africans to be slaves, and then, following emancipation, who would do the work?, and Indians were encouraged to emigrate. At last, nobody quite sure the day or time, a tipping point: the Asians outnumbered the Africans outnumbered the Europeans outnumbered the Indians. There were murders, businesses torched, lynchings, gangs, and attacks with machetes, arms and legs and heads hacked off and left in the street or tossed into ravines. And, at the same time, with everyone intermingled or intermingling, nobody could be quite sure they weren't killing their half-brother, cousin, uncle, mother, themselves.

That was my idea when I began to sketch *The Dying Indian*: all of that, all of that history and collision and violence. And, here, I brought you my sketchbook from back then, and you can see for yourself what I was trying for, what I wanted to do.

She handed me an old and well-used pad, and I flipped through the pages. The first images were line figures, as if she had something of the sculpture already in mind and was trying to work out the body position, the angles of the head, torso, and limbs. Many of these were small and hasty, and had circles and ovals drafted over the lines. Then, a long series of faces, more or less realized, some more Arawak- or African- or South Asia-looking, but with incongruous features, a broad nose with Arawak eyes and the close, clipped hair of an English colonial officer. Faces, and bodies without heads, limbs variously broken or severed, some piled in heaps, others barely attached, some of the bodies lying prone, others seeming in mid-fall, others recoiling as if struck or about to be struck. Then, emerging slowly over the course of several pages, the iconic, mythic pose of the dying Gaul, the classic image of defeat, death imminent, but still the mismatched limbs, the mismatched faces, elegant, even beautiful Mr. Potato Heads of agony, fear, defeat.

She really had done it, had created the image and logic of *The Dying Albertan*.

The Dying Indian had come first, and O'Keevan had stolen her work and refashioned it into his own and had leapt to the heights of the Canadian art world.

I sat back, and exhaled at last:

"It's all here. You worked it all out, and it's amazing, stunning, brilliant."

"I told you I would tell you the truth, and there's your evidence."

"Now what?"

"Now, I leave it to you. You can have the sketch book—I don't want it back—and you can do with it whatever you want. You can make yourself famous."

"If I publish this, people won't leave you alone. You'll be famous—or infamous—and O'Keevan will be disgraced!"

She smiled, a rich, warm, cat-eyed smile:

"Oh, well."

And, with that, she stood and ushered me to the front door of the little cabin. The truck and the old couple eating their breakfast were gone. She walked me to the rental, and wished me well:

"However it goes, I imagine we'll cross paths again, Miss Agarwal. I'll look forward to that."

I started the car, three-pointed it back in the direction I had come, and drove slowly along the narrow path leading to the road. I was spent, shocked, overwhelmed by what I had just learned, and when I reached the rural route, I turned right when I should have turned left toward Victoria and my hotel. Less than one hundred meters along, on the right hand side of the road, was a small, graceful sign:

FUNDY HOUSE

EST. 1921

Without glancing in the mirrors, I slammed on the brakes:

"No way."

It was as if someone had kicked me in the stomach.

I turned into the immaculate stone- and hedge-lined drive and followed it as it swayed through the cedars and flowering dogwoods and slowed a couple of hundred meters from the landmark.

Fundy House was the creation of Ram Finlayson, the Canadian Frank Lloyd Wright, and one of the most famous private homes in the country. Finlayson was known for his whimsy and unexpected combinations, and Fundy House looked like a magnificent Craftsman-style home, but three times the size and made out of steel, limestone, and glass. As I stared, Brionne emerged from a path among the cedars and began to stride across the perfectly-kept lawn. Standing on the limestone porch, glass in hand, was O'Keevan. Brionne glided up the wide stairs and into his arms. He was careful not to spill his rum.

15.

The studio was open and warm, with a high ceiling, tall windows along both exterior walls, and a broad skylight running the length of the room. At the front was a raised platform and facing the platform in a staggered semi-circle were a dozen or so easels. The interior walls were exposed brick, with student sketches and paintings taped or tacked haphazardly on one wall and a work bench, shelves, and storage slots along the other. Above the work bench were more slots for canvases and twin bulletin boards overflowing and layered with notices about classes, exhibitions, and scholarship and fellowship opportunities.

If the room and air were warm and inviting, the late November light filling the space was not. A cold, blinding glare slanted through the west-facing windows, stinging the eyes and wrapping the model seated on a barstool in a harsh, icy, too vivid light. With nods from the others, a couple of students dropped the blinds, leaving the room bathed in the softer, diffused rays filtering through the snow accumulated on the skylight. Another then flicked on the overhead lights, allowed the rest to contemplate for a moment, and then turned them off and waited for the verdict. Off. In the natural, suppler, less hostile light, the guest seemed smaller, less abrupt, less alien, and the ambient, slate-blue glow from above brought him into clear, yet intense relief. With the light acceptable, if not perfect, the students approached the platform, stepping up and around the model, studying his form from all angles, some taking notes or making brief sketches and talking among themselves:

“Do you see the way his ribs zigzag and all but jut out as if they were spines on a dinosaur’s back? It’s as if they were smashed and put back together with crazy glue and guesses.”

“Whatever happened to him, it must have hurt like hell. Do

you think he's still in pain? Must be, right?"

"Tore his arm and leg right off—wonder if he still feels them?"

"You see all those scars? They're amazing, the ridges and the way they radiate this way and that."

Neil, who was helping Brice prop his prosthetic against the supports of the bar stool, whispered:

"Are you sure about this?"

"No. And, do they always talk about the models as if they weren't here?"

"You're in their place, and they're working."

"Swell."

When the leg was secure, Neil stepped off the platform and took a few paces. Hornsby had put him in charge of the session—he was Brice's friend, after all—and he stood back and surveyed the stage.

Brice looked uneasy, yet composed and he half-rested on the seat and braced himself in place with his right leg. Neil had wanted Brice to sit further back, but Brice had explained that his back had been bothering him and he was more comfortable this way. He agreed to ask Neil for help if he needed to reposition himself.

Good enough.

Brice really had been smashed up. How he survived was a mystery to Neil, and how long after he had been struck or fallen—or whatever had happened—had he had to lie there waiting for help? Had he been conscious the whole time? How did he not bleed to death?

His left arm and part of the shoulder were completely gone. The impact had either sheared away or pulverized the bones and muscle, leaving the surgeons few options but to cut away what must have been a splintered, pulpy mess. Where the shoulder joint and part of the collar bone should have been was now a softball-sized divot. Below the shoulder, the ribs had also been crushed, and while the doctors had repaired several, they evidently had been forced to remove parts of the upper three so that an area of his upper chest appeared to cave inward. Scars ran up and down his back and chest, and crisscrossed his sternum and right shoulder blade. The left side of his lower torso had likewise been smashed and the soft tissue, having been reconstructed and sewed back into place as much as possible, bulged here and there and was intersected in all directions with scars from both the accident and, Neil imagined, multiple surgeries.

The left leg was also missing. What remained was crosshatched with scars and glowed scarlet in the soft light.

Neil pretended to sketch, but mostly he stared at the clock and watched as Brice squirmed now and then, trying to find a more comfortable position. Around him, Neil's peers worked busily, draughting and no doubt thinking through what sorts of angles and points of view they would take for their final projects with this model: what would he look like from overhead, from 3/4s right or left, from behind, below, either side, cubist where all sides could be seen at once?

At the half-hour break, Neil rejoined Brice:

"Weary? Had enough?"

"I'm fine. No Briony, eh? Man, she hates you."

"Very funny. And, why me? I kept trying to tell her that this was all you, and that I had nothing to do with it. She told me she thinks I want to see your nuts, hold them for you in case they're too heavy."

Brice snorted:

"I think you'd better forget about that one, brother. She ain't coming back."

Neil shook his head:

"It's your damn fault."

Brice snorted again:

"It's funny because it's you. And, I had kinda hoped she'd show up to class, naked, and be up here with me as a show of support. But, then, I'd get a boner, and the women would go crazy, be a whole wild scene."

"You have a vivid imagination."

"Yup. Here, help me sit back, my leg's getting twitchy."

After grabbing Brice around the chest and lifting him back onto the stool, Neil retreated behind his easel. He didn't bother picking up his pencil or charcoal, and he blocked Brice from view with his pad. He watched the clock.

In a daze, he heard Brice gasp and, just as he looked around the edge of his easel, slip from the stool and fall to the ground. Brice, all at once wheezing and coughing, tried with his one arm across his torso and leg to lift himself from the plywood. His arm buckled and his head drooped. He collapsed before Neil could reach him.

16.

He had played well, but not brilliantly: 1 goal, 1 assist, and 1 penalty, a minor for slashing. Not quite a Gordie Howe, but good enough: the Voyageurs had won 5-2, and he hadn't had to bring his A-game. None of the scouts had stuck around, yet the coaches seemed reasonably happy and optimistic and said that it didn't mean anything that the scouts hadn't stuck around. They were on the road constantly, driving thousands of kilometers every winter, always headed to the next game, the next small town, keeping track of dozens, if not hundreds of players from the peewees on up.

Sure, every coach wanted his players to get drafted—and, even better, actually to play in the NHL—not only because they were hoping for their players, but their way to the bigs was to start out coaching mites and work their way, quickly, up to the juniors or the U.S. college game, and from there, as an assistant or even head coach, to the pros.

Once the puck had dropped and the pills the trainer had given him had begun to kick in, Brion had begun to feel better, but he couldn't shake the headache and by the end of the game his head was pounding and he was having difficulty seeing. The trainer had said maybe a migraine, winter light, the glare, could do that, and he had given him a couple more somethings when he had come out of the showers. They had gone off like bombs in his empty stomach, and his guts were sour and he couldn't shake the hiccups. He felt awful. He struggled into his clothes and pulled the Oilers toque over his sopping hair.

The trainer said he'd catch pneumonia if he went out like that.

—I'll be home in half an hour. No problem.

—Let me give you a ride.

He waved a no-thanks and, turning up his collar, left the arena. He crossed the parking lot and began to retrace his route through the bitumen fields, a ghostly orange light from the flare stacks illuminating the low scud. He still couldn't see well, but it didn't matter. He had crossed through the bogs and sand and quaking shale a thousand times, to and from the town, to and from the rink, and he let his feet navigate.

Sister had not murmured a sound. She had not sung during the game. She was still, and not gnawing on his hat, now all-but frozen by the wind into a helmet of wool.

—I appreciate it, Sister, I do.

He kept walking, but instead of turning toward home he hobbled past the bridge and deeper into the fields, moving parallel to the river. He could hear the ice clacking and groaning as it swirled and buckled in the current and wind.

At last, he reached the tracks, a metal ribbon in the gloam. He knelt and grasped the near rail with his mitted hand. He could feel vibrations and jumps in the icy steel, and the wet wool had frozen to the alloy and he had to yank his hand away. He stood, and looked north, and then south. He could neither see the lights nor hear the rumble of the massive diesel engines, but somewhere out there was another long, heavy, unstoppable mass, running back empty and fast, or running away, chockfull and with the momentum of a living, needful, astronomic thing that must begin to slow a hundred kilometers from its destination.

About the Author

Brady Harrison has worked on the killfloor of meatpacking plants, as a reporter for a smalltown newspaper, research officer for the Métis Settlements of northern Alberta, piano mover, construction yardman, and coin dealer. He has written, edited, or co-edited several books, and his articles, essays, poems, and stories have appeared in journals and books in numerous countries. He lives in Missoula, Montana, and teaches at the University of Montana.

www.ingramcontent.com/pod-product-compliance
Lightning Source LLC
Chambersburg PA
CBHW030530310726
48979CB00010B/1860/J

* 9 7 8 1 7 3 3 1 9 4 9 6 9 *